# AS RAIN TURNS TO SNOW
# AND OTHER STORIES

# AS RAIN TURNS TO SNOW

## AND

# OTHER STORIES

Robert Morgan

BROADSTONE

ISBN 978-1-937968-29-8

LIBRARY OF CONGRESS NUMBER 2016958381

Broadstone Books
An Imprint of
Broadstone Media LLC
418 Ann Street
Frankfort, KY 40601-1929
BroadstoneBooks.com

FOR MY GRANDDAUGHTER

*Rory*

# CONTENTS

# THE BURNING CHAIR

THE BUNGALOW in the rainy woods looks as though it might be buried soon in leaves. The air is filled with great leaves floating down, and the trail through the trees is covered with wet leaves. Even the windows have yellow and brown leaves stuck like hands to the glass. Every time a gust hits the trees a new shower pounds the drifts and roof, and another flock of leaves shivers down. There is no smoke from the chimney, though there is smoke in the living room where the right arm of an easy chair is on fire.

The fire has burned a circle in the cloth of the armchair. The cotton stuffing of the cushion has caught and is smoldering also. The flames are no more than four or five inches high, but they burn steadily, almost like a lamp. They are the only light in the room except for the cigarette in the hand nearby. As the flames advance, sputtering and sending up smoke, the hand pulls back a little. But the man in the chair sleeps on, his head slumped on the back of the chair.

The phone on the nightstand by the chair rings. Its electric shriek fills the smoky room, but the man does not stir. The telephone makes the air throb and shudder, again, five times, and then stops.

The cigarette drops out of the sleeping man's hand and falls to the linoleum still smoking. Ash and bits of tobacco are scattered around it, and the tiny button of fire eats into the paint of the linoleum, and then into the felt underneath. A chemical smoke rises from the burn, but after a few minutes the cigarette goes out, and a pock is left in the floor cover.

But the flames on the arm of the chair continue, eating deeper into the cotton cushion. The fire flutters and shakes a little as the sleeper moves and brushes his hand through it, but springs up again. The flames are reflected in a bottle on the night table, a gin bottle, less than half full, with the top off. There is a glass by the bottle, but it has not been used. Drops around the rim and neck of the bottle show it has been drunk from recently. The bottle is tilted at a dangerous angle because it rests half on the corner of a magazine. There is a pile of magazines on the table beside it.

In fact the whole room is scattered with magazines and newspapers and paperback books. The other chairs hold stacks of *Combat* and *National Rifleman*, and *Field and Stream*. Six months of back issues of a daily newspaper are piled on the couch, many opened to the listings of the television schedule. The set itself sits on the floor ten feet opposite the armchair, turned off, its screen the color of wet putty but also mirroring the flames. The wires from the set run along the floor to the jack where the cable has been disconnected.

Paperbacks are heaped around the sides of the armchair and several stacks have toppled and spilled into the middle of the room. A glance at the titles shows the predominant subjects: *The Great Schweinfurt Raid, Patton, The Good War, Guadalcanal Diary*. Most of the books look old and tattered, as though they have been read many times, or purchased from a used book exchange. The room smells like old paper, ink and paper, and smoke.

The sleeping man stirs but does not move as the fire approaches his hand. His fingers will burn soon if he doesn't take his arm from the armrest. But just as the smell of burned flesh is added to the smell of burning cloth his hand falls off into his lap.

The man wears faded jeans and an old T-shirt. He might at one time have been muscular, but through lack of eating or lack of exercise he has lost most of his weight, and seems slight of build, even fragile. The tattoos on his arm look like veins circling in elaborate patterns. A cigarette pack weighs down the one pocket of his T-shirt.

But the most striking thing about the sleeping man is the lack of color in his face. He looks as though he has not been out in the sun for years, and has worked the third shift and slept during the day. His skin is white as an albino leaf grown in a cave or cellar. His forearms, except for the hair and tattoos, are equally white. His pallor is the kind you see in extended care wards. His skin and T-shirt are almost the same color.

The flame on the chair arm, as it eats down into the padding and touches the wooden frame inside, burns steadily as a lamp. It is perhaps the threadbareness of the cloth covering that makes it burn so slow, along with the soiled slickness of the fabric. Even so the fire advances toward the resting elbow, spreading sideways, advancing in one direction, slowing to dig deeper into the cotton, then moving forward again. The flame is like some small animal, say a ground squirrel, digging for nuts or roots, then turning to work in another direction. Nevertheless it progresses, a thread at a time, up the arm of the chair. Eventually it will reach the elbow and arm of the T-shirt, and spread down to the legs of the sleeper. Rain tinkles on the panes where the smoke presses, unable to escape.

The phone rings again, shaking the gloomy air. The man in the chair stirs but does not open his eyes. With his left hand he makes a gesture which might be an attempt to reach for the phone, or an effort to shrug or brush flies away. He moves as if his arm were made of lead, in the supergravity of his sleep. It would take more will power for him to move a wrist than for most of us to jump six feet. His head slumps further on his shoulder and the phone rings four more times and stops. Drops crash on the window louder than the phone.

The fire is now a circle about six inches across, draped along the arm of the chair. It eats its way at irregular speeds through the worn cloth, but shines like a bent crown or tattered ring of light. Most of the stuffing in the center has burned, but the oak frame inside has not caught well and goes out. The fire is within eight inches of the sleeper's elbow.

On the wall above the night table hangs a photograph of a soldier, dressed in a rumpled uniform and loaded down with ammunition belts and canteen. He rests his rifle on a sign that reads "Berlin 371 km." He's smiling like a kid who has won a baseball game. On his shoulder is the insignia of the infantry. Under the arrow pointing to Berlin is another arrow, foreshortened because it points to the right. In the dim light the name "Dachau" can just be made out, though if one did not know the name it might be impossible to read. The rifle seems raised in both victory and a salute to the photographer.

The soldier resembles the sleeping man, but only if you look for the resemblance. The soldier is just a teenager, and his dark hair, pressed by the straps of the helmet, curls around his ears. The sleeping man has almost no hair, but what he has is gray and disheveled. The deep lines down his cheeks make it hard to compare his features to those of the soldier, but the nose and chin are the same.

The sleeping man stirs again, and this time he moves his right hand to his lap. His fingers twitch and close, as though grasping for something. His arm lifts from the elbow, and drops back onto his jeans. The hand lifts again and clutches the air, and then drops back into his lap.

The third time the arm moves it is clear what its target is: the pack of cigarettes in the shirt pocket. The first two fingers meet the thumb, as though closing on a cigarette, and on the fourth attempt the fingers catch on the lip of the pocket, but then drop back again, unable to grasp the pack.

The flames have spread farther up the arm of the easy chair and are now within six inches of his elbow. After one further attempt to reach the pack the hand relaxes, as though the sleeper has drifted into a deeper drowse. He is unable to move, as if under the pressure of a deep ocean trough.

Underneath the picture of the soldier there are three smaller photographs in a row. The first is of a boy in a cowboy suit and aiming a pistol, as though he has just drawn on the camera. The kid, not more than eight or nine years old, glares with exaggerated ferocity. The hat and chaps look too little for him, too small to wear except for the picture. His eyes and chin resemble those of the soldier. It's clear from the Dodge in the background that the picture was made in the 1950s.

The two girls in the other photographs also resemble the soldier. The first is a school picture, just a portrait. The girl has short curly hair and smiles like the photographer has just asked her how many boyfriends she has. Her face looks young and smooth and tanned, and her pink sweater appears to be cashmere.

The last picture shows a girl in shorts and cowboy shirt with sequins. Her face is made up and she wears sequined shoes that might be used for tap dancing. She holds a majorette's baton high above her head. From the makeup and the shoes you might think she'd been in a play or musical, or taken part in a talent contest. Her legs are long and skinny and the shoes seem too big for her. She looks about twelve, at that stage where a girl gets her height but hasn't begun to fill out. On her face is the stage smile of a performer, but it is weak around the corners, as though she is uncertain of her role or performance. "For Daddy" is written on the corner of the picture.

On the back of the night stand, under the pictures and behind the magazines, are many bottles of medicine. Most are orange plastic cylinders of pills or capsules, but there are also larger bottles of syrups and clear liquids, as well as aspirin and cards of time capsules. Along with twenty or thirty prescription drugs there are also patented painkillers of every brand, and cough medicines, inhalers, and nose drops.

The phone rings again, and the sound seems to fan the flames on the chair a little higher. The room is now thick with smoke. The sleeping man twists a little and makes a vague gesture of reaching for the phone. Or maybe he's reaching toward the half empty gin bottle. His left hand falls uselessly back into his lap after the second ring. Two more rings and the room is quiet again, except for the rain on the window.

The flames on the chair reach higher, as though they have found new fuel, a spill of oil, a clot of tar on the cloth. In the brighter light the bottles along the floor are visible, mostly gin bottles, clear as icicles. Where two lie side by side they look like binoculars of clear glass. But there are a few wine bottles and also beer cans. It looks as though there might be hundreds, if you counted those in the shadows. Where the rim or the bottom of a bottle is found by the firelight it seems the wet eye of an animal watching from the floor or the corner.

Underneath the feet of the sleeping man, which are covered with corduroy slippers, some money is scattered, a number of coins and several bills. Most of the bills are ones, and they have fallen like leaves around his feet. There is nothing bigger than a five among them.

With the dollars are mixed letters and what we might take for duns, several stamped "Final Notice," and forms from the Veterans Administration, insurance statements, printouts of policies, and a document from the county sheriff's office that would appear to be a subpoena. All are thrown carelessly on the floor. Almost underneath the chair, and almost out of sight, sits a half-eaten plate of pork and beans. The beans and sauce have dried and look like crumbs of dirt or perhaps some kind of glue and brown sugar.

The flame is now within inches of the man's elbow. His skin and bare arm must be getting hot. A little closer and the flame will singe the hair on his forearm. He moves in his sleep as though dreaming, or as though he feels the pain from the fire. First he twists to the right, and then to the left, and kicks out with his right foot. Then he slumps back into his first position, back into the lagoon of his slumber.

When the phone rings again he jerks, not awake, but as though in response to some attack in his dream. His left hand reaches out toward the bottle or phone, and falls back. Just then he feels the fire under his right elbow and pulls it away, twisting to the left. He squints at the fire and jerks again, unable to stand or even move his body, except for his arms.

Straining, now with his eyes open, he lunges for the phone as it rings the second time, but cannot reach the receiver. Instead he hits the bottle and tips it over the edge of the table so gin dribbles out on the floor. There are tears in his eyes from the effort, or from the pain of the fire, and the frustration of his helplessness. Concentrating all his strength and will he stretches for the bottle and stands it upright, precariously, on the edge of the magazine.

On the third ring he reaches for the phone again, but instead of grasping the receiver he merely knocks it off its cradle. The receiver lies on the magazines.

"Elmer, is that you?" a woman's voice says, sounding tiny and far away.

"Help," he mutters, but not loud enough to be heard.

"Elmer, what are you doing?" the voice says.

He reaches for the receiver again, and this time it scoots out of his fingers to the other side of the table and slides off, to dangle by its cord out of sight.

"Elmer, are you drunk again?" the woman's voice says, coming from the dark beneath the table.

"Fire," he mumbles, and strains to sit up, touching the flame again with his right elbow. "Oh," he groans, and twists to the left side, as far away from the flames as he can.

"Fire," he says again, this time louder. "Fire!"

"What's on fire?" the voice under the table says. "You're drunk again. Have you set the house on fire?"

"Chair on fire," he says, exaggerating speech with the working of his jaw, as he strains to articulate the syllables.

"I'm coming right up," the woman says and the phone clicks.

The man pushes himself back into the chair as far as he can, away from the flames which have moved halfway up the padded arm. He is awake now to the horror of his condition, and makes futile attempts to brush away the flames, fanning them a little with his left hand, but unable to beat out the fire, and unable to reach for anything that would be helpful.

He does grab a magazine, and knocks several medicine bottles off the table. With his left hand he catches the gin bottle again and brings it to his mouth, slurping the contents and spilling some on his chest. But the bottle slides out of his grasp and rolls down his blue jeans, spilling onto the seat of the chair.

"God damn," he whispers. The alcohol is within inches of the flames on the side of the arm chair. The spilled gin could catch any second. He knocks the bottle out of his lap and onto the floor and weeps as he watches the liquid spill over the money and envelopes there.

He reaches for a magazine to beat the flames back, but drops one on the floor and another in his lap. Leaning as far away from the fire as possible he grabs another. There is lightning at the window, and then thunder, which shakes the house and rattles the panes. But there is another sound now: someone is banging on the outside door two rooms away.

"Open it!" It's the voice of the woman on the phone, hoarse now with shortness of breath. "It's locked!" she shouts.

Lightning outlines the leaves stuck to the window like moths gathered to a light.

"Elmer," the woman shouts, "It's locked!"

When the man tries to pull another magazine off the night table the whole pile slides to the floor with a crash. He cannot reach far enough to retrieve even one of them. And he cannot reach past the flames on his right, even if he was strong enough to pull himself up.

A face appears at the window and watches in horror the scene of the burning chair and the man struggling to put his hand on a magazine. She's so shocked by what she sees she doesn't bang on the window but runs around the house to the back door. She rattles the door, testing it, but it also is locked.

"Elmer," she calls, "You're locked in!" Her voice cracks with excitement and exhaustion. She bangs on the door with her fists.

With everything out of reach, and the fire closer than ever, Elmer seems to have given up and recoils into the back of the chair. With his feet he pushes himself into the cushion as far as he can, as though he weighs tons.

In the brighter light from the fire a cockroach appears and crosses the floor toward the fallen magazines. It may be headed for the plate of half-eaten beans, or it may be attracted by the smell of spilled gin. The gin has spread in a large slick on the linoleum, among the money and letters. When the man's foot kicks out the cockroach retreats just out of the fire-light. Only its long antennae, like fishing poles, can be seen. But after the foot is still for a few seconds the insect crawls back toward the chair.

"Elmer, you crazy fool," the woman says. She's at the window, rattling the sash. With a great effort she raises the window which is old and wet. The counterweights knock in the walls.

"Elmer, you crazy damn fool," she says, out of breath, and pulls herself up on the sill. She falls back and rests a moment, and a gust of wind sweeps leaves into the room and stirs the smoke that has been confined there. The flames on the chair sputter, and then revive in the new oxygen. On her second try she gets her chest across the ledge and wriggles through, falling to the floor and resting to catch her breath.

"Elmer, you damn fool," she says again. The man sees her but is helpless to respond. The fire is almost touching his knee now, and it has spread down the arm of the chair and is burning the cushion in the seat. Obviously his leg is getting hot, and he twists with the pain.

The woman pulls herself up and stumbles on another pile of magazines, knocking over an unlighted lamp. Holding onto a chair she hoists herself up with great effort and runs to the man. Because of the fire on one side, and the night table on the left, she can't reach him. She kicks the table over, making the phone ring once when it hits the floor.

"So this is what it's come to," she says, more to herself than to him. "Look what you've come to."

She tries to pull him out of the chair, but it's clear he's too heavy. In her panic and excitement she simply cannot lift him past the flames. And he's pure drunken weight, unable to coordinate himself enough to help. She runs to the front of him and tries to pull him by the left arm, but the flames are too close for her to bend over him.

She takes a copy of *Life* and begins to beat the flames in terror, or perhaps in fury. She beats the fire in the cushion close to the spilled gin, and then she beats the padded arm. After she knocks the fire out it springs up again from the stuffing, and she demolishes the revived flames with a few hard licks. In the dark smokey room she probably can't see, or perhaps her glasses have been lost in the excitement. But stumbling over magazines, and the fallen lamp, and a hidden footstool, she heads for the kitchen and switches on a light there. There is the sound of water running, and water being poured.

"Louise," the man calls in the dark, but she ignores him. The edges of the burn still glow with tiny coals, and smokes rises from the smelly mess of the stuffing,

"Louise," he calls again, sounding like someone lost in the dark calling for directions.

The woman is outlined by the light from the kitchen as she stands in the doorway with a bucket in either hand. Advancing to him she puts one bucket down and hurls the contents of the other onto the chair. Much of the cold water hits the man in the face and chest.

"Merciful lord!" he cries, under the pain of the icy water. No sooner has he wiped his face with the back of his hand than she showers him with the other bucket.

"Merciful lord," he groans again in the smokey dark.

She finds the light switch and turns it on, and there he is, revealed in the dripping clutter of bottles and fallen books, half-burned chair, and wet T-shirt stuck to his chest. The room is piled with junk like a storeroom or attic where things are put to be forgotten.

"Ain't you a pretty looking sight," she says, and leans over to kiss his forehead. Then she takes a blanket from the closet to wrap around him. Lightning illuminates the bare trees outside the window for an instant.

# AS RAIN TURNS TO SNOW

WE'LL MEET AT the holly tree by the Little River Road," Dr. Lewis had said. "That way we can approach the house through the woods and nobody will hear a thing until we open the front door."

"What if they're watching through the window?" Roy Revis said. Roy was the postmaster and one of Dr. Lewis's oldest friends, from the time the doctor arrived here from South Carolina.

"They'll have other things on their mind," Dr. Lewis said. He wore a high collar and silk cravat, but he also wore shiny riding boots. He was the only doctor I ever knew who used a motorcycle. He rode his motorcycle with a leather bag strapped to the back to visit patients in the country, in remote coves and on ridges over in Transylvania County. During the typhoid epidemic Dr. Lewis was the only doctor who'd go into the valleys where the fever was worst. And he always tried to make his patients laugh, no matter how sick they were. Dr. Lewis loved to laugh.

"What are we supposed to do when we get there?" John Huggins said. John was the druggist in town. He'd owned the drugstore since I was a boy.

"Just do what I do," Dr. Lewis said and winked. "That's all you have to do."

Dr. Lewis was so mysterious about the plans it puzzled me. I didn't know what I was agreeing to do. But I figured I owed him a favor or two. I'd worked for the Lewises as a handyman off and on for years. I'd built the back porch on his house, and every year I did some painting and repair work. I'd made stone pillars at the entrance to the driveway off Little River Road, and I'd laid a rock wall around the yard. Dr. Lewis had hired me at full wages when nobody else would. I figured I owed him too much to ask many questions.

Dr. Lewis's wife was a Mayhew from Greenville. I think he must have met her when he worked as a young doctor in South Carolina, before moving to Henderson County. She liked horses, and was always going around in riding pants and boots. Dr. Lewis kept several saddle horses in the stable at the edge of the woods. When I worked there, Mrs. Lewis often rode away and was gone for hours. There were trails all over Flat Rock and into the nearby mountains. She looked awful stylish in her tight riding jacket, with glistening blonde hair, carrying a bright little riding crop.

IT WAS A RAINY February morning when we met at the holly tree on Little River Road at nine o'clock. I expected to see Dr. Lewis coming out of his driveway to meet us, but instead he approached on the road from town. And he was not on his motorcycle, but driving the new Buick with the gold radiator cap that looked like the great seal of the nation. And he wasn't wearing riding pants, but was dressed up in his best suit and a black overcoat. He looked like he was on his way to a big medical convention.

"Gentlemen, I want to thank you all for meeting me here," Dr. Lewis said when he got out of the Buick. He was wearing bright brown gloves.

"Whatever you say, Doc," I said.

Dr. Lewis pulled a large gold watch from his vest pocket and studied it. There was a cold drizzle in the air. A cow grazing in the pasture across the road bawled mournful, the way a cow in heat will. If the temperature dropped a degree it would be sleeting or snowing. The holly tree shed drops big as berries.

"What do you want us to do?" Roy Revis said. Roy was wearing a sheepskin coat with the collar turned up around his ears.

"Just follow me," Dr. Lewis said, "and do as I do."

"We're going to freeze out here," John Huggins said, his teeth chattering.

"When this is over I'll pour us a hot toddy and we can sit by the fire," Dr. Lewis said. He pulled his hat lower to shield his glasses from the drizzle.

"Which way we going?" I said.

"Through the woods to the side of the house," Dr. Lewis said. "Then we'll go in the front door." Some mud had stuck to his shiny riding boots as he climbed the bank to the holly tree.

"We'll get wet going through the bushes," I said.

"Sorry, my friends, but that can't be helped," Dr. Lewis said. "I want you to know how much I appreciate what you're about to do."

"We'll help you any way we can," John Huggins said. I wondered if John and Roy knew more about what we were doing than I did.

As Dr. Lewis parted the bushes at the edge of the woods, drops showered off on his cashmere coat. We followed in a line and every time I brushed or shook a limb another shower came down. The cold water on my face startled me with the strangeness of what we were doing. Blackberry briars tore at Dr. Lewis's fine clothes, but he ignored them, picking his way around sweet shrubs and sumac bushes, getting wetter every time he touched a limb. A quail shot up out of the brush like a mortar round, and we stopped in surprise. A partridge always sounds bigger and more powerful than the little handful of bird it is.

"Shhhhh," Dr. Lewis said, as if he was talking to the bird that was long gone.

When we got into the big trees it was not nearly as wet, but we were already pretty well soaked. The oak trees dripped and acorns fell. A squirrel stirred the limbs above us. I shivered as the dampness sunk down next to my skin. A crow called from somewhere like it was mocking us.

We reached the edge of the yard after a few minutes and came out in the rhododendrons I'd set out for the doctor. The leaves on the bushes were rolled up like cigars from the cold.

Dr. Lewis stopped and turned to us. "Now it's important not to do anything," he whispered. "We'll just go in and see what we see. But I want you to be witnesses, and do everything I do. Okay?"

"Okay, Doc," we said and nodded.

"Shhhhh," he said like a high school boy about to play a prank. He bent over and stepped quiet across the wet grass and we followed. I saw a roadster parked in the driveway, a maroon and black model, with enormous silver headlights and a shiny grille. I'd seen it around town and thought it belonged to the lawyer named Hughes who had an office on South Main near Hatch's feed store.

Rain had attached itself to the windshield in big freezing drops that looked like snails.

Dr. Lewis walked quick up the steps and we followed onto the porch. Then he turned to us and smiled and brought his arm down like a bandleader signaling the music to start. He grabbed the front door and opened it, no longer trying to be quiet.

The living room of Dr. Lewis's house always smelled like the spice and rose petals Mrs. Lewis kept in bowls on tables and mantel. There were no lights on, and in the dark the scent was stronger. A fire in the fireplace gave the room a smell of warmth and burning oak. In the dim light the fire leaned like a dancer, circling and stepping back, quick and then slow.

As we walked on the carpet without brushing our feet, I heard glass rattle in the big china closet where Mrs. Lewis kept her fine crystal and little porcelain statues. I reached up and took my hat off as I always did coming into the house, but Dr. Lewis and Roy and John left their hats on. Water dripped off my hat and ran across my hand to the floor. Dr. Lewis didn't seem concerned about the mud on our feet and the dripping on the carpet and shiny hardwood floor.

There was nobody in the living room. The big clock beside the sofa beat like a heart. Firelight glinted off the glass face of the clock and the many whatnots on shelves around the room.

"This way, gentlemen," the doctor said.

He strode down the hallway and we followed, past the dining room. I thought we must be headed for the kitchen, but he turned beyond the dining room to the second hallway that led to the study and master bedroom. Mrs. Lewis's little terrier trotted out of the kitchen, its feet clicking on the floor. "Here, Fiddle," Dr. Lewis said. "Here, Fiddle."

The hallway was dark, but I could see light under the door of the bedroom. Roy bumped into a stand or little table and something fell to the floor and rolled under our feet, a vase or maybe a tankard. "Never mind," Dr. Lewis said. It was too dark to see much anyway. I bumped into John Huggins; his coat was wet like it had been soaked in the river.

"Knock knock," Dr. Lewis said, and flung open the bedroom door. I held back for a second, feeling it odd to be stalking into somebody else's bedroom. But Roy and John followed the doctor, and then I did too. At first I just saw the fire in the fireplace, and the fire reflected in a dressing mirror, and both men's and women's clothes on the floor. And then I saw a big bed with a naked man and woman on it. I didn't even recognize Mrs. Lewis at first because she looked so young and slim. And she was bent down with her face on a pillow while the man was behind her. How young and fair her thigh looked, and how hairy and ugly the man's behind was.

It was Hughes the lawyer all right, for soon as we crowded in he turned and looked at us in shock. He didn't even roll off Mrs. Lewis; he just froze there. And then Mrs. Lewis looked around from the pillow and screamed. It was the scream of a trapped animal.

"Good morning to you both," Dr. Lewis said. "We thought we would just drop in, like the rain."

Hughes rolled away from the woman and pulled a sheet to his waist. "You bastard," he said to Dr. Lewis.

"Am I the bastard, gentlemen?" Dr. Lewis said and turned to us.

Hughes jumped out of the bed and begun grabbing up clothes from the floor. He picked up a shirt and suspenders, socks and shoes, pants and drawers.

"Don't forget your gaiters," Dr. Lewis said. "It's raining outside."

Mr. Hughes's face was red as he collected the things under his arm. "You are a pig!" he hissed at Dr. Lewis.

"Now it's animals we're insulting," Dr. Lewis said and started laughing. Dr. Lewis was always a great laugher. He loved to tell jokes and laugh with his patients and friends. He laughed at Hughes scrambling to gather his things the way you laugh at a vaudeville show. He gestured to Roy and John and they started laughing too. I joined in, because I'd agreed to do whatever the doctor did. Dr. Lewis's laughter boomed like Santa Claus's as we watched his wife pull the sheets about her slender body, and as her lover struggled to collect his duds. Dr. Lewis guffawed like Teddy Roosevelt, and Roy and John and me laughed with him.

As Hughes ducked past us to the door, I saw the look in his eye. It was the look of a man that's humiliated, but determined not to let it show. It was a look I'd describe as dangerous, the look of a man who might do desperate things. That look sent a chill through me, but I kept laughing with the others. The little terrier ran into the room and yipped.

Beyond a certain point laughter has a life of its own. Laughter builds and builds on its own force. Laughter will forget what started it and go on for its own sake. Laughter is its own fuel and cause. Dr. Lewis looked at Hughes darting through the door and at each of us, and then he started laughing all over again, like he'd just remembered what tickled him in the first place, as if the situation was getting funnier by the second. He laughed so loud we had to laugh with him, getting a second wind. The terrier run around the room and yipped like it was going crazy.

Dr. Lewis turned back to his wife who'd clutched the sheets to her neck and pulled herself to the head of the bed. He stepped closer to her and pointed at her face and shook his head from side to side and laughed all that much harder. He turned away slightly, as if he couldn't stand to look at her, she tickled his funny bone so bad.

We stepped closer also, and kept laughing with the doctor. We couldn't stop laughing as long as he laughed. But I was beginning to wish I wasn't there, and that I wasn't laughing.

"You're going to be the death of me," the doctor said to his wife, wiping the tears from his cheek.

"Aren't you proud of yourself," Mrs. Lewis said.

Dr. Lewis kept laughing for a few seconds, and then he said, "You know, I *am* proud of myself."

"You swine!" Mrs. Lewis said.

Dr. Lewis pulled a handkerchief from his coat pocket and took off his glasses and wiped his eyes, and then busted out laughing again. When he stopped laughing he said, "These gentlemen are my witnesses. I never raised a hand against you or Mr. Hughes. And as the Lord is my witness, I caught you in the act." He laughed again.

I watched Mrs. Lewis's face. She started to say something and then decided not to. The look in her eyes was that of somebody who knows they have nothing to lose. The worst had happened and there was no reason to be afraid. It was like something firmed up and hardened inside her at that moment. She raised her chin and looked at her husband. "Aren't you the prince," she said. But her voice broke a little and lost the edge of contempt.

"Aren't you the princess," Dr. Lewis said.

With a slow, deliberate gesture, Mrs. Lewis tossed the sheet aside and stood up. In the firelight her skin looked rosy and young. Her figure was slender and beautiful. Looking her husband directly in the eye, she begun picking up her clothes, the petticoat and stockings on the floor. She ignored the rest of us and acted like she was calmly going about the business of gathering her clothes. We stepped back to give her room. I couldn't take my eyes off her and yet I wished I didn't have to look as she picked up the garter belt and blouse and lacy bloomers. The terrier danced around her feet.

John and Roy and me made way for Mrs. Lewis to leave the room. She walked by us like we weren't there. I heard a car start up in the yard and guessed it was Hughes's roadster. A door slammed down the hall.

"Shall we go into the parlor, gentlemen?" Dr. Lewis said. He was no longer laughing. But there was a smile on his lips, and his face was red as if he'd been straining to lift a great weight. We followed Dr. Lewis into the dark hallway. In a room nearby things crashed as if drawers were being opened and boxes thrown and keys dropped on the floor.

"Let's have a nice toddy to warm up," Dr. Lewis said. He led us into the living room where the fire strutted in the grate. I heard the little terrier yip somewhere in the house. My hands were cold from holding my wet hat. I stretched them out to the clean flames. There was a mirror over the fireplace and when I glanced in it I didn't recognize myself at first.

Just as Dr. Lewis brought us glasses of heated whiskey from the sideboard, his wife walked down the hall. She wore a coat and hat and was slipping on gloves. She walked slow, as if to show she wasn't scared. The little dog Fiddle followed her. We watched her open the door and scoop up the dog as she slipped out. The glass steamed in my hand.

"Gentlemen, I am in your debt," Dr. Lewis said. "Let's drink to friendship, and the future."

We raised our glasses in the firelight and said after him, "To friendship, and the future." I saw myself in the mirror again, but glanced away.

I listened for the sound of another car starting, or the hoofbeats of a horse outside, but there was only the crackle of the fire and the drip from the eaves. And through the window I saw the rain was beginning to turn to snow.

# HALCYON ACRES

FROM THE TIME she welcomed me at the door, it was clear Gloria knew what was going to happen, or it was clear she thought she knew what was going to happen. There was a boldness about the woman that was both scary and thrilling.

"I've been worried about you," she said, "all alone and still mourning." She had on a loose gold dress with flowers that shivered when she walked. And she wore several big bracelets on each arm. My wife Jean had never worn jewelry like that.

"I'd be OK if I could sleep," I said.

"You can," she said. She put on some low music, saxophone music, and brought in a tray with tea and honey and some nutty, raisiny cookies. The lights in her living room were low and hidden. When she sat down on the couch her slinky dress slid off one knee.

I'd never liked the taste of chamomile, but made up my mind to sip the tea politely and make agreeable conversation. I wanted Gloria to feel her tea and hospitality had been a success. I had no right to impose my sadness on her.

"Have a cookie," she said. "They're made from my special recipe."

I took a cookie and bit off one side. It was a very good cookie, buttery and nutty and chewy, with bits of raisin and chocolate, and honey that seeped out on the tongue. The taste was partly in the texture. There was subtlety in the mixture of flavors, a hint of salt with the honey.

"That's mighty good," I said. I took a sip of the tea and the flavor of the cookie on my tongue made the tea taste better. "That's a perfect combination," I said.

"It's one of my specialties," Gloria said and smiled. In the low lights she was beautiful, not much younger looking than her sixty-eight or seventy years, but beautiful. I hadn't noticed a woman in that way for months.

Gloria moved a little closer to me on the couch. The low music and the lights made me think of 1950s movies.

"I think you're trying to seduce me," I said.

"A lonely widow has to make the most of her opportunities," Gloria said.

Maybe it was my lack of sleep, or the emotional dimness I'd been living in since Jean died, or maybe it was the tea or something in the cookies, but suddenly I noticed the colors in the living room were more vivid and the lights were mellow as fruit. The flowers on Gloria's shivery dress seemed to flutter and sway, and the air in the room was warm and golden. I sipped the tea again and it tasted like wisdom from the east in warm drops on the tongue. I could hear blood humming behind my ears.

"I feel better," I said. My words sounded like they came from another part of the room, but were precise and firm.

"I knew you would," Gloria said. Her dress had slid back showing much of her leg. The limb was lightly tanned and smooth.

"Do you have all your neighbors over to tea?" I said.

"Only the ones I like," Gloria said. She slipped closer and laid her hand on my shoulder. Her hair smelled faintly of almonds.

"So this is my turn," I said.

"You're quite a catch," she said. She lifted my arm and put it around her.

"How so?" I said. She felt so strong and soft at the same time.

"Have you noticed how few men there are here?" she said, and put her cheek on my neck.

"There *are* a lot of women."

"Only twenty percent of Halcyon Acres residents are men," Gloria said, "and look at the shape most of them are in."

"I haven't really noticed," I said.

"I have," she said. We rested that way for a while. Holding her made me feel connected to things. She placed my hand on her breast. The nipple was hard.

"You are a prize," Gloria said.

"I don't feel like a prize," I said.

"You will when the ladies at Halcyon Acres are finished with you."

"You flatter me," I said. There was a prickle in my veins and a stirring in my lower belly.

"Not in the least," Gloria said. "Do you see any young men around here? Do you see many men as fit as you?"

"I've tried to take care of myself," I said.

"Indeed you have," she said and rubbed her hand across my chest.

"You mean there are affairs going on here at Halcyon Acres?"

"Not enough," Gloria said. "Too many lonely women and not enough men to go around."

"I never would have thought of that," I said.

"Men are such teases," Gloria said. She moved into my lap. I felt myself getting serious down there.

"And all I've seen is people playing shuffleboard and golf and riding bicycles," I said.

"Riding bicycles is good exercise," Gloria said. "Wouldn't you say?"

The air pulsed like a bass string as we led each other toward the bedroom. "You put something in those cookies," I said.

"They are my secret recipe," she said and slid off her dress. Her body was even younger than her face.

We made love as I had not in decades, hot, intense, giant, breathless love. Not the best kind of lovemaking, perhaps, because wasteful, but thrilling because I never thought I would do anything like that again. I'd assumed such a rush and crowding of passion were only a memory, and here I was in Florida reliving a rift of my youth, out of breath, urgent, soaring, hell-bent for relief.

THE SADDEST THING that ever happened to me was the death of my wife Jean. I'd just retired and sold my interest in the chain of suburban groceries around northern Indiana and bought the condo here, when Jean began to feel the pains in her hip. I thought maybe she'd torn something loose in all the work of moving. The moving was harder than either of us had dreamed. We'd lived in the same house for thirty-four years and become set in our ways. There's a lot of difference between going on a long vacation, and selling up and moving lock, stock, and cardboard box. But it had been the plan of our middle and late years to move to Florida where we would never have to shovel snow, and the condo outside Boca Raton seemed perfect for our lifestyle. We assumed we would have lots of sunset years. "I want to live where I can play golf on New Years Day," Jean said. Halcyon Acres had its own golf course on the grounds.

But after we got to Florida, the pains in Jean's hip wouldn't go away. She put a heating pad on it at night, and tried to ignore the throb by day. We took our clubs and played a round every afternoon, in the glorious winter sun. But Jean's face lost color and she started to limp. She tried to cover up the limp by walking slower, but the pain in her face could not be concealed.

"I think I must have broken something in there," she said.

When she finally conceded the pain was not going away and went to a doctor and took a series of tests, the news was the worst that could be: cancer in the hip and pelvic bones, cancer that had already begun to spread.

I don't need to tell you the rest. You know the plot: the regime of chemo, hair loss, the periods of recovery, radiation that left her exhausted, tumor counts, the waits, steady weight loss, the wonderful courage a woman has within her, the awful sight of her hip rotting away, the pain that requires self-administered morphine, the pain that even morphine can't reach, the giving in, the final kiss, and the end.

I decided to bury Jean in Florida where she'd wanted to end her days. I chose a graveyard not far from a golf course, where the stone would get both morning and afternoon sun. The children and grandchildren came down from Indiana for the funeral. It was a numbing three or four days.

"Pop, did Florida make Grandma sick?" my grandson Willy asked. His question suggested he'd heard one of his parents say something to that effect.

"Grandma started getting sick before she came to Florida," I said.

"You'll be returning home with us?" my daughter-in-law Margaret said.

"Maybe later," I said. "I'll have to think about it."

"You need to be closer to your family," my son Jason said.

AFTER THEY WERE gone and I had the apartment to myself, I tried to sleep. I knew the thing that would heal me would be sleep, wide, floating, nurturing sleep. I wanted Halcyon Acres to live up to its name. I needed calm and rest. I needed to forget the sight of Jean wasting away in pain, the sleepless nights, the drip of morphine.

But the more I pursued sleep the farther it fled from me. Sitting in front of the television I could feel slumber approach and the sweet fizz of numbness rise in my veins and limbs. But soon as I lay down in bed I was wide awake again, staring into the dark. Sleep was farther away than ever. I got up tired and went to bed again tired. Sleep would threaten to overtake me as I was sitting at the table or driving to the grocery store. But soon as I closed my eyes in bed sleep laughed at me and vanished into the tedium of time.

When I closed my eyes at night I saw Jean's hip eaten away. When I opened my eyes I saw the gray light of the bedroom and the wallpaper Jean had chosen. My son Jason advised me to take a cruise, a trip, or come home to Indiana for the summer and go to Georgian Bay with the family. But I knew my insomnia would travel with me. I didn't want to carry my sleeplessness long distances at great expense. Either I solved my problem where I was, where Jean had left me, or I wouldn't be able to solve it. That was clear to me.

I wooed sleep and coaxed sleep and tried to bribe sleep with exercise. I lured sleep with warm milk and pills and spoonfuls of honey. I tried to trap sleep in my thoughts, but it vanished through the walls of my skull as a ghost might. I humbled myself and begged sleep to come to me. I offered to go like a pilgrim on my knees over rocky miles to receive the absolution of slumber. Sleep whispered in my ear like a lover and then disappeared.

WHILE JEAN WAS SICK some of the neighbors had stopped by to ask about her. But we never had a chance to really get to know many people here. And after she died, several neighbors brought casseroles and desserts. But I had the impression the neighbors at Halcyon Acres were concentrating on health and living, and wanted to stay away from sickness and dying. And who could blame them? Most of the residents were in their seventies, and a few in their eighties. They had come to Florida to live, not to be sick and disabled.

In the weeks after Jean's death, I stayed away from the pool and recreation room, the golf course, and tennis and shuffleboard courts. It didn't seem right to impose my mourning on the other residents. Many ate in the cafeteria, where they snickered and gossiped till long after the meal was over. I fried eggs and warmed up chicken pot pies in the apartment, when I did feel like eating. I knew I should keep my grief to myself.

It was in the area of the mailboxes that you were most apt to meet people. Residents sometimes congregated there in the morning as the mail was put up around nine-thirty. And between nine-thirty and ten you would see almost everybody in the condo show up to check their mail and stand jawing in the lobby and corridor opposite the wall of mailboxes. Around the first of the month, when Social Security checks and pension checks came, there was more cheer and socializing than ever.

My closest neighbor was Gloria Swenson. She had visited Jean twice in her illness and brought a basket of fruit after the funeral. Gloria was a widow, like so many of my neighbors. But she had kept her figure and her brown hair. I hated the blue rinse so many of the women put on their hair. I usually went for my mail around ten-thirty, to avoid the earlier rush. But one morning in March I ran into Gloria in front of the mailboxes.

"Good morning, Raymond," she said. "Are you taking care of yourself?" She wore a yellow jogging suit, as though she had come in from a walk or bicycle ride. Many of the residents had three-wheel bikes they took into town or out to the park.

"I'm fine," I said.

Gloria looked at me, her eyes dark as chinquapins. "You look like you haven't slept in weeks," she said.

"I've had a little trouble getting shut-eye," I said.

"I'm not surprised," she said, "after what you've been through."

We walked back to our wing together and she asked me to come over after dinner that night for tea. "Chamomile will help you sleep," she said.

"Nothing will help me sleep," I said.

"I wouldn't bet on that," Gloria said.

All day I worried about going over to Gloria's apartment. I'd hardly seen anyone since Jean's death, and I hadn't been alone with another woman for years. I thought of phoning her with some excuse. Are you chicken? I said to myself. Yes, I'm chicken, I said to myself.

"That was *something*," I said to Gloria later in bed and wiped the sweat from my forehead.

"Glad you liked it, sir," Gloria said. She pushed up against me and rested her leg on top of mine. I felt I was floating in a river of chocolate soda water and the current was soaking through my skin into my veins and sweetening my blood all the way to the tips of my toes. I could see Jean standing on an island far out in the river. She was watching and smiling. I couldn't hear what she said, but knew she approved of what I was doing.

I must have slept four or five hours, for when I woke it was almost morning. Gloria was asleep beside me, but woke soon as I stirred.

"I've been asleep," I said.

"You're beautiful in your sleep," she said. "I could watch you for hours."

"You were right about the tea," I said.

"Home remedies are always best," she said.

I felt cleansed by the sleep, as though every cell in my body had been scrubbed and rubbed with lotion and was making a fresh start. And then an ugly thought hit me with a jolt. I must have jerked with the pain.

"What is it, baby?" Gloria said.

"We didn't take precaution," I said.

Gloria looked me in the eyes. "Well, I'm pretty sure you haven't slept with anybody but your wife in years," she said.

"That's true."

"And I've been very careful," Gloria said.

"I hope so."

"I have," she said.

We lay in the comfort of our tangled bodies. It was almost morning. I heard a garbage truck in the parking lot whine as it lifted a dumpster.

"But you must be careful from now on," Gloria said.

"What do you mean?"

"You don't think I think I can keep you all to myself?" Gloria said.

"Why not?" Gloria was a wonderful flatterer.

"The other girls will be all over you as soon as they hear."

"Hear what?" I said.

"That you're a lover," Gloria said. "And what a lover."

"I'm not going to tell them," I said.

"Oh yes you will," Gloria said. "You'll tell them by the way you walk into the clubhouse, and the way you flirt with them, and the way you ignore them sometimes."

"I never was promiscuous," I said.

"You're a rare commodity at Halcyon Acres," Gloria said, "a nice man with a hard dick, if you'll pardon my French."

"I prefer love," I said.

"So do I," Gloria said. "But most of us take what we can get. And you're going to get a lot."

"You astonish me."

"You've wandered into paradise, widow man," Gloria said, and kissed me on the lips and on the ear.

I didn't conquer my massive insomnia at once, but after I began seeing Gloria I started sleeping in wonderful snatches and patches. And because I was sleeping some, and was not numb, I began to work out in the gym two mornings a week. I got out my golf clubs and played a round with Gloria and a friend of hers named Rachel, and Rachel's husband Richard. Richard had owned a tire company in Cleveland, and we talked about the changes in business since the 1950s, mostly about tax laws and how they affected retail.

"Boys will always talk shop," Gloria said.

"What do girls always talk about?" I said.

"Wouldn't you like to know," Gloria said.

To play golf again was to discover its special rhythms, the drive and then the walk on the fairway, the waiting and watching and standing aside, the deferring to others, the tense pitching and the intense putting, the sunlight on the green and on the sand traps, the glitter of pines in the breeze and water surfaces stiffened by the breeze, the precision and luck of the putt. I began to play well on the sixth hole.

"What did you say your handicap was?" Richard said.

"Raymond was being modest," Gloria said.

One reason to love golf is that every hole is different, and each hole leads immediately to another, as one minute or hour leads to another. Golf is the metaphor for time, the time of a life. Suddenly I saw how much I wanted to play again, on and on, hole after hole, day after day. I was flushed with desire for play.

I'd read that a golf ball flies so far because of the little pits on its surface. The dimples break the resistance of the air. A smooth ball would not go half as far. I tried to think how they would have ever discovered such a thing. And the way a wedge would loft a ball to plop right on the green and hardly roll seemed almost a miracle.

"Raymond has been fooling us," Gloria said. "He was really a professional golfer before he retired."

IN THE CLUBHOUSE afterward we had gin and tonics and I met a number of the other residents of Halcyon Acres. Gloria had been telling the truth. There were few men around the place. In a room of two dozen residents there were maybe eight males, all my age or older.

But the mood was neither gloomy nor restrained. Women returning from their bicycle rides into town wore colorful scarves and straw hats and came to the bar for margaritas and whiskey sours. They embraced each other and called out to each other across the room. Some went around from table to table trading gossip and plans for bridge parties, trips into town for shopping.

Most stopped at our table, and I met Ann and Linda, Hortense and Martha, Prue and Florrie, and a small dark woman with huge brown eyes named Maria. Some put a hand on my shoulder and said they were sorry about Jean's death. Catherine Steele asked me if I liked bike riding. She said her late husband's bike was sitting in the storage room and I was welcome to use it. Dannie Purvis, who had been a professor of chemistry, asked if I played chess. And Theresa Thorne asked if I would like to join her book discussion group. I looked at Gloria and she winked at me.

The next day I got a call from Gloria. "I was wondering if you'd like to come over for dinner this evening," she said.

"That's mighty thoughtful of you."

"You don't have another date?" she said.

"Only with you."

"Then I'll expect you around seven," she said. "Do you like Chinese?"

"I'll eat anything."

At dinner Gloria told me she'd been a secretary who married her boss in Tulsa. He was twenty years her senior, and had died two years ago. Since he had a family with his first wife, most of his estate had gone to his children. What he'd left Gloria was the condo, and it was hers for life.

"I'll never have to leave," Gloria said as we sat down with our drinks before the picture window.

"Are you happy here?" I said.

"What is happy?" she said. She was wearing lavender pants and a lavender blouse that went perfectly with her hair. "I'd rather be doing things than be happy. I'm so busy I don't think about happy."

"Maybe I can learn from you," I said.

"Maybe."

Gloria was bold, but she didn't brag, and she didn't conceal her humble origins, or her luck in marrying Mr. Swenson. "I had to borrow a dress to graduate from high school," she said.

"I couldn't afford a class ring," I said.

"And now look at you."

The gin began to work on me, giving me that light, ethery feeling. I hadn't really enjoyed alcohol since before Jean got sick. I hadn't let myself enjoy it. We watched the sun set over the palm trees at the edge of the golf course.

WE WERE HAVING decaf and lime sherbet for dessert when the phone rang. "Must be a solicitor," Gloria said. But her face went pale when she answered. "Oh my god," she said.

"What is it?" I said.

She put the phone in its cradle, then quickly picked it up again and began dialing. "Send an ambulance to Halcyon Acres, apartment C-34," she said.

"What's wrong?" I said when she hung up.

"It's Richard. He's had another attack."

"What kind of attack?"

"Bad heart," Gloria said.

When we got to Rachel and Richard's apartment other neighbors were already there. Catherine Steele was holding Rachel away from the center of the living room where Richard lay on the shag floor. Dannie Purvis bent over Richard saying, "Just lie still." Richard's face was the color of wax paper, his temples wet with sweat.

"The ambulance is on its way," I said.

Rachel and Richard must have had people over for dinner, for the coffee table was heaped with plates and glasses, cups and saucers. A movie was running on the television and no one had thought to turn it off. Presents had been unwrapped and ribbons and paper lay on the floor.

I knelt down beside Richard. His body jerked in mild spasms, little seizures, and he stared straight at the ceiling. "The ambulance is coming, old boy," I said.

"Just lie still," Dannie said.

Richard kept jerking as if he was cold and couldn't stop. He ignored us and didn't seem to be in any pain. "Take it easy," I said and patted him on the shoulder.

When the ambulance attendants arrived they lifted Richard gently onto a stretcher and strapped him to the pad. Catherine Steele found Rachel's purse and she and Rachel followed the stretcher to the elevator.

After they were gone, I helped Gloria and Dannie gather up dishes and glasses and cups in the living room and carry them to the kitchen. We scraped everything into the disposal and loaded the dishwasher.

"Richard was so happy playing golf," Gloria said as we left the apartment.

"I'll call the hospital and let you know how he is," Dannie said.

I thought of all the tires Richard's company must have sold over the years, of the mountains of tires that must lie heaped in junkyards and landfills, vacant lots, and scattered as rubber dust along highways.

LATER IN BED, when Gloria got on top of me, she told me about the death of Mr. Swenson. He had had a bad heart and had been short of breath and short of temper. But after they'd moved to Halcyon Acres he had open-heart surgery, and the operation rejuvenated him, for a while. He exercised like a young man, and made love like a young man. "Like a young man that knows everything an old man knows," Gloria said.

She moved above me slowly. "Buster changed after he married me," she said.

"We all change when we fall in love," I said. "Love humbles us."

Gloria put her fingernails on my nipples. "And love gives us confidence," she said, "and slows down time."

"I wish I could make time run backwards," I said.

"You wouldn't want to go back," Gloria said.

"Probably not."

"I'm in love with the future," Gloria said.

"What does the future taste like?" I said.

"Open space with sunlight on wood and cool air, and a little savor of salt."

She leaned sideways so her hair fell on her shoulder, and the look on

28

her face was as serious as the expression of a woman sewing a colorful pattern in a quilt. And just then the phone rang.

"Don't answer it," Gloria said.

The phone rang again, searing the darkness. It's astonishing how much authority a ringing phone has.

"It might be about Richard," I said.

Gloria reached for the phone and said, "Hello." When she hung up she said Richard was dead.

"I must go sit with Rachel," she said.

"I'll make you some coffee," I said.

# THE CHURCH OF
# THE ASCENSION

I NEVER THOUGHT I'd see thirty naked grownups in an Episcopalian chapel. They huddled together and held each other, and some cried on others' shoulders. Some had cuts that were bleeding and most were smeared with mud from falling in ditches or the creek. An older woman panted and streamed with sweat, as though she might be having a heart attack.

"I demand that you do something," their leader, a bald, powerfully built man named Mr. Sherman, said. "I demand that you contact the authorities," he added, as though he blamed me for their predicament.

"First I must get you something to wear," I said. I had no special dislike of nudity, but I knew it would be better if they were all covered. I thought of the choir robes hanging in the vestry.

"Please call the police," Mr. Sherman said. When he jerked with the assertive request his masculine equipment jiggled. I tried not to look. I knew there were only sixteen choir robes hanging on their hooks. What could I use to cover the rest of the nude guests? Were there costumes left from the Christmas pageant? I'd have to go back to the rectory to gather some of my own clothes.

"First, I will find some clothes," I said.

"We don't need clothes, we need justice and protection," Mr. Sherman bellowed.

I didn't take time to explain to him that they were likely to be arrested by the county sheriff if found in a church, even an Episcopalian church, as naked as Adam and Eve in the Garden and no fig leaf in sight.

"We will take these savages to court!" Mr. Sherman shouted.

A young woman with freckles on her back broke into a sob by the altar, and another woman put her arms around her. I didn't want to look at their nakedness. Some faces were flushed and some were pale. The woman who was sweating so badly sat down on a pew, her face gray as cement.

"I should call an ambulance," I said.

"First get the police," Mr. Sherman said through clenched teeth.

Nothing I'd been taught at divinity school had prepared me for this particular challenge. Dr. Bowers, my mentor, and others, had warned me that I would need to counsel those in crises of faith and crises of health, those going through divorce, drug rehab, bankruptcy, loss of income. No one had suggested I would face a church full of panicked nudists, and a mob shouting outside for their blood.

I'd been warned that local Baptists and Pentecostals might not approve of a woman priest. But they didn't approve of Episcopalians in general, so I saw their disapproval as no special barrier to my ministry. I'd served as a deacon in Kentucky and West Virginia, and felt I knew the mountain people well enough. I understood how they feared outsiders, change, were threatened by the unfamiliar. Their country had been invaded by tourists and retirees. But most of my parishioners were those retirees from elsewhere, and summer folk, three doctors, a school principal, and a hip- pie-type who lived in a cabin on Callahan Mountain and produced poetry and organic vegetables.

"Will you please call the state police?" Mr. Sherman said in a cold, quiet voice. "I don't trust the local deputies."

The phone was in the tiny office to the right of the chancel. I was so distracted I didn't know which to do first, make the call or try to get the crowd of nudists dressed. I was glad that none of my communicants was there to see the mess that had dropped into my lap. I wondered how I would report this incident to the bishop.

I was about to run to the vestry to collect choir robes when there was another loud bang on the front door. It was a stout oak door which I'd painted red. As soon as the desperate nudists had poured inside I'd bolted it.

"Open this devil door," someone outside called.

A rock crashed through one of the small apostle windows in the rear of the church. Pieces of stained glass tinkled to the floor. I looked at Mr.

Sherman and knew he was right. I headed to the office to call the state
police barracks in Tryon.

IT WAS DURING my first month at the Church of the Ascension when I
heard about the nudist enclave on Panther Creek. I was serving sherry to
some of the older communicants at a get-acquainted gathering, and Mrs.
Prestwick, her blue hair perfectly coiffed above a deep purple tailored suit,
asked if I'd heard of Rainbow Acres.

"Is it a commune?" I said.

"Sort of," Mrs. Wilson said. She said it was a colony of nudists mostly
from Atlanta, who built the retreat here in the mountains to worship the
sun and meditate, eat only vegetables, and practice New Age religion. "Of
course I only know it by hearsay," she added.

"If they don't bother us we won't bother them," I said. I wanted to
be the kind of priest with a sense of humor.

"It's not the nudists I'm worried about," Mrs. Prestwick said. "It's the
locals." She said the local preachers had denounced Rainbow Acres from
their pulpits, and teenage boys had thrown firecrackers, snakes, and stink
bombs over the fence into the compound. A dead buzzard had been hung
on the gate outside Rainbow Acres.

Later I met Mr. Sherman by chance at the grocery store in Saluda. He
looked like a distinguished man, perhaps a lawyer or a surgeon, in his
Emory University sweatshirt and jogging pants. I thought he could be a
senator or governor. I asked him where the light bulbs might be, and then
introduced myself and invited him to the Church of the Ascension.

"We have our own fellowship," he said.

"Which denomination?" I said.

He described the life at Rainbow Acres as devoted to health and freedom, friendship, diversity, and mutual trust. I wished him well and told
him I was pleased to meet him.

It was both my duty and my pleasure to read the local newspaper. Each
morning I skimmed the accounts of weddings and arrests, the features
on the largest pumpkin grown in Polk County, the fight for zoning in the

32

Green River Cove, the opening of a new white water rafting camp. Twice I'd seen references to incidents at Rainbow Acres. Once there was a fire which Mr. Sherman suggested to reporters had been set by an arsonist. The fire department arrived too late to save the recreation building. Another time shots had been fired into the compound, perhaps by a hunter. There was to be an investigation, but I never read about the results. There were no indictments.

"YOU MUST come to the rescue of these people," I said to the sergeant who answered my call.

"What people, ma'am?" the trooper said.

"A group attacked by a mob."

"In Polk County?" the sergeant said.

"At Rainbow Acres," I said.

"Oh."

I knew the police were reluctant to get involved where voters' emotions were stirred up. It was lose-lose any way they considered it. And many of the troopers were themselves local boys, kin to those outside with flashlights, torches, guns, and clubs.

"They are gathered in my chapel," I said. "They're in real danger." I swallowed. It all seemed so hopeless and ridiculous as I looked through the door at Mr. Sherman watching me.

"Tell them to get the morons off us!" he shouted.

"The situation is serious," I said into the phone. I told the trooper again my name and the name of the church. I tried to think what would be most persuasive.

"They have broken a window," I said.

"The nudists?" the sergeant said.

"No, the vigilantes, the attackers."

"It may be thirty minutes before we can get there," the desk sergeant said.

I DIDN'T KNOW I wanted to be a priest until I was already married and divorced. I'd gone to law school, and had a job with a law firm. I had a husband who was fun to be with, who shared my love of architecture and history, and late night talk over herbal tea. I imagined we would have children, and buy a vacation home near the beach. My parents were fond of Jim. I thought I might someday run for office, put my ideas into action for my fellow man, as I liked to say pompously in my own mind. I saw my life unfolding to a plan.

It was not part of my plan to come back to the apartment one evening and find a note on the kitchen table, just a note on yellow paper. "Dear Karen," it said, "I must make a change in my life. I cannot go on this way. I will love you always, but I must have my freedom. Please understand."

My husband didn't say where he'd gone. He'd taken his clothes and the CD player and his golf clubs. I called his parents. I called his office. I called our friends the Wallaces. No one could or would tell me anything. "Perhaps he needs to be alone," his mother said.

"He's my husband," I said.

"You must be partly responsible," she said. She was the kind of mother who thought her boy could do no wrong. I cried for days, and when I called his office his secretary wouldn't put me through.

It was in the shocked aftermath of his leaving, when friends told me I would find another love, another apartment, another life, that I found my call to the ministry. Though raised a Presbyterian, I'd been an Episcopalian since I married. I'd been devout at times, thrilled by church music and architecture, by the poetry and drama of the *Book of Common Prayer*. But it had not occurred to me to be more than a communicant, more than a volunteer, more than a vestry woman, if you will. I was just a consumer of worship, and perhaps a modest giver of tithes and service.

I remember the morning I knew I wanted to be a priest. I sat down to coffee and toast, planning my day and the next week. I had to pay bills and arrange for the steps to the basement to be repaired. I looked at the paper and saw that tomorrow was the Third Sunday of Epiphany. The word Epiphany caught my attention. The word lifted and soared, in a luminous aura. And I thought: what a privilege to have another calendar, a map of days laid out beside the secular calendar. What a blessing to have

34

an alternate year within and around and above the regular weeks and months, to measure time by feasts and Ash Wednesday and Good Friday, by Ember Days and the Ascension. The year was enriched immeasurably, as were the days and hours, by matins and evensong and compline.

I saw what a wonderful inheritance the church calendar was. It transformed ordinary time into significant dates and occasions. It gave the flow of time drama and symbolic value. The words of Cranmer rang in my mind: "As it was in the beginning, is now and ever shall be, world without end." I'd heard them all my life, but now heard them as though for the first time.

And my next thought was that I wanted to share this gift with others. Instead of merely struggling to be independent, to work and fight my way ahead into the future, I saw I must also serve others, in a greater purpose than the merely personal, and the merely secular. I saw that the church and the love of Christ were the greatest romance I'd found. I saw that the church did not exclude the rest of life but embraced it, included it, informed and enriched the secular, the physical, the financial, the sexual, the intellectual and emotional. I saw that the church was about love, allied to human love and even sexual love.

I knew that I would be the poorer if I did not seize this opportunity. The choice was so obvious I almost felt guilty, selfish, in seizing upon it. Why had I not seen it before? Why had it taken the shock of my husband leaving to show me what I most wanted to do? I saw what a gift of self-knowledge I'd been given.

At the same time I knew there was no need to hurry. The goal was to serve as I went along. I would serve even while I was studying Latin and Greek, theology, and church history. The goal was to be of use, while indulging myself in the luxury of ecclesiastical history, while trying to write sermons. I could serve as a lay volunteer to the parish, the rescue mission, assist the chaplain at the hospital, the prison. I could visit the sick and the bereaved.

"The church is your new toy," a friend said when I told her of my decision.

"That may be true," I said. "But work is no less important just because it can be enjoyed."

I knew it would take me years to finish my studies, to be ordained as a deacon and then as a priest. I would relish every step and stage of what I called "the pilgrimage." The smallest act of kindness or learning was important. My ministry would not be just in the pulpit, but every hour of every day. It would be in my acts as much as in my words. I'd been shown and given a pearl of great price. I would not lose it or throw it away. I would not hide my talent or bury it. I'd been given a lamp and I would keep it trimmed. I saw that answering the call would not make my years easier, but would give them infinitely more meaning.

As SOON AS I put down the phone I gathered the choir robes and began handing them out to my guests. Many were reluctant to put on clothes designed for a sacred purpose.

"The cloth is harmless," I said to them.

"I'm not ashamed of my body," said a big blond man who looked as though he might be an athlete.

"Please put these on," I said. "The police will be more cooperative if you're dressed."

"We're not the law breakers," said a short woman with black hair and large breasts.

The old woman who was sweating so badly took a robe, but her eyes told me she was very ill indeed. She was almost certainly having a heart attack.

"Lie back on the bench here," I said. I helped her recline and spread a robe over her. And then I returned to the office and called 911 and asked for an ambulance.

There were still fourteen people who had nothing to wear. Someone pounded on the door with a rock or piece of metal.

"Episcopalians are the devil's helpers!" a voice cried out.

I saw that dashing to the rectory for more clothes was out of the question. With the mob of angry vigilantes gathered around the chapel I might well be attacked myself. I didn't want to give them a chance to do something they would later regret, when they'd calmed down. With time they might see reason.

I walked to the broken window and shouted through it, "Would you trespass upon a place of worship, neighbors?"

"This is a place of Satan worship," a voice called back.

"Your candles and smoke and silk robes are an abomination," a woman called out.

I looked at the stunned and frightened nudists gathered near the altar and sitting on the pews. One held the old lady's head in her lap. Never had I dreamed of finding myself in such an absurd predicament. I'd sought to show my neighbors I as one of them, a friend and a laborer in the Lord's vineyard, never mind the differences of service and denomination. My ministry was to all, not a select few. And yet the nudists, by rushing into my chapel, had made it appear I was their ally, or at least a fellow traveler to their eccentricity. But there was no question I must give them sanctuary from a lynch mob. And they might have taken the sanctuary anyway, with or without my permission.

"I'm not afraid of these grits," the big blond man said and picked up a candlestick from the altar and held it as though it was a club.

"Please put that down," I said. "The police will be here soon."

I hurried to the box in the vestry where the costumes for the Christmas pageant were kept. There was a white gown for an angel, with glittery wings attached, and three robes for Wise Men made of sateen. I found three more gowns for shepherds and the dress for Mary. I recalled that Allen Cantrell, who played Joseph, had brought his own bathrobe.

The young woman who got the angel gown put it on and shook her torso so the wings flapped. "Buffy, you were always an angel," the big blond man said.

Several of the group still had on no clothes. There was the cloth on the communion table, and my own cassock and surplice hanging on a hook in the office, by the back door. I'd forgotten the back door. I ran through the office and quickly locked the rear entrance.

As I hurried by the door of the restroom I saw a towel hanging on the rod. But it was a hand towel. It would take two pinned together to make even a loin cloth.

37

A woman rushed into the bathroom and closed the door and I heard her vomiting. Mr. Sherman stood outside the door and asked if she was OK.

"She is upset," I said.

He turned to me with fury in his eyes, as though I had accused her. "You don't need to tell me she's upset," he said. "You religious people are responsible for this kind of hate." He stopped, as though he could say more but chose not to.

I was going to observe that it was not Christianity that attacked people with dogs and clubs and shotguns, and that it was the church that had opened its doors for their protection. But it seemed better not to argue. A hound bayed outside, and another dog barked and clawed at the door. Something heavy hit the roof and rolled down the slates. I looked at my watch. It would be another fifteen minutes before the police arrived.

"How did they attack your compound?" I said to Mr. Sherman.

"They held a prayer meeting," he said.

"A prayer meeting?"

He described how two local preachers held a prayer vigil at the locked entrance to Rainbow Acres. They sang hymns and preached through a bullhorn, and members of the colony had taunted them back with their own bullhorn and hard rock music played full blast. Mr. Sherman had called the sheriff, but the sheriff said he had no authority to break up a prayer meeting, that the law guaranteed freedom of worship and the right to assemble. A patrol car was seen watching the events.

"I knew there was no help from local law enforcement," Mr. Sherman said.

The dueling with music and derision continued until someone in the crowd threw a large firecracker, or perhaps a stick of dynamite, over the wall. The big blond man, who had been a professional football player, stood on the wall and hurled a rock that hit one of the preachers in the chest. The minister fell off the truck bed, and after that the crowd went wild. They attacked the fence with pliers and wire cutters. They rammed a pickup truck against the main gate. They threw torches onto the roofs of buildings.

Luckily there was a back gate out of the compound, and the members fled through that into the woods, and found their way, as it grew dark, to the Church of the Ascension.

"This is a savage country," Mr. Sherman said through clenched teeth. To a neutral observer, looking at his dirty and half-dressed flock, there might have seemed some irony in his statement.

I PULLED the curtains off the walls of the office and gave them to four guests. And I handed my cassock to a heavy woman who had had a mastectomy. Only the tall blond man was left without any garment. He'd chivalrously passed all the clothes to others, and now he alone stood like Adam on the day of creation. I could not help but notice he was hung like a much smaller man. Perhaps his member was shrunken by anger.

"I will find something for you, sir," I said.

"Don't need your threads," he said.

Only then did I remember the hanging behind the altar. It was a kind of reredos of brocade and watered silk, an image of St. Cuthbert taken from an illuminated manuscript from Lindisfarne, the plain stylized face staring through huge eyes out of the dark at the congregation. It was perhaps the single finest thing in the church. Climbing on a chair I took the hanging off its hooks and handed it to the big blond athlete.

"Who is this dude" he said.

"St Cuthbert, the first Anglo-Saxon saint," I said.

"Looks like a junkie," the blond man said.

I didn't tell him that when the Norseman attacked Lindisfarne, three hundred years after his death, Cuthbert's body was carried by monks to the mainland of northern England and, according to legend, was found to be uncorrupted, as whole as on the day of his funeral.

"No!" someone screamed.

There was a flash at the rear of the church and I saw a fire where a coke bottle had been tossed through the broken apostle window and landed on the floor with a whoosh. Luckily the Molotov cocktail hit the stone floor and not the carpet. Flames leapt shoulder-high.

"Give me some water," Mr. Sherman called.

There was no water in the font, but there was water in the bathroom. But I couldn't think of anything to carry water in, unless it was the mop bucket in the basement. And then I saw the carafe of communion wine behind the altar, I hesitated for a moment. Could I pour out the blood of Christ on burning gasoline? It was only symbolic of the blood when consecrated in the act of communion, and besides, what was left was supposed to be poured out on the ground. I grabbed the carafe and spilled the contents on the burning pool, and for some reason thought of the libations in temples of antiquity, the pouring out of wine in honor of the pagan gods.

"Ooooogh, ooooogh," a hound bellowed just outside the window.

"I call on you to stop this devil worship," a voice yelled. I recognized the voice of Rev. Silas Pritchard, who had his own church and congregation two valleys over, the Green River Cove Full Gospel Tabernacle. I knew his voice from his radio program every weekday morning. I heard him as I listened for the weather and local news. "They'll bust hell wide open," was his favorite phrase. He liked to list those who would bust hell wide open, and his list included politicians, Methodists, scientists, Catholics, and even some Baptists. He had a great voice and personality. I envied his preaching ability.

"Preacher Pritchard," I called through the broken window. The hound bellowed again. I called Rev. Pritchard's name again.

"What does *she* want?" a woman said.

"Are you listening, Preacher Pritchard?" I called. In the dark all I could see outside were flashlights and torches.

"Yes, ma'am?" the preacher said.

"We are told to love one another, not attack one another," I said. "Is that not Christ's new commandment?"

"Yes, ma'am," Rev. Pritchard said. "And sometimes we show our love to children by punishing them, and by protecting them from Satan's forces, to save them from hell."

"Attacking unarmed people on their own property is not the Lord's work," I said.

"We was only witnessing to them," the preacher said.

"Then leave them alone," I said. "The police are coming."

"Ma'am, I'm afraid for you, locked in among those devil worshipers and whores," the reverend said.

"I believe in loving all God's creatures," I said.

"Looks bad, lady, you harboring infidels in your church."

"Burn them out," someone yelled.

Another rock crashed through the window and a piece of flying glass nicked my neck. A spot of blood appeared on my blouse.

"Come get me, you scum!" the big blond man shouted.

"The police will be here any moment," I said. I hoped nothing else would be broken. Our budget was stretched beyond its limits already. I tried to recall if our insurance covered acts of vandalism.

"This is how Christianity has always treated innovators," Mr. Sherman said, glaring at me. Wearing a curtain, he looked like a Roman senator in a toga. His bald head glistened in the light.

"I'm glad I was able to help you," I said, trying to keep all irony out of my voice.

"She's gone!" a woman cried on the front pew. I ran to her and saw the older woman lying there jerking faintly. Her eyes were closed and her face was the color of a wet napkin.

"Can we give her mouth to mouth?" I said.

"Only thing that would help would be a defibrillator," Mr. Sherman said. Several women began weeping, and some comforted each other. In the dim light the scene made me think of stories of the early church, of Christians huddled in caves and catacombs, hiding from Roman soldiers and angry mobs. It was an odd sense of deja vu.

"She died peacefully," I said.

"She died of fright," the woman holding the old one's hand said.

Some of the colonists were so scared they seemed in shock. One man sat in front of the altar with his legs crossed, in the posture of meditation. His eyes were closed and his lips moved slightly. Another rock hit the roof and rolled down the slates.

"Where are the police?" Mr. Sherman said.

I looked at my watch. It was 9:17, but I couldn't remember exactly when I'd called the state troopers. Had it been twenty minutes? Thirty minutes? "They should be here by now," I said.

"Did you really call them?" the woman with short black hair said.

"I beg your pardon," I said. "I know you've been upset and frightened."

The situation was hideous and getting worse. Nothing I'd studied or even heard of had prepared me for this crisis. My love of Cranmer's cadences, of the Great Litany, my admiration for the words of Lancelot Andrews and the embroidered prose of Jeremy Taylor, had not conditioned me for such an absurd mess. I'd merely taken the fleeing victims in, and yet had assumed responsibility for them. Now they seemed to blame me, as those outside blamed me.

"You will call the police again," Mr. Sherman said.

"I will try again," I said.

"No, I'll call myself this time," he said. "And then I'll call the U.S. Marshal or the FBI. We can't depend on any justice in this hick county."

As he stepped toward the office I yelled after him, "Call directory assistance."

They were banging on the front door with a pole or heavy instrument. I thought I heard wood cracking. If they broke down the oaken door it would cost two thousand dollars to replace it. If they did enough damage the church would be bankrupt. If the mob got inside there could be real human blood on the altar. And if someone was injured or killed the story would taint the Church of the Ascension for decades. It would always be a joke: nudists finding refuge, being wounded at the altar.

Someone screamed as another rock broke through the other apostle window in the back.

"You morons!" the blond man yelled and brandished the candlestick like a bat.

I stepped to the pulpit, as though it was my natural place. I thought of Silas Marner rushing to his loom in his grief, seeking his accustomed work. I stood behind the lectern and said in the strongest voice I could muster, "My friends and neighbors."

Some looked at me and some ignored me. I remembered that Emerson once said the test of a speaker should be his ability to quell a riot. Surely one test of a minister's ability was to comfort those afraid and injured.

"My friends and neighbors," I said again.

"Look at her," someone yelled.

"The police will be here shortly," I said. "In the meantime we must all be calm."

"And get beaten by neanderthals?" a man said.

"No one will beat you," I said. "The police will be here and escort you to safety." It was the first time I'd stood in a pulpit wearing slacks and a sweater. I was glad I didn't have my robes and surplice on.

"And we have your word for it," the heckler called again. I was being mocked in my own church by those I was trying to protect. And I was being accused by those outside of practicing Satanism.

"You are human beings and I want to help you," I said.

"That's big of you," the heckler said.

"And little of you," I said, my temper beginning to weaken.

"I called the fire department," Mr. Sherman said.

"That was wise," I said. But I remembered that the fire department was all volunteers, and some of those outside might well be members.

"We'll see how wise," Mr. Sherman said.

When another bottle came crashing through the window and spread flames near a pew, I ran to the bathroom and wet three hand towels, and threw them on top of the blaze.

Just then I heard a siren in the distance. I hoped it wasn't just a patrol car on the Interstate two miles away. The siren got louder, and then I noticed there were at least two sirens, coming seemingly from opposite directions. That would make sense if the police were approaching from the barracks down near Tryon, and the fire trucks coming from the station in Saluda.

Even the wet towels didn't put out the flames of the gasoline.

"Bring me more towels," I said.

One of the women brought me four more hand towels, but they were dry. I ran back to the sink to wet them.

"The Lord sees all and judges all," a voice said on a bullhorn outside.

With the last two towels I was able to smother the flames before they touched the pew or the carpet. The squeal of the sirens got louder. And the donkey horn of a fire truck brayed so loud it echoed off the mountains. The police were coming down the connector road from the Interstate, but the fire engine would be winding along the little county road from the village.

The woman who'd brought me the towels was shivering, probably more from excitement than from chill, for the evening was mild. I wished I had an extra sweater or cloak to throw over her shoulders. "They will be here soon," I said.

"We're grateful to you," the woman said. She was the only one of the group who had thanked me.

I'D BEEN IN the chapel office when they knocked on the door. I'm almost embarrassed to say it, but I was praying. I often, after a hard day, sat in the office at sunset, watching the evening's alchemy turn the mountaintops to gold. It was my favorite part of the day in those troubled times of my first parish. The parish was short of funds, and the membership falling off, and I was uncertain about how to reverse the trend. It was whispered that a woman priest had driven some away. We were too small a parish to have evensong except on Sunday. I'd poured myself a glass of sherry and prayed as I watched the fiery sky in the west.

The light behind the mountains seemed so big and close I felt I could reach out and touch it. I could step across the threshold into a vast and luminous world. It looked as though all eternity was just behind the ridge, and the ground in shadow was a transom to a glorious future. I prayed for guidance and confidence. I prayed for humility and compassion. I prayed for courage to prepare myself for the task of rebuilding. And I felt the firmness you sense when you're heard.

The knocking at the church door wrenched me away from my reverie. There were shouts and violent blows on the wood. I hurried to the entrance of the church and when I opened the door saw the frightened, breathless, dirty crowd of naked people. And I heard shouts and shots in the distance.

"The lunatics have attacked us," Mr. Sherman said.

"What lunatics?" I said. But I guessed all too quickly what must have happened, for just then men with guns and dogs emerged from the woods below the parking lot. A pickup truck roared up the drive and slid to a stop in the gravel. I was going to say to the group we needed to calm down and talk rationally. But then I saw a man step out of the truck holding a shotgun. I backed aside and said, "Come on in."

The nudists poured inside, and I stood at the door as the men with dogs and guns ran up to the steps.

"Won't do you no good to protect them heathens," one said.

"There must be some misunderstanding," I said.

"How low can you get, protecting infidels and Satan worshipers?" the first man drawled.

"Take your guns and dogs away from the chapel," I said.

"Either them heathens come out and leave this county peacefully, or we come in and get them," the second man said. "We don't want to hurt you, Miss Clemmons."

He reached for my arm to pull me aside, but I stepped back quickly and closed the door and locked it.

The flashing strobe lights on the police cars and fire trucks threw their crazy dance on the windows, and through the broken windows onto the walls inside. There was a loud knock and someone yelled for me to open up.

"I'll handle this," Mr. Sherman said, and brushed past me to the door.

The officer who stood on the steps wore a uniform so starched it looked like Teflon. He was weighted down with badges and holsters, handcuffs and radio on his collarbone. Another officer stood behind him, and I saw most of the local people had stepped back into the shadows. Only Preacher Pritchard had stood his ground.

"We were driven from our private property," Mr. Sherman said. "I want you to arrest these hooligans for trespassing."

"Looks like you all are the ones trespassing here," the officer said.

"I let them enter the church," I said, "for their own protection."

"Is there any law in these woods?" Mr. Sherman said.

"Sir, I know you're upset," the officer said. He took a tablet out of his pocket and stepped inside the church. When he saw the crowd in choir robes and pageant costumes and curtains he shook his head.

"Tell me how this started," the officer said.

45

"We were attacked with guns and firecrackers, bullhorns," Mr. Sherman said. "One of our members has died." He led the officer to the front pew where the old woman lay with her head in the lap of her friend.

The officer called out to his associates to bring a stretcher. I hadn't seen the ambulance behind the fire truck, but the attendants rushed in with a stretcher and took the old woman away. Her face quivered like jello as they rolled her over the stone floor.

As the ambulance squealed away from the parking lot the nudists crowded around the officer, several talking at once. The policeman stopped them and asked them to speak one at a time. He began to write down notes, and it got quiet outside. After he'd written down a page of comments the officer asked me if I would like to make a complaint or file charges.

"These people were desperate and I wanted to help them," I said.

"Aren't you going to arrest these thugs?" Mr. Sherman said. "They must be charged with murder."

"You are free to file charges in county court," the officer said. I admired his calm. He acted as if someone had lost a wallet, or a fender had been nicked.

"We will file federal charges," Mr. Sherman said. "Our civil rights have been violated."

The trooper nodded and closed his tablet. When he opened the door the fire truck lights and police car lights were still revolving in the yard. But Preacher Pritchard was the only one of his flock still in sight. The rest seemed to have melted back into the woods.

"Do you know the names of your attackers?" the officer said to Mr. Sherman.

"You can put my name down," the preacher said. "I ain't ashamed of fighting the forces of the devil and the Antichrist." He glared at me as though I was the lowest worm, a traitor to the gospel, the poorest excuse for a minister and disciple since Judas.

"We will prosecute you to the full extent of the law," the big blond man said to the preacher.

"The cowards have slunk back into the shadows," Mr. Sherman said.

After a lot of starting and stopping, snarling and accusing, it was agreed that the colonists would ride in the police cars and on the fire trucks back to Rainbow Acres, and that a trooper would stay at the gate of their compound the rest of the night. The nudists would press charges in the county court, and I would go down and make a deposition the next day. They would bring the choir robes and costumes and curtains back tomorrow morning. The Reverend Pritchard watched them file out of the church and climb into the vehicles. The wings on the angel costume flapped as the girl climbed up on a fire engine.

"The devil has his fallen angels," the preacher said.

"You imbecile redneck!" the big blond man hissed at him.

WHEN THEY WERE all loaded up in the fire trucks and police cars, I watched the vehicles turn in the parking lot and drive back down the road. I closed the door and saw the mess in the church. Broken glass, burned towels, spilled wine and water covered the floor. Mud had been tracked over the aisle carpet and there was vomit on the floor near the bathroom. The altar was bare and the communion table bare. My sherry glass still sat on the desk in the study, a pupil of liquid in the bottom.

The church is a shambles, I said to myself. I didn't want to even try to make sense of what had happened that evening. It would be days, weeks, maybe years before I could see the consequences of what I'd done and what had been done to the church. I was exhausted by the dangerous farce, the absurdity, the surreal invasion of the sanctuary. I sat down on a pew and looked at the mess around the altar. The spot of blood had dried on my blouse.

"Don't imagine the church is a refuge from the world," my mentor at Sewanee had said. "The church is not a cloister or asylum. The living church is in the middle of the world and of the world. The church is a human institution as well as a divine one. The only way out of the world is through the world. Our business is not avoidance but participation, the testimony of our acts, the example of ourselves. Where we touch the pain around us we find the work most needed."

I'd been drawn to the church partly because I loved the traditions, the words said by millions for centuries, the practice of humility and compassion. I loved the architecture and the cloth, the music and the candle flame. And I loved the faith that went hand in hand with work. But I saw I had a lot to learn about myself, as well as about my use to the world. And I saw that much of my learning would be forced on me, not chosen.

I rested a few minutes, and then took the broom and dustpan from the closet and began to sweep up the broken glass. I'd have to find some plastic in the rectory to tape over the broken windows. As I worked I began to compose in my mind a letter to the bishop describing the events of the evening.

# BIRD WARS

WHEN MATTY SAW the first dead blackbird under the walnut tree she thought nothing of it. There was talk that birds were being killed by pesticides and this might be the victim of all the bean dust and orchard spray used in the valley. She'd seen a news program on TV about all the damage to wildlife from the poisons put on weeds and crops, and had just read in the paper about the balsams dying on the tops of the high mountains from acid rain.

The grass and weeds under the walnut tree were lush in the shade and from the recent rains. You wouldn't think they would grow so thick under the tree, but the ground was deep in crabgrass and ragweed. Of course this used to be the chicken yard, thirty years ago when she still kept chickens, before she went to work in the new instrument plant, and the soil must still be rich. Every time she took a step her foot seemed to turn on a walnut buried in the grass thatch from last year. She hadn't had time for years to gather and crack them for cakes and cookies, the way she did when the children were growing up.

The special thing about the old chicken yard was the way a mulberry tree had volunteered and grown right up into the branches of the walnut. Most trees wouldn't grow in the shade of a black walnut, but the mulberry had thrived there, almost unnoticed, until it reached into the limbs of the walnut and mingled its branches with those of the nut tree. Now they seemed meshed and mutually supporting, walnut leaves among the mulberry leaves crowding to the light.

It was a paradise for squirrels in the fall and birds in summer. The trees were filled in the hot months with the songs of birds feasting on the berries. It was thrilling just to hear the chatter and chiming. But as you got close to the trees you realized many of the birds were fighting, threatening and chasing each other away from the ripe harvest. They fought

49

over clusters and twigs, over sections, over hemispheres of the trees, some-times flying out and circling in a chase like tiny Spitfires and Messer-schmitts diving sideways and chattering their threats. You would have thought they had nests in the trees to protect, or that they had chosen sides according to their different colors.

Right beside the base of the mulberry Matty saw a goldfinch, its chest feathers torn away. Had the quarreling over the fruit got so rough the birds were actually killing each other? Had the cat gotten into the tree? Or a blacksnake? A blacksnake would certainly have eaten the birds, not left them to rot. And then she saw another blackbird in the weeds by the old chicken house. Bending closer she adjusted her glasses and saw the blood on its breast. It must have been shot.

At almost the same instant she remembered that her sister's grandson, Willard, had gotten a new rifle for his birthday.

Not wanting to accuse anyone falsely, she talked it over back at the house with Art who said he'd heard shots just the day before. Matty felt a coldness in her arms and in her stomach. Jerry, Willard's father, had had so much trouble since his wife left him, and with a lawsuit over property, that she didn't want to burden him with yet another worry. And Willard's grandmother, Matty's sister Alice, was recovering from a stroke in the nursing home, and it would not be fair to involve her in whatever mischief Willard had done. Matty would have to be careful. She would listen for any more shots and talk to Willard herself.

"You be careful with him," Art said. "He's just a boy but he's bitter after the divorce. And he's took all them lessons in karate and thinks about nothing but his bow and arrow and now his rifle."

"He's still our kin."

NEXT MORNING while she rinsed and dried the breakfast dishes she heard shots coming from the old place. Not loud reports, but more like puffs and hammer blows. Tying her house robe more securely she rushed out-side, and once she reached the field above the garden she heard the shots distinctly, coming from the walnut tree. She hurried across the dew-heavy grass, getting her slippers soaked.

Willard was standing under the mulberry tree aiming straight up.

"Why on earth are you shooting the birds?" She tried to keep her voice calm.

He whirled around but didn't point the rifle at her.

"The birds are our friends, Willard. They eat insects and sing for us."

"I'm just target practicing," he said. "Moving targets."

"There must be something better than birds to practice on. Besides, it's illegal to kill songbirds."

He didn't answer her again. And she walked back to the house getting her feet even wetter.

The next day she found two more dead birds on the road bank below the walnut tree, this time a wheatbird and a mockingbird.

"I'm going to have to call Jerry," she told Art.

"I'd go ahead and call the law. That boy's dangerous with all his karate and study on killing."

"He's still family."

MATTY CALLED JERRY that evening after he got home from work. The first time she dialed there was no answer. And then she saw Jerry's Camaro pass and knew he'd taken Willard and the younger children out to Mc-Donald's for supper. When she finally reached him later Jerry said, "I keep telling him not to kill birds. But he's a big boy and I'm not here to watch him."

"Well Art's awfully worried about his birds. I'm afraid he'll have a heart attack."

AFTER THE CALL MATTY felt as though she'd accomplished nothing. She sat on the porch with Art and watched the mist rise from the spring hollows on the mountain, in places where the hollows were otherwise impossible to see. They had sat on the porch on summer evenings ever since the children were little, after the milking was done and the eggs gathered.

When Rachel and Johnny were growing up they used to sing, as the mist rose off the creek and out of the folds of the mountain. The air was cool coming up the valley, after a long work day in the beanfields. Just at dark the whippoorwills would start calling from the pines down at the end of the pasture. The whippoorwills had disappeared years ago, killed by crop dust it was said. Because of his heart Art hadn't put in a crop for several years, but he kept a nursery of pines and hemlocks and boxwoods. Every two or three weeks he mowed out the shrubbery with the garden tractor.

The evening stillness was broken by the buzz of a hornet. They looked around the porch and saw no insects. There was not even a hummingbird around the feeder.

"Where is that thing?" Matty said. "They must have built in the ceiling where I saw one go into a hole."

But even as she spoke the sound grew louder and broke into a deep roar, and she realized it was coming from a distance. Art adjusted his hearing aid and leaned over the porch railing. Matty recognized the sound was coming from around the hill toward Jerry's house. And then they both saw the motorcycle emerge from the trees behind the barn and sweep into the field of white pines. Willard was riding it, leaning low over the handlebars. In the late sun the cycle spurted blue smoke that hung in a tattered trail behind him as he raced up and down the rows Art had kept mowed. The noise was harsh as twenty chainsaws, grating the air and echoing off the ridge, filling the valley end to end.

"Where you reckon he got that?" Art said.

"His daddy bought it on credit like everything else, I'd guess."

"That boy's a criminal; you mark my word."

"He's just a boy, not halfway raised."

"He better stay out of my pines. That's all I can say."

The motorcycle continued its laps across the field. Willard took off from one end and accelerated in a blast of smoke and popping barks until near the other end where he braked and slid sideways on the dew-wet grass, coming to a stop already turned around to head back down the next row. He was threading every middle of the two acre field, running like a shuttle back and forth as the evening advanced. It was after dark when the engine coughed out.

"I never thought that boy had over half sense," Art said as they went inside.

"Well he's our blood kin, however much sense he has."

NEXT MORNING ART found only three little pines had been broken by the motorcycle, all near the ends of rows where Willard had skidded into his turn. "I expected worse," he said.

"At ten dollars a tree that's still thirty dollars," Matty said. "I'll just have to call Jerry again."

That afternoon when Matty called, Jerry said he didn't think Willard had damaged any trees, but he would tell him to stay out of the nursery. "He's awfully careful," Jerry said before hanging up.

They'd not finished supper when they heard the buzz again. Art fiddled with his hearing aid as they walked out to the porch. There was no sign of the motorcycle in the nursery field. The noise grew louder, then waned, and revved again. They looked from the barn to the garden to the creek road. Suddenly the bike burst out of the pines in the far pasture and shot up the hill. As the slope got steeper it slowed, roaring and smoking, and came to a stop just below the brow. The cycle turned over and both it and Willard rolled over a few times. But in seconds he was back on and coasting down to level ground.

Again and again Willard roared up the hillside. Even from the porch they could see the red clay scars where the grass had been torn away by the tires.

"That'll wash away in no time," Art said.

In the distance through the evening air the machine sounded like a maddened gnat bashing itself on the hill, swooping up and then down. They could see the smoke boil up and the bike start moving, before the sound of the revving motor reached them.

"He's angry because his mama's gone and left him," Matty said. "I hate to think of somebody that unhappy."

"He unbalanced."

"He may outgrow it," Matty said.

"The pasture may not if it comes a big rain. I've a good mind to go over there and put a stop to it," Art said.

"You'll do no such thing."

"That boy will end up in the pen."

Art turned down his hearing aid and went inside. Matty was worried about the way he walked lately, as though his legs were uncoordinated with his upper body, giving him an odd twist and lurch as he took his steps. Had he had a light stroke? He'd turned eighty-five in February. She worried that she might die before him, and then who would take care of Art? He'd never been able to look after money, and the children had their own lives so far away. She thought of Art in a nursing home, ignored and lonely on a long hall smelling of urine and rubbing alcohol.

THE NEXT MONDAY was check day, the third of the month. They drove to the post office where many other older people also waited in their cars and pickups for the mail truck to arrive with their Social Security checks. They could wait a few more hours for delivery to their mailboxes, but then it would be too late to drive up town, go to the bank, and have lunch at the cafeteria in the mall. Margery the mail clerk would oblige them by giving them their checks as soon as they arrived.

"I hear that McCall boy has been tearing up your field and pasture with his motorcycle," Willis Stamey said quietly from his pickup parked next to Art and Matty.

"He's just a boy," Matty said.

"I hear he's going into the Marines," Willis said.

Matty hoped it was true. It would be such a relief if Willard went away.

After they'd driven to town, cashed their checks, eaten lunch at the mall, and bought groceries, Matty drove home. She stopped by the barn to leave a bag of sidedressing for the garden in the shed. Willard and another boy were standing under the walnut tree as she drove around the curve by the arborvitae. When he saw the car the other boy ran off through the field, but Willard stood his ground, gun in hand.

Matty rattled her car keys as she walked up the bank toward him.

54

"Willard, what do you think you're doing? We've asked you not to kill birds and here you are again."

"We wasn't shooting birds. We was just target practicing. And this is not even a gun; it's just an air rifle."

Sure enough, she could tell from the size of the barrel it was not a .22, but a pellet gun. It looked almost like a toy.

"Well we don't want any trouble; we want to get along," Matty said.

Willard followed the other boy through the field, the air rifle on his shoulder. She watched him disappear into the woods, and had started back to the car when she saw the mockingbird under the hawthorn bush. Looking closer, she saw there were four or five other birds there, of different colors and sizes, pushed back almost out of sight.

"I'm not going to call the law," she said to Art. "I'm not going to call the law on kinfolks."

"That boy needs a whipping."

"He needs his daddy to discipline him."

"I just might do it myself," Art said.

"You'll do no such thing."

MATTY DID NOT CALL Jerry again. She thought about it all day and decided it would do no good. She wondered if there was any truth to Willis's rumor that Willard was joining the Marines. If only it was so. It would be a blessing for her and Art to have a little peace in their old age. But Willard must be too young to join up. Maybe Jerry had signed for him. Or maybe he'd lied about his age.

A day later they heard the popping of the motorcycle on the mountain behind the house. There was a trail over the ridge and down by the chicken yard that also led from the field on the north side of the mountain. The field had long since grown up in poplars but the trail was still used by hunters and dogs and anyone climbing the ridge. Because the path threaded through the trees and rhododendrons around the steepest part of the slope it had not washed away, but drifted full of leaves each fall and then was packed by the intermittent traffic.

Again they had trouble at first placing the source of the racket. Matty was just finishing the dishes when she saw Art start from his chair on the porch. He looked around the horizon as though scanning the sky for a crop duster or helicopter. Once she got out to the porch she understood the difficulty of locating the noise. The roar and crackle seemed to come from the ground itself and then from the sky, and again from the trees across the valley. They looked down into the shrubbery patch, and over to the pasture hill. It was as though something was on fire but they couldn't see the flames.

Gradually she realized the motorcycle was on the mountain behind the house. That was why the noise seemed to be in the tops of the trees. The engine was roaring on the straight places, then quieting on the turns and drops in the trail.

"What will that fool think of next?" Art said.

It sounded as though the motorcycle was coming right down through the trees onto the top of the house. Then the machine flashed out of the trees beside the chicken house, and smoked along the garden edge toward the barn.

"Well ain't this a pretty come off," Art said.

There was an uproar inside the chicken house. The hens, which settled down clucking on the roost poles as dark approached, were cackling and flogging around as though ten foxes were among them.

"We won't get no eggs for a week," Art said. He usually gathered the eggs from the pinestraw nests after supper as the chickens were settling down for the evening. They were used to his coming in, and though they might protest with a cackle when he pushed one aside to get her eggs, they soon quieted. Now they would be upset most of the night.

But even as Matty and Art stood listening to the hens in their pandemonium, they heard the motorcycle ascending the ridge again and coming around the slope with its hysterical chatter. Art hurried in his lurching gait toward the chicken house, and Matty followed him.

As the awful sound increased, working nearer through the trees, Matty wondered what they could possibly do, just standing there by the chicken house. Willard burst out of the trees, and Art stepped into the path. Whether he was trying to flag Willard down to talk, or strike the helmeted rider, Art himself probably did not know; but he reached out toward the figure as it blasted past in a gesture like a wave. Perhaps surprised by seeing Matty and Art beside the chicken house, and thinking the gesture a blow, Willard jerked the motorcycle aside and went into a skid on the damp grass. The engine kept revving though the wheels left the ground as he slid sideways and around on his leg, finally coming to a stop a few hundred feet below in the weeds at the edge of the garden. The engine coughed out and there was no movement from the rider.

Matty and Art walked toward the overturned machine. But before they reached him Willard wrestled himself up, righted the cycle, and began pushing it across the garden, through rows of tomatoes, squash, and okra.

"We didn't mean for you to get hurt," Matty called.

But Willard didn't look around or answer. He kept walking the motorcycle through the vegetables, trampling and knocking down row after row.

"Well ain't this a pretty come off," Art said again, and twisted the little knob on his hearing aid. Almost as soon as they reached the house Matty heard the phone, and out of breath she answered it.

"I never thought you'd try to hurt Willard," Jerry said.

"We didn't…"

"I'm taking him to the doctor and if his leg's broke it will be your fault. As if I didn't have enough worry already." The phone clicked. As Matty hung up she could still hear the racket in the henhouse, though it was almost dark.

MATTY DIDN'T SLEEP much that night, or the next. She didn't understand how things worked anymore. The elements of her life, of family and community, had been twisted and would not return to their familiar patterns. The ties of fellowship and work were gone. Art thought of nothing, and talked of nothing, except Willard and his doings, even while watching television.

"I always said he wasn't normal."

"He would be normal if he'd been half raised," Matty said.

"From the time he was a kid you could tell he was unbalanced."

"Oh hush up. He's as normal as anybody, except he's angry his mama's gone."

On the third evening, as they sat on the porch, they heard the motorcycle again. Matty was relieved that Willard must not have broken his leg. The snore grew louder as it came popping along from the direction of Jerry's house. Willard turned off into the weeds along the garden and came roaring across the field into their driveway. Instead of going on up the mountain trail he slid to a stop in the gravel and sat there, both feet on the ground, revving the engine. Smoke boiled up around the machine and drifted across the yard smelling of burnt oil. He beeped the little horn on the handlebars, and gunned the motor again, looking straight at them.

"I'll get a baseball bat and run him off the place," Art said.

"You'll do no such thing," Matty said.

"I ain't afraid of him."

"You come in the house with me. Let him go." Matty took Art by the arm and practically pulled him back into the livingroom. Art was shaking.

"Nobody's going to come and insult me in my own yard," he said.

"Just calm down; I'll get your heart pills."

The windows rattled as Willard gave the motorcycle gas and let off, juiced it and let off. He beeped every third or fourth rev.

Art was shaking so she dared not let go of him, even to get the pills from the kitchen. She was afraid he might lunge out into the yard. After what might have been minutes but seemed like hours Willard backed the motorcycle around and roared down the driveway and out the road. Art was flushed and shivering as she handed him a glass of water and a pill.

THE NEXT AFTERNOON they drove to town for groceries. It was Friday and the Community Cash store was crowded as Matty pushed her cart into the close aisles. Art always stayed in the car while she bought the groceries. If brought inside he'd try to choose the most salty and fattening items, so she made sure he remained in the car. She was deciding whether or not to get a picnic ham when she saw Jerry turn into the aisle at the other end. Matty wanted to back away and get out of the store, but Jerry had probably already seen her. She would not let her own nephew think she was afraid of him. And this might be as good a time as any to have it out with him. Matty placed the ham on the upper rack of the cart and pushed ahead, tightening her stomach muscles to keep panic down. Jerry had apparently not seen her, or at least acted preoccupied with choosing a can of coffee.

"Listen, Jerry," she said. He turned in surprise and blushed slightly. He was wearing a wide western belt and a T-shirt cut off at the midriff showing his weightlifter's muscles.

"Listen, Jerry, I never wanted no trouble in the family."

"We don't want any trouble either," Jerry said, putting the coffee back.

"And we didn't want Willard to get hurt."

"He's OK, except for some bruises."

"I'm glad to hear it." Matty felt sweat accumulating in her armpits. "Art has been so worried over this I've been afraid he'd have another heart attack."

"Willard's joining the Marines; that's what he came out to tell you all last night. But you wouldn't talk to him."

"He just set there in the yard roaring his engine and beeping that little horn."

"He was too shy to come in."

"We wish him well in the service."

"I think it'll be good for him," Jerry said.

"You all come see us," they said to each other as they parted and continued shopping.

Matty felt weightless as she pushed down the other aisles, stopping and selecting almost unconsciously. She felt easier than she had in weeks as she paid the cashier and led the grocery boy to the car. Art got out to help her load the bags in the trunk. When she told Art about her meeting with Jerry he said, "That boy needs discipline if anybody ever did."

"It will all turn out OK; blood is thicker than water."

They stopped to eat an early supper, as they always did on Fridays, at the cafeteria in the mall. For once she let Art pick the steak and onions that he liked, and the strawberry shortcake with whipped cream he was not supposed to have. They might as well celebrate once in a while. She herself indulged in French fries and chocolate pie, along with chopped steak. They saw several of their friends in the cafeteria, and everybody seemed to be feeling neighborly.

AFTER SHE TOOK the groceries to the house Matty drove on down to the barn to leave the rye seed in the shed. They were going to sow a cover on the garden for the winter. It was a fifty pound bag, and it took both her and Art to lift it out of the trunk and drag it across the weeds into the shed. At one time Art had been able to lift two two-hundred pound bags of fertilizer and carry them, one under each arm. It was near dark, but as she closed the car trunk she saw something on the bank under the walnut and mulberry trees. It looked like empty feed sacks or fertilizer bags thrown there. "Who could have left them there?" she said. Jangling her keys she climbed the bank by the hawthorn, watching her footing in the weak light, on the damp grass. She was right over them before she recognized the row of dead birds. There must have been dozens, sixty, seventy, a hundred, lying in the wet evening weeds, redbirds, robins, blackbirds, mockingbirds, sparrows, wrens, bluebirds, joreets, a meadowlark, and a rare indigo bunting. Even in the failing light she could make out the colors, the yellows besides the blacks, the oranges, and mottled grays, and iridescent blues. The bodies were stacked neatly as kindling wood.

# THE DULCIMER MAKER

THE BABY SYLVIA had run a temperature for two days, and in the August heat her little body seemed to glow red hot. Her mother Annie had not been worried at first; after all, babies often had fevers. Sylvia was now more than a year old and had had several infections in her short life. But this time the fever wouldn't go away, even when she crushed baby aspirin in a spoon and mixed it with juice in Sylvia's bottle. The baby had cooled off a little in the early morning, but as noon approached the little girl's skin burned hot as the top of a stove. Annie took her temperature again and saw the red ink in the vein touch 105 degrees. It was time to take her child to the doctor.

The problem was that Annie and her husband Frank lived far out in the country and had neither car nor pickup truck. Town was ten miles away, and in the years after the war doctors had quit making house calls out in the county. Frank farmed a little on their land along the creek, and sometimes did carpentry and masonry. But what he did mostly was make fine mountain dulcimers from maple wood and ash and walnut. He was the best dulcimer maker in the region. He made instruments for local musicians and for tourists. And sometimes he got orders from as far away as New York City for his uniquely crafted dulcimers.

But Frank had never made much money from his craft because it took so long to fashion each instrument. Every dulcimer was made somewhat differently, with its own design and combination of woods, and each had slightly different shape and tone. "A good dulcimer is like a person," Frank liked to say. "Each one has its own personality." Frank said he never made two instruments alike, and he had no intention of doing so now. Because it sometimes took him weeks or even months to find the right wood and the perfect shape and size, he produced few examples. And more than once he'd refused to sell an instrument he especially liked. "I don't feel to

61

sell this one," he'd say, and place it on a shelf in his shop, to be taken down and played when visitors came on a Saturday or Sunday afternoon.

Annie had to rely on her brother-in-law Cyrus or her brother Edward, who did have trucks, to take her to town, when she could get them to take her. If they were going already to the feed store or to sell chickens or produce, she got to ride along. They were usually too busy with their own farming to carry her to town otherwise. Before Sylvia was born Annie had sometimes started walking along the road to town, and had been offered a ride by a neighbor or even a stranger. Other times she caught the bus from the store on the highway a mile away.

Annie changed Sylvia's diaper and powdered her red splotchy skin to prevent rash in the summer heat. She pulled a clean gown on the little girl and wrapped her in a light blanket. Annie put on a fresh dress herself, changed her shoes, washed her face and combed her hair, and then grabbed her purse. She knew there was exactly $3.47 in her pocketbook, enough for bus fare to town and back. Maybe the doctor would wait to be paid later.

Stepping out into the August heat, Annie carried Sylvia to the door of the shed in the back yard which served as Frank's workshop. He was sanding a long strip of maple wood which he would bend to make the sides of a dulcimer. He caressed the wood as if it was a lover's body. It was wood from an old table that had belonged to his grandma. He believed this instrument was going to be special.

"I'm taking Sylvia to the doctor," Annie said.

Frank didn't look up from his work. "Is that really necessary?" he said.

Annie looked around the shed cluttered with planks and shavings, tools, and boxes, and the fine varnished dulcimers on the shelf that Frank would not sell. "Her fever is 105."

Frank took up an oil cloth and rubbed the smooth maple wood. The strip shone as if it had lights inside the grain. "I think she's just got the whooping cough," he said.

"Whooping cough don't last five days," Annie said. Turning away from the shed door she looked into the woods that were loud with jar-flies. Every limb of every oak tree and poplar seemed to shrill out with cicadas making their love calls. There was no use to talk to Frank, since he didn't have a car or truck. She'd only meant to tell him what she was doing, hoping for his approval and support. Without looking back she strode across the yard, as her husband continued to stroke the smooth wood, making a deeper shine.

As Annie came out of the trees into the road sunlight blinded her. The air was luminous and late summer haze hung like chalk dust over the tops of the mountains. With both hands around Sylvia she couldn't shade her eyes. Grasshoppers and crickets clicked and chiseled in the dusty weeds along the road. Annie stepped carefully on rocks that rolled like balls under her feet. She turned aside to follow the fence up to her brother-in-law's pole bean field on the hill above the pasture. Her brother-in-law Cyrus was usually reluctant to drive her to town, but today he was picking beans and would be going to market anyway. Cyrus did not like her, but he didn't have as bad a temper as her brother Edward. Cyrus was usually calm and courteous.

Annie skirted weed clumps, looking out for copperheads that crawled blind this time of year and would bite anything that ventured near them. She also kept an eye out for hornets that built their nests close to the ground in big ragweeds and hog weeds.

Cyrus's field was on the very top of the hill, and because the early part of the summer had been rainy, his beans had thrived. In a wet season the roots of pole beans will rot in the moisture of the bottom land. The bean rows on the hill were dark green and beans almost a foot long hung in clusters from the vines. Cyrus had a bumper crop and he and his whole family were busy picking. She found her brother-in-law putting lids on hampers at the end of the field.

Cyrus always had tobacco in his jaw, and a tiny bit of tobacco juice darkened the corner of his mouth. He smelled like apple flavored tobacco. "There's my little fixin," he said. That's what he always said when he saw Sylvia.

"Sylvia is sick; she has a temperature," Annie said. Cyrus didn't answer. He stretched a wire across a hamper lid until it was taut as a dulcimer string, and tied it off. With a grunt he heaved the lidded hamper onto the bed of his pickup truck. The wood of the hamper smelled fresh, the slats rougher than the pieces of dulcimer hardwood.

"I need to take Sylvia to the doctor," Annie said. Sweat stood out on her forehead and ran like tears into her eyes.

"Be lucky to get all these beans picked by dark," Cyrus said and spat into the weeds. Grasshoppers flicked around his feet.

"She's had a temperature of 105." Annie hated to beg. It seemed like she'd spent much of her life begging people to do things they didn't want to do.

"Ain't nothing but the whooping cough," Cyrus said and wiped his mouth with the back of his hand. He picked up an empty hamper and started down a row into the bean field. "Nobody ever died of whooping cough," he called back over his shoulder.

The air boiled like crazy ghosts and barely visible specters over the weeds and over the bean field. Annie wiped the sweat out of her eyes and stood for a minute, trying to think what to do next. Sylvia whimpered in the light blanket. The pickup truck beside her smelled of oil and gasoline and hot metal. It could take her to town to the doctor, but without a key, without a driver, it was useless.

"Hamper!" someone called in the field, meaning they had a full bushel basket and needed an empty one. Sylvia fretted in her arms but didn't cry out. It was a sign of just how sick she was that she wasn't crying. In the hot sun the baby's face was the color of a red rose petal.

Picking her way among the rough clods and big weeds, Annie started downhill the way she'd come. From the edge of the field she could see the church pushing its white spike into the haze, and cattle huddled under the shade of a few trees in the lower pasture. Farther out the road she spotted her brother Edward's army surplus truck at the end of his pole bean field. Hot air above the pasture dervished and tied knots in itself. The currents and swirls in the air seemed to match the churning and seething in her head.

At the bottom of the hill she passed the old molasses furnace, and saw a hornet's nest in the weeds by the rusty evaporating pan. Watching out for water moccasins, she crossed the miry grass beside the stream that murmured and tinkled between the sedge and water weeds. She did not try to hold Sylvia close to her, hoping to keep her cool as possible. There was a tiny breeze in her brother's pasture, washing up the slope from the creek.

Edward had the worst temper of anybody in her family. He'd had ty-phoid when he was a boy and her mama always said the fever had ruined his nervous system. While he was working he was often mad as a yellow jacket. "He has the most even temper in the family," Frank liked to say, "always in a fury."

Edward's bean field was not as lush and healthy as Cyrus's. It had been planted in lower ground, along the spring branch below the barn, and during the wet months of June and July the vines had suffered from root rot and water scald. Nailhead rust dotted the leaves, and some of the vines near the ground had yellowed. The beans that hung in the rows were short and crooked.

Edward was sorting beans in a hamper at the end of the field. Unlike Cyrus, he'd already finished picking, and he had only eight or ten bushels loaded on the army truck. Many of the beans he'd picked were culls, too fat and tough to be sold. He was selecting out the worst ones and throw-ing them into the weeds. From the flair of his nostrils Annie could tell he was already angry. There was no use to try to be friendly with him.

"This baby is sick and needs to go to the doctor," she said.

Edward slapped a big bean against his overall leg like it was a whip. "Ain't got time to run to no doctor," he said, like he was out of breath and smothering with anger.

"Her temperature is 105."

"Fever never hurt a baby," Edward snapped. He packed the best beans he could find on top of the hamper, lining them up to make them look neat. He fitted a lid over the top of the basket and crossed wires tight from rim to rim.

"You don't care about nobody, do you?" Annie said.

Edward spat onto the hard red dirt.

"You go to hell," Annie said. The sun crashed down on the baby in her arms, and on the top of her head. The ground at her feet seemed to heave sideways, bleached and blinding, then tilt and drain away. She took a step to steady herself, then shifting her hand bag to the hand that held Sylvia, she circled around to the side of the army truck, opened the door and climbed onto the high seat. As she waited while Edward loaded the rest of the hampers, she took the bottle of juice from her purse and put the nipple in the baby's mouth. But Sylvia was half asleep, her cheeks swollen by fever, and she didn't drink.

WHEN ANNIE MARRIED FRANK in 1941 he'd been working as a carpenter. In the early years of the war he had several jobs helping to build army barracks and other rough buildings at bases in the Carolinas. He made some furniture also. He could make fine tables out of walnut and chairs from maple wood. He built coffee tables from wild cherry, and bookends, foot stools, cutting boards, shelves for whatnots. But what he liked to do most was make dulcimers. As the war wound down he began to make instruments again, and even got a write-up in the Asheville paper, with a photograph of him holding a dulcimer in front of his work bench.

"Mountain Craft and Mountain Music Live On" read the caption under the picture.

Though he collected hardwoods and seasoned them in his shop and on the porch, Frank said the best wood for an instrument was older wood. He preferred wood from boards in old buildings, beams from ancient barns, pieces of furniture found in attics. He said the wood acquired character from aging, as if the grain stored up the storms and seasons it had passed through, absorbed the human stories, the joys and sorrows it had witnessed. And a craftsman's hands could draw out of the wood some essence of those memories, that knowledge, for the player to summon forth into the living air, from delicate wood and wires, the pain and moan of witness, the testimony of love. A dulcimer was a living thing, that in the right hands could connect the past with the present, the living and the dead, the player and the listener.

EDWARD DID NOT speak to Annie as they drove to town. He kept his eyes steady on the highway, cursing the tourist sedans and convertibles he passed, and that passed him. Annie held Sylvia and rocked her, and finally when they came out of the pines of the Flat Rock section she could see the dome of the courthouse above the town ahead.

Her brother didn't drive her to the doctor's office, but when he stopped at the bean market, and parked in the line of trucks at the auction shed, she slipped out of the cab. It was a half mile to the center of town. She hoped the doctor was in his office, and not at the hospital or on vacation.

Doctor Montague's office always smelled like alcohol and some other chemical, and maybe faintly of pee or other bodily odors. The receptionist said the doctor was running late. He'd just returned from the hospital. She told Annie to take a seat with the others waiting in chairs around the room. There were about a dozen people there, some reading magazines, some looking at their hands. An old lady in a polka dot dress smiled at her.

"My baby is awful sick," Annie told the receptionist. "She has a terrible fever." The woman behind the desk scribbled something on a pad, and Annie sat down in the nearest chair.

Most people in the waiting room avoided looking at each other, but one boy with a bandage on his jaw stared straight at her. Annie turned away, but when she looked again the boy was still staring. Sylvia fretted in her lap, and Annie lifted the blanket away from her face and neck. The doctor's office seemed so clean, after the cab of Edward's army truck, and compared to her own kitchen. There was no dirt on the carpet. And then Annie noticed a stain on her dress. It looked like grease, or maybe tobacco juice. She pulled her skirt to the side so the stain didn't show.

There was a big blue fish mounted on the wall opposite her. It had a fin like a wide fan on its back and a long spike for a bill. She thought it was the kind of fish called a swordfish. It curved in an arc as if it was jumping high out of the water. Annie wondered if Dr. Montague had caught the fish himself. She wondered if the fish was a sign of some kind, having to do with medicine, like the three gold balls that hung over the door or window of a pawn shop.

A woman came out of the inner room carrying a piece of paper and wiping her eyes with a handkerchief. The woman didn't stop at the desk but walked right to the door. The receptionist stood and disappeared into the inner office. With a dozen people ahead of her, Annie figured it would be at least two hours before she got to see the doctor. Edward would be long gone by then. She'd have to walk to the bus station, and when the bus dropped her off at the store by the highway she'd have to walk a mile back to the house. But that would be OK, because at least she had gotten Sylvia to the doctor's office.

The door from the inner room opened and the receptionist beckoned to Annie to come. Without looking at anyone in the waiting room, Annie stood and hurried to the back. The light in the examining room was bright, and everything there, sink and bowls, table and towels, was white, white enamel, porcelain. A nurse came in and told Annie to lay Sylvia on the table. Sylvia's cheek looked hot as a red pepper among all the white things. The nurse wrote down her age and name and then took her temperature. She shook the thermometer like she was flinging degrees off it, jotted something down, and then disappeared. Annie stood by Sylvia and noticed a wheeze, a faint rattle, coming from the little chest.

Suddenly the doctor entered carrying a clipboard, the skirts of his white coat flapping. He was a slender man with a stoop in his shoulders, but with a big voice like a radio announcer's. He always looked you in the eye.

"How is our girl?" he said in his large voice.

"She has a terrible fever."

"She has a fever of 106," Dr. Montague said.

"The fever wouldn't go away," Annie said.

"This little girl has pneumonia," the doctor said as he listened to the baby breathe, then put his stethoscope to her chest. He touched Sylvia's forehead, then went to the cabinet, slid open a door, and took out a hypodermic needle.

"Will she be alright?" Annie said.

"I'm going to give her an antibiotic," the doctor said. When he stuck the needle into the little girl's hip she cried out a weak sob, half a sob.

The doctor took off Sylvia's gown and rubbed her with cotton soaked in alcohol. "Do this every four hours and give her plenty of fluids," he said. "And more important, let her sleep."

Annie was afraid he would say Sylvia needed to be in the hospital. But the doctor didn't mention the hospital. She and Frank didn't have any insurance. The doctor said to take Sylvia home and give her juice and water. And he gave Annie a prescription to fill at the drugstore.

When she stepped out on the sidewalk holding Sylvia to her chest, Annie couldn't remember at first what direction to go in. The town looked different in the afternoon sun. She'd been in the doctor's office less than an hour, but the buildings and sidewalk seemed to have changed in some way she couldn't describe. But when she saw the drugstore on the corner of Main Street she remembered where she was.

Annie was afraid the prescription would cost more than $3.47. She asked the druggist behind the counter how much it would be, and he frowned and didn't answer her. He waited on two other customers and then came back and took her prescription.

"That will be $1.98," he said and stared at her. She was relieved because that left enough for bus fare to the store on the highway, if she had to take the bus.

"Do you want the prescription filled or not?" the druggist said, looking at her over his glasses.

"Yes, I do," she said.

WITH THE BOTTLE in a white paper bag tucked into her purse, Annie hurried down the street toward the produce market at the south end of town. She passed Greasy Corner, where old men from the country liked to stand and talk and spit tobacco juice on the sidewalk. She passed the Jockey Lot where pickup trucks and even a few horses and wagons were parked. There was not a second to waste, for she still might catch Edward before the auctioneer sold his beans and he took the money and drove home. If Edward was already gone, she'd have to walk to the bus station at the north end of town.

A block away she could hear the chant of the auctioneer over the loudspeaker. "A three and a three and a quarter. A quarter a quarter and a half and a half. Who'll give me a four and a four and a four? Sold to Rubin from Miami."

Pickups and bigger trucks were lined up to drive through the auction shed. The drivers sweated behind steering wheels, nervous as they waited to put their samples of produce on the block. She looked for Edward's army truck in the line but didn't see its olive drab color. Sylvia coughed and stirred in her blanket in the terrible heat of the afternoon sun.

Annie looked around the parking lot where the big trucks were parked, waiting to load the beans and summer squash and bell peppers that were being sold. The motors on the trailers hummed and grumbled, keeping the cargoes cool. Women who rode with the truckers to Miami or New Orleans lolled in shorts and halters on running boards, or sunbathed on hoods.

Annie had decided Edward must have sold his beans and already gone home when she spotted the color of his army truck at the far corner of the lot. Edward was unloading his beans into the van of a trailer truck. She started running in that direction, and was almost hit by a truck moving out of its parking slot. The truck's air brakes screeched, and the diesel engine rattled under the hood after it stopped. Without looking at the driver Annie ran on.

Edward ignored her when she climbed into the cab, but Annie was relieved. The cab was dusty and dirty and cluttered, but she didn't care. Now all she needed was to get home and give Sylvia her medicine with a dropper and wash her in alcohol every four hours.

When Edward got in he was clutching a check. His face was red and his shirt soaked with sweat. He appeared angrier than he had been coming to town. The price of beans must have gone down today.

"These buyers from Miami are bastards," he spat. He started the motor and jerked the truck into gear, then swung the steering wheel to the left, and as they exited the parking lot he ran over a curb and bounced into the street.

Edward had never been able to control his temper. Once he started getting mad he kept getting madder. It was like an ugly chemistry began to work inside him. The anger seemed to rise out of his bowels and out of his bones and fill him and spill out of his mouth and into his arms and legs.

Edward slammed the steering wheel with his fist and kicked the floorboard, and the truck lurched to the left. A passing car honked at them.

"You be careful," Annie said and clutched the baby closer.

Edward turned to stare at her and shouted, "*You* don't tell me to be careful. This is my truck. *You* don't tell me nothing!"

70

It was no use to argue with Edward when he was like that. Anything she said would just make him worse. Her mama said his nerves were burned out and he couldn't help himself. Annie looked down at Sylvia who was sleeping. There must have been something in the shot the doctor gave her to make her sleep. Annie looked straight ahead as Edward whipped the heavy truck around a corner and plunged into the parking lot of the feed and seed store beyond the railroad tracks.

When he got out and slammed the door and went into the store, Annie didn't mind the heat and dust in the cab. It was a pleasure to be alone with Sylvia. The quiet was sweet as cold vanilla ice cream. She rolled down the window, but it stuck halfway. Men were loading sacks of feed and fertilizer on the platform nearby. The place smelled of molasses in dairy feed, and the biting scent of nitrate of soda. A train rumbled by on tracks at the edge of the lot, shaking the ground. When the train horn tore the air, Sylvia jerked but didn't wake.

Something crashed into the bed of the army truck, and twisting around Annie saw Edward and a man with a pencil behind his ear loading hampers onto the bed. The truck shuddered each time they dropped another stack onto the boards.

Edward had not calmed down when he got back into the truck. He'd cashed the check and stuffed the bills into the bib pocket of his overalls. But the money had not cheered him up or soothed his anger.

"Man can't afford to farm anymore," he said and clenched his teeth. He had to wait until the train passed before leaving the lot, and the clanking cars and distant whistle seemed to rile him even more. Annie thought of mentioning that Sylvia had pneumonia, but decided not to. Edward would only snap at her and insult her. He slammed the steering wheel with his open hand as the caboose finally rattled by, then gunned the engine so the truck leapt across the tracks.

"Everybody uses me," Edward said and turned and glared at her as he drove toward the outskirts of town.

"I ain't used you," Annie said. "You were already coming to the market."

"Someday I ain't going to be here to be used," Edward yelled. He swerved the truck to the edge of the highway, then whipped the steering wheel to the left so he almost ran into a line of oncoming traffic. His face had gone pale and his eyes looked white. There was something about his look that reminded Annie of a dog with its ears laid back.

"You don't have to run off the road," she said.

"I'll do what I damn well please," Edward shouted. He ran through a red light and there was a screech of brakes and horns sounding behind them.

"Everybody cheats me," Edward snorted. "The buyers cheat me; government cheats me."

During the war Edward had been called up and given a physical, but was never inducted into the army. He said the government had kept him out of the service to deny him a pension and the GI Bill.

"I ain't cheated you," Annie said. But she quickly wished she hadn't said anything. Whatever she said would only aggravate Edward's fury.

They'd reached the pine woods beyond town, and entered the Flat Rock district with its big white houses and wide lawns and hedges. They were a third of the way home, and if she could just get back to the house and give Sylvia her medicine, Annie's mission would be achieved.

"You think you can use me," Edward screamed and turned toward her. She winced at the wild look in his eye and kept quiet. The truck veered into the weeds on the shoulder and then bumped back onto the pavement.

"You think you can use old Edward any time you want to," he yelled. "Well I just may be crazy."

"Stop and let me out," Annie said.

"I'm liable to run this truck off the road and kill us all," Edward screamed. "I'm liable to drive this thing into a trailer truck."

"Stop and let us out," Annie said firmly, only a little tremble in her voice.

To her surprise Edward hit the brakes and slowed the truck into a driveway and came to a stop. She opened the door and slid out quickly, holding Sylvia to her shoulder. The truck began moving again before she touched the ground and she had to jump free. Once she gained her balance she turned to face oncoming traffic. A big truck roared past and shoved her face with hot wind. She would have to watch out for the bus whenever it came by and wave for it to stop. She had more than a dollar in her purse to pay the driver. The ditch beside the road was littered with bottles and cans and candy wrappers, and a broken toy guitar that had belonged to some child.

AT THE WORKSHOP Frank bent the strip of maple into the perfect shape for the new dulcimer, set it in clamps and began to mix the powder to make the best wood glue. It was possible, even probable, that this would be the finest instrument he'd made yet. It was wood that had been in his family a hundred years. The wood would be scintillant under the varnish, with the special rich tone the plucked wires could summon from the best material. He would be more careful than ever with each step. Carving the face, tightening the bolts. Nothing was certain until it was accomplished, but he felt already that, with luck, this one example would take his work to a new level, and lead to things that heretofore had not seemed within his reach. He felt the rightness in his hands with every move they made.

# THE DISTANT BLUE HILLS

1752. THE BOY HOEING corn beside the creek is powerfully built though not tall. He is probably about five foot eight with blue eyes and light brown hair plaited and hanging to his shoulder. From time to time he pauses in his work and glances up at the distant hills, shading his eyes against the crashing sun.

The hills to the west look blue and cool, rolling in gentle waves that go on repeating themselves into the haze. Just looking at the far ridges makes him feel less the sun pounding on his back. He takes off his felt hat and wipes his brow and continues hoeing. Crows call from the chestnut trees at the far end of the field.

The soil that he rakes and smooths around the corn stalks is loose and dark, the loam of a creek bottomland. He rakes a collar of warm dirt around the base of each stalk. A few rocks and roots lie in the rows. Rotting stumps stand like pedestals and statues across the patch, showing how recently this ground was cleared.

A blacksnake bright as hot tar pours itself across the row ahead of the boy. He stops to watch the serpent, but doesn't raise the hoe against the rat catcher and bird catcher. The black racer drapes itself over clods and roots and drains out of sight into the weeds.

The corn stalks are high as the calves of the boy's leggings which are covered with beads and Indian designs. He wears a linen shirt that comes almost to his knees and the buckskin on his legs. He wears moccasins tied with whang leather. In the distance he can hear the tinkle of the creek on its rocks, and the dirt he digs is moist and dark, as if there is water just below the surface of the field. To cool his feet he takes off his moccasins, digs two holes in the dirt, and puts his feet in the damp under-earth. Minutes later he wipes the dirt off and ties the moccasins back on.

After this hoeing, the corn will be laid-by to grow and mature on its own until harvest time. He cuts ragweeds off at ground level, and nettles that already have lavender and yellow flowers. He chops plantain with the sharp hoe blade, but spares a morning glory vine that still has morsels of dew on its leaves and deep purple flowers.

The boy looks to see how many rows he still has to work. Among all the stumps it's hard to count accurately. There are either seven or eight more columns of stalks marching from the woods on one side of the field to the woods on the other. The rows seem to go on for miles, though the woods are only a hundred yards away.

A mockingbird calls from a poplar along the creek, imitating the ring of his hoe on the rocks, and the chop of an axe. It mocks a catbird and quotes a cardinal and a rain crow. The mockingbird flies to a persimmon tree and repeats the catbird call.

The boy looks far into the sky and sees a chicken hawk soaring on the uplift of hot air from the valley. The hawk floats light as a leaf on the high spiral of air. From where the hawk hangs it can see the mountains beyond the hills. The boy knows the hawk's eyes are so good it can spot a mouse in the field below, or the eye of a dove in the brush along the creek.

The sun seems to thunder in his back of his head. He hoes slowly to calm himself, to clear his thoughts in the riot of heat and blinding sun. The sharp hoe swings too far to the left and slices a corn stalk. Sweet sap oozes from the cut stub and the lush leaves begin to wrinkle and wither at the tips even as he watches.

He steps into the woods at the edge of the field where day flowers, wild carrots, butterfly weeds are blooming. He pushes yarrow and day lilies aside and steps onto a trail completely hidden from the field. Concealed by weeds and brush, the path could be found only by someone who knows it's there. The trail slips through poplars and maples and down a mossy bank to a spring hidden by laurel bushes. The fountain shivers out of the hill into a pool dammed by wet rocks. The boy kneels by the spring and takes a gourd from a stick and dips a drink. As he drinks, water spills down both sides of his mouth and drips onto his hunting shirt. Something gleams in the brush, in the spotlights of sun from the canopy of trees—the barrel of a long rifle.

With the rifle in his right hand and the shot pouch and powder horn slung over his shoulder, he climbs out of the branch hollow to a path through the oak trees. Dodging spider webs stretched between brush, he steps quietly into the woods, his eyes sweeping the trees ahead where birds and squirrels are busy.

The trail leads around a gentle hill and takes him down toward an opening in the trees. The opening is a river between low banks, the stream called the Yadkin, swinging wide around a bend between overflowing forests. Trees crowd along the banks and reach over the water, each stretching to get more sun, more free space. The bank where the trail comes down to the water is muddy, traveled by deer and raccoons, foxes, hogs, cattle.

Quickly the boy lays down the rifle and shot bag and powder horn and strips off his shirt and leggings, his moccasins. All he has left is a breech clout bound to his waist by a thong. A knife in a leather sheath is hung from the thong. Wrapping all his things in the linen shirt, he holds the bundle to his chest and wades into the river. Feeling his way from rock to rock, exploring with his toes the sandy bottom, he reaches the middle of the stream before he has to swim, holding the bundle on his head with his right hand.

The river puckers and wrinkles, tears its fabric on a snag and heals itself, goes rocking and shifting its scars in the sun. A duck takes off in a mighty splash, and fish dart like shadows around the pools. The boy remembers the Shawnee story of the underwater panther, but knows it's just a tale to scare children and white people.

When he touches bottom and begins wading again, river water dripping from his shoulders, his feet stir up clouds of mud and sand that fog the pools with little dust storms. Crawfish and minnows flit out of his way. He steps without splashing onto the rocks that lead down to the ford and climbs, not pausing, into the protection of the cane that grows along the bank there. The cane looks much like corn, but is thinner and taller. Stalks reach twice as high as his head; they swish and rasp as he steps through the giant grass.

Hidden from the river, he slips on his leggings and the hunting shirt. Brushing sand off his feet, he slides on the moccasins and ties them, as cane rustles and nudges in the breeze. He listens, then picks up the rifle and shoulders the horn and shot pouch.

The trail out of the cane follows the contour of the hill around the slope, on a kind of bench that curves away from the river. As he walks, the boy listens and looks from side to side, bent over slightly, as though keeping his center of weight closer to the ground. The trail is worn deep and smooth by the feet of men and horses, by the buffalo that traveled this way from valley pastures for thousands of years. Here and there the charred wood of old campfires litters the side of the trail, sign of the many hunters and travelers who have passed this way. Bones of animals killed and eaten bleach around the camp sites.

The trail winds over a hill and comes down into a little clearing, covered not with grass or cane, but wild peavines. The vines are tangled on the ground and draped over bushes and roots, hanging from trees. The lush vines are crushed together, swarming over every inch of the clearing, blooming white and pink. The air over the clearing is smothered with the scent of blossoms, smothered with a mist of bees shaking the peavine flowers and swelling the air. Grape vines swing from limbs far up at the brow of the forest. The boy stops in the clearing as though listening to the hum of the bees, and then steps into the shadow of the woods. Kneeling behind a sumac, he seems to soak into the dapple of leaves and shadows, the gun held low so its barrel won't show in a splash of sunlight. His head perfectly still, he listens to the bees and the faint breeze in the trees above.

Three men appear on the trail coming from the direction he was headed. They are Indians, the hair on the tops of their heads raised in single tufts, the rest of their heads bare. They wear paint and beads and no shirts. Their leggings and moccasins are covered with beads. The three stop on the trail and look into the clearing. They don't see the boy only a few feet away from them. One Indian has a flask covered with leather which he drinks from and passes to the others. The one with the flask mumbles something and the others laugh quietly. Each carries a hatchet and a musket and has a powder horn and shot bag slung over his shoulder. One has a bloody blond scalp tied to the thong around his waist. The tawny hair is plaited and dirty. He turns to look into the brush exactly where the boy hides. He leans closer and it appears certain he sees the boy, but instead he lifts a praying mantis off a twig and shows it to the others. They each say the same words and he drops the creature into a little bag tied to his waist.

As the Indians move on down the trail toward the river, the boy waits until they're out of sight. He waits several more minutes, and then he waits some more. Finally he steps out into the path and glances both ways before starting again in the direction he was headed before. The path leads around the low hill to another small creek and tall sycamores and poplars line the stream, marching up the flat valley out of sight. The trees are enormous, the poplars sixty, perhaps seventy feet straight up before the first limbs. The trunks are straight and thick, as much as fifteen feet across at the base, the sycamores chalk white and shedding bark, upper limbs running out like lightning in the sky. A squirrel leaps through the far limbs and the boy raises the rifle as though to shoot, but he lowers it again, saving his powder for larger game. Besides, this time of year squirrel fur is full of grubs called "wolves."

THE SYCAMORES form a barrier tall as a hill, but once he crosses the creek and follows the trail into another canebrake swishing and whispering in the faint breeze he emerges into a humming peavine meadow where a farther ridge is visible to the west, ragged and with a few rock outcroppings here and there. The ridge slumps against the sky in a massive wall. An eagle soars far above the ragged humps of rocks and trees.

The boy hears a sound and stoops to listen as he eases ahead. A crunch and a snort float on the breeze and he slips into the brush along the trail and parts limbs as he works quietly ahead. Easing to the side, hardly breathing, he melts his way through the heavy undergrowth until he can see into the meadow beyond. Five deer are cropping peavines and clover there, a buck, three does, and a spotted fawn. Their skin seems to shine in the sun. They graze like cattle, tails bright as torches. One of the does raises her head as if she smells something or has heard something. The boy slips closer without making a noise. But the deer are nervous; they pause in their cropping and look around, great eyes glistening. The buck lifts his head and turns and begins to run, and the others follow. The boy raises the rifle and pokes the barrel between branches of a sumac and fires. A doe stumbles and falls and the rest run on into the woods.

The deer has dropped into the peavines and blood seeps out through the hide near her heart. The way she has fallen the doe's udder is exposed, tight as though inflated. The boy takes the knife from under his shirt and cuts the throat so blood streams out. He slits the udder, then bends down and drinks milk directly from the flesh, as though swilling from a spring. Some blood gets on his lips, but he drinks long and full at the udder. When done he wipes his lips with the back of his hand. Flies already circle the eyes and the wound on the chest. He lifts the body and carries it to a nearby tulip poplar. Leaving the deer lodged on the branches out of reach of wolves, he steps to a stream close by. With sand he scrubs the blood off his wrists and dries his hands on his shirt.

Placing the knife under his shirt, carrying the rifle in his right hand, he starts again up the trail toward the looming ridge. Startled birds challenge him as he steps back into the trees. The trail steepens and swings over rocks and between dogwood trees. Winding around stumps and boulders, the trail comes to a very steep slope and runs out along the incline. As if impatient with the path, the boy leaves the track and mounts straight up the ridge. Balancing from one foot to the other, hooking an arm around a sapling here, elbowing a tree there, he lifts himself a foot at a time up the slope, never letting go of the rifle. He ducks limbs and eases between rhododendrons, his knees almost rubbing against the steep incline. Some places he negotiates on his knees, and then stands again. The very top of the hill is intimate and narrow, just a few feet wide, and the ground falls away sharply on either side. The air is cooler up here, the breeze stronger. He parts the limbs of a white oak with mistletoe in its top and steps out on a boulder that juts into the open air.

The boy squats on the boulder and rests the rifle on the rock, looking out over the tops of the trees, to the valley draped from ridges for miles ahead. A cloud shadow swims across the depths of the valley unbroken by clearing or road. And beyond the valley another ridge rises like a great ocean wave about to spill over, and above that ridge another, blue not green, and beyond that another, hazy with distance, as if fog or smoke were lifting out of the valley between the ridges. And beyond that mountain still others rise higher and higher like steps, wave on wave breaking in haze so high they seem to float among the clouds, the hunting ranges of the Cherokees, the gateway to the west, to the wilderness of the interior, to the edge of the world, lost finally in mist at the edge of infinity.

The boy drinks in the far distance, the blue summits and knobs and crests, and the passes, the defiles, the gaps in the mountain chain, where a path or an old buffalo trace might slip through the heaped wall to the world beyond that sends a glow into the sky above the ridges.

THE SUN IS dropping in the west, gilding the lines of ridges and making the leaves on nearby trees glow. He picks up the rifle and thinks of the deer he has killed and cached. For supper his mother will broil some of the tender meat over the fireplace on a spit of sweet shrub or sassafras. The long walk has made him hungry. He takes a last look at the waves of the mountains in the west and turns back down the slope. Picking a way carefully between rocks and saplings, finding footholds on logs and tufts of moss, lichened stumps, and weathered sticks, he descends the ridge quickly, turning this way and that to avoid limbs and spiderwebs.

He is almost to the valley floor where the shade is deep and the woods dim as the bottom of a pool in the river, or a cellar, when he hears a thud behind him, a jolt, as if a sack of corn meal had fallen against a log. He stops to listen. A rain crow calls from somewhere across the valley. He stands at the bottom of a lake of shadow, and looks behind him. But there is only deep shade and late sun bronzing the peak above him, coppering the hills on the other side of the valley. He starts walking again, joining the path toward the canebrakes and the river. The trail is a line of shadow between lush grass and weeds. He hears something again, a twig breaking, and stops. He listens as a step crushes a leaf and strains his eyes to stare into the shadows.

A scream tears the air like the cry of a woman in childbirth, harsh as the sound of a saw cutting glass, a withering, shattering cry.

Stopping on the trail, he pulls the stopper from the powder horn with his teeth and fills a measure made from a buck horn, pours black powder into the barrel of the rifle. Then he tears a piece of linen from a greased rag in the shot pouch and wraps it around a ball of lead, and drives the shot down the barrel with the hickory ramrod. With the rifle loaded and primed, he scans the woods behind him, then continues down the path. From time to time he looks back over his shoulder and then ahead, as if expecting to see someone on the path. There is a thud in the trees behind him and a swish of limbs brushing in the hickory trees, as though a great weight had dropped from one branch and caught on another. The bone splintering scream comes again, a scream that freezes the spit at the back of his mouth. And the pad of feet and crash of leaves on the ridge above are closer.

Stopping near where the deer is lodged on the poplar limbs, he backs away from the trail, stepping to the side, and slipping into the brush without disturbing a twig or leaf. He pokes the end of the rifle through the sumac limbs and waits.

The panther trots out into the open and stops. It stands with one paw raised the way a cat will, looking down the trail. The mountain lion stands perfectly still, as though listening or sniffing, then trots quickly down the path toward the tree where the deer lies. Just as the big cat reaches up for the deer with its paw, the rifle cracks and the side of the panther's head bursts in a spray of blood. The heavy cat rolls over in the grass as if hit by a log, trembles for a few seconds, and lies still.

Slipping out of the brush, the boy lays the rifle in the grass and takes the knife from under his shirt. Lifting the panther's bloody head, he slits the throat. Blood streams hot into the weeds. Working quickly, he slices the hide along the belly and cuts out the warm heart. He bites the heart as though it were a dinner roll, chews and tosses the rest of the organ into the weeds. Wiping his mouth with the back of his hand, he goes to work cutting the hide off the legs and from the neck. After ripping the skin along the belly he cuts the hide loose, stripping the skin from the flesh as if opening something glued and sealed. He works the blade carefully under the skin to keep from damaging the hide. And then he rolls the body over on the other side, stripping away the tawny hide an inch, two inches, at a time.

Once the skin is free it is long as he is tall, but not very wide. He wraps the deer in the skin and drapes the body over his shoulders. With the rifle under his arm he hurries down the path toward the canebrake and the river. The smell of blood in the clearing has already attracted a wolf which watches from the edge of the trees.

# DANS LES HAUTES MONTAGNES
# DE CAROLINE

IF DANNIE WOULD come home I could tell her. If she just flew back for a day and took a taxi from the airport and sat with me fifteen minutes I could fill her in on all the details. And I'd know where to begin too, with exactly how much we're paying these heathens to torture me day and night and starve me and leave me filthy. If my daughter would just surprise them at the most unlikely hour she'd see it all, what they feed me and call it food, how they leave me stinking for hours, sometimes for days at a time, without putting a washcloth on me.

It was different when Jean was still here to keep an eye on them. We had only been married a year, and she sat most of the day and read to me and tidied up the room herself, and told them to change the bed and bring me the painkiller.

"Mr. Morris, you dropped your soup," the big fat nurse says. "Shame on you." But she doesn't pick it up. She just leaves it lying there for one of the attendants to clean up later. I've never seen such lazy people. If they could just knock you over the head and still collect your fifteen hundred dollars a week they'd do it. As it is they have to keep me breathing to collect the money.

"How is the pain, Mr. Morris?" I don't answer the fat nurse. I've found it doesn't pay to communicate with these people. They'll use everything you say against you in some way. There's no persuasion or pity that affects them. As soon as you pay your money and your folks are gone they pack you away like meat in a locker.

"Is the pain worse, Mr. Morris?" The pain never goes away, and she knows it was well as I do. When I was young I never heard that strokes give you pain. I thought paralysis just made you numb. But the blocked nerves hurt as though they are being torn and smashed in a vise. It's unrelenting, though it can ease off and go away at any time, the doctor says. I don't know if he says that to give me a false hope. I don't trust any of them anymore.

She knows I need the pills, and that what I really need is a whole bottle of them. Back when I was still talking I asked Jean to get me a bottle, and she shamed me for it. And once I asked the nurse, as one human being to another, to let me have just half a bottle.

"I'll pretend I didn't hear that," she said, and stalked her two hundred and fifty pounds out.

Today she says, "I'm warning you, Mr. Morris, if you won't talk I'll have to cut out your prescription. And they tell me you're not cooperating with the therapist. Unless you respond to therapy you'll never walk again."

I try to laugh as she sweeps out of the room, but my face is too stiff to crack a grin, and the soup is all over my chin and neck. One of the farces that medical people always go through is the pretense that their procedures and policies work. An eighty-five year old man paralyzed with strokes will not walk again. They know that, I know that. Yet they want to keep up the charade of therapy, of treatment. After all they're getting paid to do that.

When the physical therapist comes in and works my legs it's like sledge hammers are hitting my knees. They can hear me yelling all the way down the hall to the reception desk and out in the yard. "Mr. Morris, you'll have to stop that," she says in her Northern accent.

"Or what? You'll punish me?" That was when I still talked to them.

"You'll have to behave," she says, and starts peddling my leg again. I scream as loud as I can lying flat on my back with lungs only half-filled.

"Shame on you," she says, standing up. "I'll be back next week to see if you have calmed down." Everybody acts as though they expect me to feel shame, as I lie helpless in great pain, as though I am perversely interrupting their procedures.

The painkiller must have made me drowsy for when I wake it's late afternoon. There is a light in the mountains this time of year that sometimes reaches even into this hell-hole. It's the late sun hitting the haze in the air, the smokiness that makes the mountains blue-white. In the autumn sun all turns to gold, the burnish on the peaks and on the hickory groves, in the poplars, and the browning fallen leaves. Even the early explorers noted it, the Midas touch of late summer and early fall.

When the French botanist André Michaux came through over two hundred years ago he found a number of flowers and shrubs that have not been seen since. But one flower, the *shortia galacifolia*, was rediscovered about a century later by assistants of Asa Gray. Michaux had taken the dried flower back to a museum in Paris, and had written under it simply "Dans les hautes montagnes de Caroline," and everybody took that to mean he'd found it on the highest peaks. So they looked in vain on the mountaintops, but finally found the shortia by accident, almost at the foot of the mountains. Local people had known it all along as the Oconee Bell. I used to think there was a moral in that story, about looking too high when the truth was down around your feet, but I'm not sure anymore. There used to be a joke in high school that went: "He who keeps his eyes on the stars will step in shit."

When I was just out of college and a young teacher I got the idea of retracing Michaux's route across the mountains, and keeping a journal of my hike, listing all the things I saw along the way, comparing my notes with the Frenchman's notes. I wanted to write a book, as all the young do. Then the Depression hit and I was lucky to find work in the summer, and a school teaching job in the fall. Who could afford to gallivant through the mountains looking for the tracks of some romantic Frenchman?

THE NURSE'S AIDE, who must have been late to work and didn't have time to put on her uniform, comes in with another cup of soup and coffee. The cups have covers and spouts, the kind toddlers use. But then I am a child, more helpless than a baby in its crib. She is wearing blue jeans and a tank top. If the manager catches her out of uniform he will fire her. But then again she is a comely thing in her tight jeans. Maybe she has special privileges.

I'm sure she notices the smell, but she ignores it. They like to change me once a day, and since I'm the only one who has to smell my shit in this private room, they put if off as long as possible. The thing is I don't even know when it happens, unless I hear my guts moving, until the smell reaches me.

I could ask her to change me. But I don't speak, even to her. Brenda, I think she's called. If there was a chance she'd bring me extra pills I might try to ingratiate myself with her. But I'm not even sure she has a key to the pharmacy closet. What does an old man have that would interest her except money, and I don't even have that anymore.

I can handle the coffee, though it's still too hot. With my good hand I bring the cup to my chin and suck. The liquid warms my tongue and throat and belly, as far down as I can feel. Good coffee is something to live for. In fact it's the only thing I've had to live for this past year, since Jean went to the hospital. Even though this is just an instant imitation of coffee, with non-dairy creamer, the cup I get three times a day is my only connection and remembrance of life, of desire. How the same dull room lights up a little when I feel the coffee in my veins. The painkiller makes me sleep and dream and remember a little what the world was like. The coffee makes me feel faintly alive again.

All the coffee is gone before I touch my soup. Now that it's half cold the soup is truly repugnant. The painkiller is wearing off and the throb returns to my legs, all down my left side. I bite down on the spout and the lid pops off the cup. Soup pours down my chin and neck, soaking into the sheets and pajama top.

It will be another two hours before they bring me more pills. Even when I still talked to them and asked politely for something to stop the pain, they always said, "Mr. Morris, you know you have to take your medicine on schedule. We don't want to wear out the drug before we have to. It's for your own good you know." But I'm the one in pain; they think my body should respond to their schedule. I have to study about my problem again. I've always believed that when the mind really applies itself it can find a solution. It's only a matter of concentration. But for more than a year I've been unable to solve this conundrum.

When I offered the fat nurse money to bring me a bottle, I could tell she was tempted, for half a second. But she said, "Shame on you. That would just get us both in trouble."

"I am in trouble," I said.

"Not with the creator, yet."

For hundreds of days and thousands of hours I've run my mind over the contours of the problem. I've felt into the cracks and niches, pulled back and examined from a distance. I've looked longingly at the cord on the blind, and at the few feet from the bed to the floor. I've thought of gnawing my own wrist, of choking myself on a bottle cap, of inducing a heart attack by tearing into the electric clock on my stand. The very strength of my heart, that tough old friend, is my enemy.

The truth is my hope ended when Jean went to the hospital. I thought I could persuade her in time to bring me a prescription of sleeping pills, or to smuggle in a gun. She has a tender heart, and I could have worn her down.

"Don't talk that way, Stephen," she said. "It breaks my heart. I feel as though I've failed you."

Then one day she didn't come back, and they told me she'd had a heart attack in the night. Her son took her to the ICU in Asheville. And since then I haven't had a card, or a word from her. "She's in the hospital," they said when I asked. Now I don't talk to anyone. Her son never approved of our marriage.

"Mother has a bad heart," he said to me, man to man. Jean and I asked the doctor if it would hurt her heart to marry. The doctor winked. "You know what I always say to seniors," he said. "No sex is bad." And he laughed at his joke, as he had so many times before.

"Routine sex can strengthen the heart," he added.

"Routine, hell," I said, and took Jean's hand.

"NAUGHTY, NAUGHTY," the nurse's aide says when she sees the spilled soup. "You've been naughty again."

One of the things Andre Michaux is credited with is teaching the settlers in the mountains to gather ginseng. Before that the few people here either didn't know what it was, or didn't know it was valuable. But Michaux knew the Chinese would pay dearly for the dried roots, and he started a dozen generations of mountain boys on their quest for sang. At times it was the only thing you could do for a little money, though you can only find it in late summer and early fall, this time of year, when the leaves or the berries are still visible. It's mostly gone now, they say, hunted out.

I've often thought ginseng was like any other valuable thing you seek. At first it may be all around, at your feet, and you have a honeymoon, beginner's luck. But soon it gets scarce, and you really have to work to find any more, going far back in the mountains, looking for places no one has thought of. You have to use cunning, and stay out longer, and try to imagine where it might be.

It's interesting that Michaux's "lost flower," the *shortia galacifolia*, was unrelated to anything except one rare mountain flower in China. That always seemed romantic to me, the kinship between these mountains and the Chinese highlands. I meant to follow up that connection someday, but never did.

The Depression interrupted everything for my generation. Just when I'd worked my way through college and got a master's degree and had my first teaching job I was fired. People with PhD's were fired by universities and ended up teaching high school. And people teaching high school ended up teaching grammar school. Or unemployed. Since I was the most recently hired I was let go, and I came back to the farm to live.

At this cheap boarding house in Wilmington, where everybody on the second floor used the same bathroom and shower, I'd caught athlete's foot. No medicine I got, no powder, and no amount of pampering, would cure it. Back home I just went barefoot in the hot cornfields, and the dry dirt took care of the athlete's foot, the dryness and the sunlight which fungus can't stand.

AND CAME the fall, when I didn't have a school, I took a spade and hunted for ginseng, tramping far back to the Flat Woods and the other side of Long Rock, over into South Carolina, and back up on Mount Olivet. What a change, after years of school. I built up my muscles, and ran into moonshiners, bee hunters, deer poachers, coon hunters, and berry pickers.

And nobody else ever claimed to be hunting sang. They'd admit to prospecting and liquor making, but never to looking for ginseng. By the end of October when the leaves were gone I'd dug maybe two or three pounds. But by the time the roots dried only four ounces were left. I think I got ten dollars for the lot from Wilbur down at the store, just in time for Christmas you might say. And then in the spring I got the job teaching at the CCC camp.

To think of all the times in my life I could have stored up hundreds of aspirin or sleeping pills against this need. In the woods in the old times they would have just left me out to die and I'd be rid of the misery. And forty years ago I'd have just died at home, without such fuss and torture, not to mention expense. This old body isn't worth it.

If only Dannie knew how bad it is she'd come. She's still mad at Jean, and doesn't know Jean has left me to stay in the hospital.

"Daddy, there's no reason to get married at your age," she said when she came with the two boys. "You can keep seeing Jean as you have been."

"Whose business is it?" I said.

"It's mine if I have to look after you," she said. "And you may end up nursing her."

"I ought to kick your rear end," I said. I'd never spanked her since she was three. She looked real serious then, and got her things together and left with the boys.

"I don't need you to direct my love life," I said all the way to Buffalo, in my thoughts. And she was listening, though I never got a phone call or letter. Dannie and I always did understand each other. That's why she never got in touch. She must know how much I want to see my grandsons, and how much I want to get out of here. It's that Morris pride, that standing on stubbornness, the same as gave me the stroke in the first place.

But I won't give her the satisfaction of calling first, even if I could call, which I can't. And I won't speak again to the apes and heathens here. My hate is the only focus I have left, and focus is my only weapon.

"Ain't we been busy," Norman the orderly says when he comes in to change me. He doesn't even take the earphones off as he rolls me over and brings the pan of water to the side of the bed. "Ain't we been busy today."

89

I can hear the orderly rubbing and wiping, and then rinsing the cloth. The sound from his earphones is a tinny hiss, with a beat. It's a terrible cliché I'm sure, used by editorial writers everywhere, but everybody seems tuned to their own world now. With earphones on they listen to a private music and not each other. All you ever notice is them humming to the beat they hear. They'll take the earphones off for a few seconds and talk, then put them on again, impatient to get back to their own music.

The last year I was principal I outlawed radios in school. That was so long ago they just had the little pocket transistors, not the big blasters with handles they got later. But even so they listened to them in class, and turned up the volume in the halls and on the playground. I confiscated a half dozen of the little things, and had no idea there was worse ahead.

"There now, you're all cleaned up," Norman says. He rolls me on my back again. "Clean as an Irish spring," he laughs.

He rolls me once more to put on fresh pajamas, then takes a mop and wipes up the place the soup spilled. "We've had another accident," he says, using the imperial plural that makes medical attendants feel even more superior to their patients. And what can the patient say, guilty after all of his sickness? But I'm glad he cleans the floor.

All that summer when I worked in the cornfield I thought of the library at Chapel Hill, of the cool clean floors of the reading room. Sweaty, standing in dirt and weeds, I daydreamed about the marble and mosaic floors, so cool under the polished tables and high ceilings.

"Now you have a nice day, Mr. Morris," Norman says as he loads up his cart to head for the washroom. "You have a good one now." He doesn't look back to see if I answer. He knows I don't talk anymore, and his earphones are in place.

It's another hour before my next dosage, and this pain is a straitjacket, a cramped closet I can't get out of. I feel I'm crawling through a duct underground that gets smaller and tighter. Pain is hot, but this pain is hot like ice on a raw nerve. This must be the way burn victims feel.

When I was young how I feared death. I'd lie out in the field and look up at the sky and imagine I was falling into it, falling right through the clouds and blue and the nothing beyond forever. As I thought of all that nothing I closed my eyes, and then got up and ran to the shade.

90

It's not in the open we feel comforted, but in the shadows, ever notice that? The place of worship is always covered over, closed in, the tent, the chapel, the gloomy grove, or cave. The columns in the church are like the trees under which our ancestors worshiped, they say. I read that somewhere. We can't feel at home with the infinite sky above and around us. Space must be limited, shaped, defined, to comfort us. From cradle to coffin it's enclosure that defines us.

When I was a kid the preacher terrified me with all his talk of hell and the hereafter. And when I grew up I was as afraid of death as anyone. I wanted so badly to survive, to learn to live into a better time, beyond the Depression and the war. I drove carefully and used seatbelts before anyone else. And I quit smoking and watched cholesterol before anyone on television talked about it.

And I still fear death, but as a starving man fears the meat he finds may be poisoned. I'm afraid of death as a woman in a burning building is afraid of the height but jumps as the flames tear at her hair. I remember watching my dog die when I had to shoot him, and thinking, as his lungs emptied and his eyes set, that he hadn't gone anywhere. He was still here, and not. Had slipped through the door to another dimension. There are thresholds we can't see, right here where we are. When we die there's no long journey, no soaring to a faraway city. We just slip inside the here, out of the now.

"You hush that, Mr. Morris," the nurse's aide says. She has her uniform on now, and she quickly pulls the blinds to kill the sun on the wall and bed.

"They can hear you hollering all the way down to the office. There's visitors here."

It surprises me that I have been screaming, for I never meant to speak again. Then I realize she's just trying to trap me, to distract me. She wants me to protest, no, I haven't been shouting, and then she'll have me talking again.

"You're hollering like a scared mule," she says. "A grown man like you."

But I don't fall for her trick. I keep my silence, hold my peace.

"We'll be around with your pills in no time," she says.

The blinds throw gold bars of sun on the bed and on the wall. It's a golden prison, I laugh, or a tiger skin decor. The room is sliced with sheets of light almost horizontal, like an MRI. If it was lasers it would turn the whole place into plywood or layers of debris.

As the pain changes color, red then purple, green then black, I imagine blasting the place with a laser gun, or with heavy artillery. I'd like to get back on the hills and level the nursing home room by room with all its stinking old patients and silly staff. The director I'd like to incinerate. I'd use baseball bats and chainsaws. As it is I can't even destroy myself.

"You hush that up," the nurse says as she slips through the ropes of light. "I never heard such carryings on."

I won't be tricked by her into answering either. I turn away from the lit ribbons.

"They can hear you all the way to Hendersonville," she says, slapping on the cuff to take my blood pressure." I wouldn't be surprised if they can hear you in Brevard."

She writes on her clipboard, and puts down the little paper cup with the pills in it, then fills the water cup.

"I hear you spilled your soup again. You must be hungry. That's what happens to bad boys."

She heaves herself out of the room and closes the door. The lines are fading now, orange to pink to gray. The lamp by the bed comes on automatically. They must have a timer somewhere in the office.

There are three pills instead of two in the little crimped cup. Does that mean the nurse is being generous? Does it mean she wants to help me build my collection by saving the extra one each day? Probably they just want me to sleep extra sound, if I have been hollering, which I haven't.

If Dannie would come I'd tell her about the CD in the little bank in South Carolina. Before I married Jean, before I had my stroke, I took forty thousand dollars and placed it in a CD in the tiny town just across the state line. Even when I was maddest I set aside money for Dannie and her boys. But she'll never know unless she visits. Let the little bank keep it. With so many banks going broke they may need it.

When the painkiller starts to work it makes my mind function clearly for a while, before I get sleepy. I think of the fibers in the pith of a corn stalk, and how sometimes when you break a dried joint the fibers stick out the end like whiskers, like the wires inside the insulation of an electric cord. If I could take the wires out of the base of the lamp, peel them back, and hold the copper when the lights come on at dark, it might stop my heart. The old thumper can't be that good anymore.

Or put the wires in a pan of water, or the pitcher of water, and my hand into the liquid. That would give much fuller contact with the current. They would come in with the supper muck and I would have slipped through their bars. It's the first good idea I've had in months. All I need is to free the wires from the base of the lamp. It would work if I could get the wires out. It's the happiest thought I've had since Jean left. The pain is now a cool blue, turning down like a Bunsen burner, and then a pilot light, a shining blue seed.

When Michaux crossed the mountains the first time there were still Carolina parakeets around. By the time his son Francois Andre returned, many years later, the parakeets were gone. There were still passenger pigeons, but the elk and buffalo and who knows how many birds, such as eagles, had begun to recede into the West. I haven't heard a mockingbird in months. Even though there are trees outside the nursing home, I never hear any birds except the rain crow, squawking before a wet weather spell.

The strangest thing I ever saw in the woods I never found corroborated by Michaux or Bartram or anyone. It was a spring night, the year I was living back home unemployed. I came in late from the barn and looked up the ridge. The whole side of the mountain was lit with something like lightning bugs or glow worms, except they were maybe a foot off the ground, just hovering there making a soft green light. I walked up to the field to view them, and they glowed under the trees all the way to the top of the ridge. Never found if it was something coming out of the ground like swamp gas, or electrical charges in the air, or living creatures, but it looked like the whole mountainside was shining in the dark, just before the rain started.

# THE WEDDING PARTY

IT WAS ONE OF those old mansions in Flat Rock, maybe the oldest one, built by rich flatlanders in the last century. You know the kind of place, with white columns and a third or fourth story, and cupola like the top layer of a wedding cake. There were porches all around, and more windows and gables than you'd want to count. The problem with houses like that is they need so much upkeep even rich people don't want to pay for the painting and roofing. I reckon they were built back when wages were near nothing.

Bowman Ward, the caretaker, was showing me what needed to be done. The owner, some mill owner from Atlanta, hadn't come up there since the stock market crash. "Several windows need caulking, before you paint," Bowman said. "And the roof leaks in a dozen places."

"I'll need scaffolding to reach those dormers," I said.

"Can't you use a ladder?"

"Can't reach them," I said.

No need to tell Bowman I didn't have any insurance because of my bad back. I'd been hurt on a job down in Greenville and couldn't get insurance anymore. After the fall they gave me a one-time settlement, which was soon spent, and they wouldn't hire me again. That's why I was taking whatever I could find, at wages below scale. I was a minister of the gospel on Sundays at the Full Gospel Holiness Church, but I couldn't get any insurance because of the back injury.

"Can't you rent scaffolding?" Bowman said.

"Might be able to rig a platform out of two-by-fours for the dormers," I said.

We walked around the front of the house where the boxwoods lined the walks and the porch was wider than most houses. Just looking at the porch made you think of ladies in low-cut dresses dancing to an orchestra, and men in high collars sipping from frosty glasses. My grandpa had told me how the rich people in Flat Rock lived in those days, with garden parties and banquets in tents. He'd worked as a carpenter at this very place, and he said the young women back then wore dresses so low you could see their bosoms. He said they chilled champagne with ice from the cellars and danced till it was morning.

"Why are the front windows still covered with shutters?" I said to Bowman.

"Because the owners didn't come this year. Since the Depression hit they haven't been back to Seven Oaks."

I'd forgotten that the place was called Seven Oaks. In the vast front lawn there were several big oak trees, and evergreens lined the driveway. It was a circular driveway made for carriages.

"This is the house where the girl is supposed to have disappeared," Bowman said. "Disappeared on her wedding night and never seen again."

"I don't believe such a tale," I said.

"It's supposed to be true," Bowman said. "They say the house is haunted."

"People like to tell stories," I said. "A tale gets started and just keeps growing."

Wind swept uphill from the lake, tossing leaves along the walkway and flowerbeds. Water sparkled in the distant lake like brushed steel.

"It was some kind of French count that built this place," Bowman said. "I think his name was de Choiseul, something like that." We walked along the driveway and climbed the front steps out of the sunlight. Our feet drummed on the wide porch, and my teeth chattered a little as Bowman unlocked the front door. Bowman's wife had just up and run away about five years before. She and Bowman had always quarreled and it was thought she had a lover. It was rumored Bowman was glad to get rid of her, but nobody ever mentioned the scandal around Bowman.

"How could a girl disappear with a hundred wedding guests around her?" I said. I'd heard the story several times since I was a boy.

"Let me show you which windows need caulking first," Bowman said. "Then we'll look at the roof later."

The great parlor inside had carpets and a gleaming hardwood floor.

But the furniture was covered with sheets. It gave me a chill just to look at all those ghostly white cloths draped on sofas and chairs, bureaus and highboys. I saw something move and jumped, then realized it was us in a tall mirror.

"Where do you go to church now?" I said. I wanted to think of something more cheerful. Bowman's family had always been Baptists, but I heard they had a fuss at Poplar Grove church and split off.

"We still go where we always went," Bowman said.

"You'd be mighty welcome at the Full Gospel Holiness," I said.

Bowman led me to a high window at the end of the long parlor. There was a water stain on the wallpaper beside the window frame. "This one needs caulking the worst," he said.

Through the glass I could see the tall hemlocks swaying and twisting outside. There was a whisper where air came through a crack around the window. It felt colder inside, among the mirrors and chandeliers, than it had outside. "What was the girl doing when she disappeared?" I said.

"She was in her wedding dress," Bowman said."She was only sixteen the day she married the Frenchman. They had the ceremony at St. John in the Wilderness church, and then there was a feast and dancing on the front porch. I reckon the celebration went on all day, and then along about dark the girl and some of her friends started a game of hide and seek."

"In her wedding dress?"

"She was only sixteen," Bowman said. "I've heard she still played with dolls and toys."

We climbed the big winding staircase up to the second story. The stairs were as wide as a highway. At the top was a hallway running the length of the house.

"There's a window in the master bedroom in bad shape," Bowman said. It was so dark I'd have to bring a flashlight or lantern to see what I was doing on the inside. The second floor smelled like dust and old face powder, or talcum powder.

"How long has it been since they lived here?" I said.

"Like I said, they came up the summer before the stock market crash," Bowman said.

"Don't seem like a friendly house," I said. Any two of the bedrooms were bigger than the house I grew up in, or the house I still lived in with Mabel and our four younguns.

"People say it's still haunted, and that's why the owners don't want to stay here," Bowman said.

"People like to talk that way," I said. The bedroom doors were all closed. In the master bedroom the furniture was covered. I saw a water stain on the wall that looked like tobacco juice.

"This window will need a lot of work," Bowman said.

There was a brass telescope pointed through the window, and a globe the size of a washpot in the corner. And there was a dead squirrel on the floor below the window, dead so long it was dried flat and it eyes looked like daubs of glue.

"Died of heat in the summer time," Bowman said and pushed the fur with his foot.

"Where were they playing hide and seek?" I said.

"Do you want to tell stories or start work?" Bowman said.

"You're the one that started telling," I said.

Bowman patted the water stain like he thought I might not have noticed it. "They was hiding all over," he said. "They hid behind boxwoods and in the hedge. They hid in closets in the house, and under the porch. I've heard they giggled and shrieked as they run out of the dark. I reckon boys and girls rassled and put their hands on each other as they'll do in fun. It was a wedding party, but the bride and her friends flirted like sixteen year olds will, while the groom smoked his pipe and the older guests watched the young folks romp and holler from the porch and parlor."

"The Frenchman was much older?"

"He was at least twenty years older than the girl," Bowman said.

I looked out the window toward the lake. The glass was so old it seemed to ripple and stretch. There were crows in the oak trees.

"So when did she disappear?" I said.

"It was long after dark and many of the guests had called for their carriages and gone home. The groom suggested to his bride it was time to stop the game, but she only laughed at him and run away. The boy who was It counted to a hundred and hollered and hollered that he was coming to look. There was screams and laughing as young folks run into the shadows and everybody was found one by one. But they couldn't find the bride. At first everybody laughed, and then they started calling her name. Everybody went looking. Even the Frenchman went looking."

"And she was hiding?" I said.

"Nobody knows," Bowman said. "They looked among the boxwoods and all the shrubbery. They lighted torches and looked in the woods and around the lake. They even looked in the well and among the barns and stables."

"And they searched the house?" I said.

"Of course they looked in the house. They searched the cellar and all the rooms and closets. They looked in the attic and on all the porches. They even took a lantern and looked in the cupola."

"And they searched the road?" I said.

"They sent parties along the road as far north as the French Broad," Bowman said, "and south to the state line. They questioned drovers and travelers, and nobody had seen her."

"It's just a story," I said.

"You better get to work," Bowman said, "if you plan to get anything done today."

Bowman wanted to act like a boss man because he was caretaker for the rich people in Atlanta. "I know how to earn my pay," I said. I'd learned a long time ago it won't do to let somebody boss you around or low-rate your work. Once they start running over you they'll never stop.

"Reckon there's a lot of carpenters out of work," Bowman said.

"I do a day's work for a day's pay," I said.

"Don't your church pay you nothing?" Bowman said.

"They give me what they can," I said. "These are hard times."

"And times will get worse before they're better," Bowman said.

Before Bowman left to go to town for roof paint and a roll of tarpaper, he told me to take a flashlight and climb up to the attic. "You'll see where the old roof is leaking," he said. And then he was gone.

I got the ladders and started to caulk the windows. I'd get that done before I looked at the attic. Caulking windows is almost as dull as painting. I cut the end off the nipple on the tube of caulking and squirted the white paste into the cracks around the windows on the first two stories.

I filled every split in the old wood, and knocked away loose putty around the panes. I spread fresh putty and smoothed it with the knife.

As I scraped and brushed, caulked and smoothed, I kept thinking about the girl in her wedding dress playing hide and seek among the boxwoods and shadows of lantern light. Bowman said she was just a girl that played with dolls and toys. I kept thinking of a child playing children's games on her wedding day and night. Had she dreaded the wedding night and was putting it off with the children's games? Had she fallen in the lake and drowned? Had she been kidnapped by highway robbers? Had she run away with a younger boyfriend to the West? The old turnpike was now U. S. Highway 25. I heard a police siren go by on the highway. There were pine trees at the end of the lawn and I could see red lights flashing beyond them.

When they held the torches over the well and looked in that night could they see all the way to the bottom? It's just a story, I reminded myself. Think about how you're going to pay your bills. Think about what you're going to preach on Sunday. Think about poor Bowman whose wife left him.

I'd finished the windows Bowman had showed me by lunchtime. The breeze under the trees was so cold I shivered once I got out of the sun. It was cold in the big house, but at least it was out of the wind. I ate my dinner in my Model T truck because it was warmer there. As I ate biscuits and sipped coffee from the thermos, I looked at the dormer windows on top of the house. They stood out like raised eyes on a frog. They would indeed be hard to reach. I'd have to build some kind of platform beneath them.

But I could put off the dormers until the next day. Why not do what Bowman had said and check the water damage in the attic this afternoon? Find out where the leaks were, and worry about the scaffolding later.

The sun had gone in and it was getting colder even in the Model T. I reached into the glove compartment for my flashlight. The batteries were weak, but maybe they'd give me enough light to see the underside of the roof. I hadn't been able to afford new batteries.

When I entered the house it felt cold as an ice box. Freezing air seemed to tumble down the stairs as I climbed. I didn't look at the furni-

99

ture all covered with sheets, and I didn't look at the mirrors as I passed them. It was darker in the house than it had been that morning. I shivered as I climbed to the third story. Something rustled behind a door but I figured it must be a mouse, or maybe a bird that had come down a chimney. There were fireplaces in most of the rooms.

Bowman had said the stairs to the attic were in the closet at the end of the hall. I opened a door and somebody in white stood there facing me. But it was just a dummy or manikin, like dressmakers use to fit clothes on. My breath was short. You're acting silly, preacher boy, I said to myself. You've let that silly story get to you.

When I found the stairs and started climbing, I felt my way in the dark. I didn't want to use up the juice in the flashlight until I had to. The air in the stairwell smelled like old tobacco and something else: rat pee? sour rags? When I reached the attic door and opened it I was relieved to see there was a little light from the dormer windows. They were small, and only threw light close around them, but it was better than no natural light.

I paused to get my eyes adjusted, and looked away from the windows. There were boxes all around the attic, and old chairs and benches. I looked into the dim corners, and I looked at the chimneys. Strings were stretched between the rafters and old leaves were tied to the strings. I walked between boxes to look closer. That's where the tobacco scent was coming from. Somebody had left tobacco up there to cure years ago and forgotten it. Something fluttered against my cheek and lips. Was it a moth? Cobweb? I wiped a hand across my face and slapped it away.

You idiot, I said to myself. It's just an old attic. You're alone in the house. Nobody is going to hurt you. You're a minister of the gospel. Don't be silly. All I had to do was switch on the flashlight to look at the roof. Nobody was going to see me or do anything to me.

The floorboards creaked as I walked on them. Something else fluttered in the darkness. Probably a bat. Most old attics had bats in them. Keep yourself steady, Reverend, I said.

I switched on the flashlight and pointed it at the roof above. But the rafters and braces up there were in the dark, and the boards so blackened with age the dark swallowed up the beam. The flashlight was so weak it threw a pitiful spot into the blackness. I strained my eyes to see water stains on the underside of the roof. It was hard to see much of anything without a stronger light. I'd have to get Bowman to bring a new flashlight, or furnish new batteries if I was to make any kind of inspection of the roof.

It came to me that any leaks would drip on the floor below. You could tell where all the worst leaks were from the stains on the floor. I turned the flashlight on the floor, and sure enough, among the old books and papers, the jars and cigar boxes, I saw circles and craters in the dust where the drips had splashed. There were circles big as elephant tracks where puddles had spread and dried up. There were little circles and runlets where one puddle had touched into another. There were so many splash tracks it was hard to tell where the leaks were exactly. And I recalled how water from a leak will run down a rafter before it drips off. So the drips might not be exactly under the leaks. I'd still have to get a stronger flashlight to examine the roof.

That's when I saw the shoe print in the dust. Holding the weak yellow beam closer I could tell it was a man's shoe. Somebody had walked through the dust recently. My heart jumped into my throat. I swept the flashlight ahead but couldn't see anything. Something brushed my cheek like a wing. I slapped it away and heard a flutter in the air toward the chimney. Calm yourself, preacher, I said.

Bending closer I saw the shoe prints were so fresh you could spot nail holes in the heels. I followed them around a chair and between boxes to the chimney and under the tobacco. And then I busted out laughing: they were my own tracks! They circled past the strings of tobacco and right back to where I first noticed them. You fool, I chuckled to myself.

I laughed again to make myself feel better. On Sunday I'd be standing at my pulpit describing this dusty, spidery attic in the house of the rich. I shined the light on the floor again and saw that my tracks had disturbed older tracks in the dust. They were dim tracks, like tracks in snow that have been covered by later snow, tracks so vague you could hardly see their outlines. I followed the old tracks toward the far end of the attic. They must have been made by Bowman or others bringing boxes up there, or looking for things, or by other carpenters coming up to inspect the roof and braces. There were tracks that might have been made years ago, still showing through the dull coatings of dust.

I shined the light around a box and saw an old trunk. There were no tracks in the dust around it. It was an old steamer trunk, covered with leather, and the leather was mostly eaten away by rats. And then I saw there *were* tracks going up to the trunk, but they were so dim you could hardly see them.

The trunk was not locked, but a pipestem had been stuck in the latch holding it tight. With childish curiosity I pulled out the pipestem, and saw it was so old the clay had cracked. I lifted the lid to see what had been left in the trunk. The flashlight was so dim that at first I couldn't see a thing. Holding the light closer I found lace, like the lace of a wedding dress. And then I saw the yellow hair and a skull with the mouth opened in a scream. And I saw the finger bones holding a doll clutched to the smoldering bosom of the fancy low-cut wedding dress.

At first I thought it must be a trick Bowman was playing on me, after telling me that story about the bride. But when I looked closer I saw the bones were real, and the hair was real. And the bones didn't look a hundred years old either. For I could see dried black stuff on the bones that must have been flesh. My hand shook so bad I could hardly close the lid. And I wondered what I would tell my congregation later about the moment I had opened that trunk and found Bowman's wife.

# THE CLIFF

THEY STILL HAVEN'T found out who did it, though both the sheriff's office and the police have been poking around, asking questions and taking fingerprints and offering a reward for information. But they can't come up with a thing. I mean how do you get fingerprints off a bulldozer when half a dozen operators have been driving it and others have changed the oil and refueled it. Not to mention boys climbing up to play on it during the weekend. They even took my fingerprints off the panel and shift of that big Caterpillar and came around asking questions, trying to make something out of it.

"Hell, I'm the one you ought to thank," I said to Sheriff Dixon.

"I know that, George," he said. "But we've got to do our job. We've got to check out all the leads."

"I don't see how a fingerprint is a lead if you know how it got there," I said.

The sheriff took off his hat and wiped his forehead and put the hat back on. I could tell how much he was enjoying this. Usually he didn't have anything to do except sit at The Blue Guitar Café and drink coffee and flirt with Mary Lee. That's why he was giving me a hard time because he knew it was me she was sweet on. He was throwing his weight because he could, for once, and even the town police had to let him do it. For the whole thing had started outside the city limits where they are building the overpass and intersection on the superhighway. And that made it the sheriff's jurisdiction, if you follow me. He had to figure out how it all started because it happened in his territory and almost right under his nose. It was Dixon's shots to call and there wasn't a thing the police and the mayor could do about it. And since no firearms had been used and nothing had been carried across state lines the FBI couldn't be called in either. Not that any local law enforcement wanted them called in.

"Where were you at noon on Thursday," Sheriff Dixon said, "at approximately twelve twenty?"

"You know damn well where I was," I said. "For you were there."

"I've got my job to do," Sheriff Dixon said.

"Then do it," I said, "and quit bothering me."

"Don't get smart with me, boy," Sheriff Dixon said. "You might need a friend before this is over."

"And you may need all the help you can get," I said.

Dixon's daddy had been sheriff before him was how he got the job. It was a family business. They'd been sheriffing so long they didn't know how to do anything else, and nobody so far had been able to throw them out of office. Their real talent was for visiting people back in the county during election time and eating fried chicken at homecomings and bringing boxes of canned food to shut-ins during bad weather. Sheriff Dixon once drove Kelsey Wyman's girl that was about to have a baby through deep snow to the hospital in Asheville, and he reminded people of it at election time.

"I was at The Blue Guitar same as you when it happened," I said. And that was certainly the truth. There was a big lunch crowd there that Thursday. Mary Lee serves fried shrimp and the best hushpuppies and the coldest iced tea in town and everybody goes there. You'll see Dixon there almost every day and Mary Lee will keep his cup filled and bring him special slices of pie. There's a long window on the side where the booths are and you can look out on Main Street across town to the bluff above the river where the railroad runs, and way across the river valley to the orchards and dairy farms in the next county. You can even see the smokestack of the power plant out toward Asheville puffing like a long cigar.

I was eating my coleslaw and shrimp and thinking I hadn't used enough soap on my hands for I could smell grease on them. There's a burned smell that gets in your skin when you touch the graphite in axle grease. I'd replaced the brake rotors on a Pontiac that morning. When I washed my knuckles they looked clean, but every time I brought a hushpuppy to my mouth I smelled a little tang of grease.

People in the diner started getting up and going to the window on the west end. I didn't notice at first, and I didn't hear anything special.

"What is it?" I said to Judd at the next booth, but he had already gone to look.

"Now what is it?" Mary Lee said, trying to make her way through the crowd with a platter in each hand. She and I didn't talk much in the café. She said it was better if we just met after hours and acted like no more than friends in The Blue Guitar. She hadn't agreed yet to be engaged.

"Look at that," somebody said. "Now just look at that."

"My god!" somebody else said.

I saw the sheriff get up from the counter and head toward the push of people. He had to shift his gunbelt a little because it had twisted while he sat. "What's going on?" he said.

I was sure it was a fight. There had been a lot of lay-offs lately and people hung around town looking for work. You get too many old boys in town with nothing to do you'll have a fight every day. You might see a circle of men gathered anywhere in front of The Dugout Grill, or The Blue Guitar, even at the filling station on Grant Street where I work. Any time you see that ring of men you know a fight is at the center. The circle will shift sideways and backwards and forwards, as the fighters push and claw and roll over.

I wasn't even going to get up, for the last thing I needed was to see two boys busting their knuckles and bloodying each other's noses. I'd done it too much myself, and I didn't want Mary Lee to see me involved in any trouble. Fighting is contagious. Besides, I had to eat my shrimp and drink my tea and get back to work on that Pontiac. I wanted to be done early for I was driving Mary Lee over to the new mall in West Asheville that evening.

"He's plumb crazy," somebody shouted.

"What is that damn fool driver doing?"

"Stand back," Sheriff Dixon said, but nobody paid him any attention.

"Who is that?" one man at the window said.

"It ain't nobody," another said.

That's when I jumped up to see what was going on. Two boys fighting was one thing, but a runaway machine without a driver was another. I thought of eighteen-wheelers and pickup trucks and Pontiacs loose on the hill. The crowd was pressed so tight to the window I couldn't see a thing. Mary Lee couldn't even get back to the coffeepot.

I was going to have to run outside if I wanted to see anything. Much as I hated to leave my shrimp and iced tea I had to have a look. But it was like everybody decided to go out at the same instant. You would have thought they all followed me out of The Blue Guitar. I had to elbow somebody aside just to get the door open. As I dashed onto the hot sidewalk the whole clientele of the café poured out behind me.

Everybody was looking to the left, and at first I couldn't see a thing. The haze of late summer and heat wrinkles and exhaust in the air made it hard to spot anything. And then I saw the bulldozer. It was the biggest kind of Caterpillar there is, the kind with a canopy over the driver's seat and a blade as wide as the whole road. The blade itself was tall as a man. The bulldozer was coming right down the street, crossing the lanes of traffic at a slight angle, and cars were honking and skidding and stopping. Some swung around the big Cat. Those that didn't make it got pushed aside and rolled over and pushed again. People left their cars in the street and started running. But the big dozer just kept coming, edging toward the other side of the street and knocking everything out of its way. And there was nobody in the driver's seat.

We learned later the bulldozer had come all the way from the construction site on the Interstate. At lunch hour the drivers stop their machines and turn the motors off, leaving the keys in the ignition. Only some of the big trucks keep their motors running because their cabs are air conditioned. Some of the men working on the highway come into town to eat at The Blue Guitar and Taco Bell. But most bring their own coolers and lunchboxes. They sit in their pickup trucks and turn on the air-conditioning and listen to the radio or tapes while they eat. I guess music sounds awfully good after sitting behind a diesel engine all morning.

We heard the driver of the bulldozer had a computer in his truck and he and his buddies liked to play video games on it. They would sit there in the air conditioning and play electronic poker or something, betting on themselves and each other. This time there was a big game going on and a bunch had gathered around the cab and in the back to watch. The stakes had gone so high there were hundreds of dollars changing hands. Almost all the crew were betting.

The bulldozer driver was sure he didn't leave his machine running. A big diesel engine will idle so quiet it's just a mutter and low grinding sound. Maybe he left the motor on and it threw itself in gear and started crawling. But there was a lot of bad feeling in the county about the highway taking people's land, and it's just possible some old boy, for the hell of it, climbed up on the seat and started the dozer, then jumped off. That fits what I saw later. But I don't think they'll ever know, no matter how many fingerprints they get off the ignition and controls. Whoever it was must have known how to turn up the throttle. Maybe it was one of these environmental agitators that are always protesting new roads and factories and anybody cutting down a tree.

The crew gathered around the truck to watch the computer game never even heard the bulldozer until somebody saw it climbing the high bank they were building for the overpass. They looked up, and there it was, blasting diesel smoke and crawling right up the steep embankment. It lurched a little on a long steel beam they'd delivered for the new bridge and tilted up on one track, then started down the other side. That's why they didn't catch up with the dozer. It was too far away when they noticed it and going full blast.

That yellow mother roared down the other side of the embankment out of sight before most of the boys watching the game ever saw it. The big tracks reared on some culvert pipes along the roadway and crushed them to dust. The jolting seemed to push the throttle even higher. The dozer knocked right through a chainlink fence along the right of way and headed through a line of trees toward the French Broad Shopping Mall.

People in the parking lot of the mall saw the bulldozer coming through the trees and probably thought nothing of it at first. Somebody was always grading there as they expanded the parking lot. The big Cat came clanking along like a tank, crashed over the wall into the parking lot, and revved its motor even higher. They looked on helpless as the dozer headed right toward the rows of parked cars. I think some people tried to run and move their cars, but there wasn't time. Mostly people got themselves out of the way.

A woman had left her baby in its seat inside her car. When she heard the bulldozer she was almost at the door of K-Mart. She came running like she was berserk because the dozer was headed straight toward where she'd parked. She pushed past people screaming. Her car was locked and she had the key in hand. "Stop it," she shouted to nobody in particular. I think it's against the law to leave a baby by itself in a car, but people do it all the time.

"Get back!" somebody yelled at the woman, but she pushed her way past. Her car was a new Neon, the color of pearl. The baby was asleep in its chair strapped to the front seat. Just as the mother reached the car and tried to insert her key the bulldozer slammed into a jeep Cherokee parked alongside. A track reared up over the 4x4 and the bulldozer turned slightly, hitting the rear of the Neon and spinning it around. Then it roared past, clanking and crashing into other cars. The woman got her baby out but it was crying. She clutched it to her breast and bawled herself.

The bulldozer crawled up over a few small cars and mashed them flat. But mostly the wide blade pushed cars and trucks out of the way. A compact pickup caught in the center of the blade was pushed almost across the parking lot into the traffic of Main Street. And then it too spun off to the side.

Drivers on the four lanes of Main Street didn't see the bulldozer at first. It roared down the sidewalk knocking over parking meters and shoving parked cars. Drivers honked at the dozer and swerved as it edged into the right lanes. A policeman in his patrol car came screeching up and spoke through the loudspeaker: "Stop that machine. Stop it or I'll shoot." And then he saw there was nobody driving it. Some people said he got out his pistol and tried to shoot at the controls, but if he did it didn't have any effect. In the excitement it was hard to know what was happening.

There is a building at the third block of Main Street called the Ewbank Building. It reaches out over the sidewalk on pillars and has a room almost above the street. It's against all regulations, but because the building is old and owned by the mayor's brother nobody has ever torn it down. There's a doctor's office there now, Dr. Shuford, who is a baby doctor. People saw the dozer going right toward the pillar of the building and knew there were children and their mothers in the doctor's office. Some honked and some hollered. There was a gasp from everybody watching as the machine kept coming and hit a corner pillar with the tip of its blade. They could see kids looking out the windows of the doctor's office.

The blade knocked down the pillar and shook the building. Everybody expected to see the top story fall. But after the bulldozer went by the top story was still standing on one of its pillars. The floor sagged a little and the roof tilted. Women and children screamed inside but only the first pillar was hit.

As the bulldozer edged into the outside lane on Main Street, traffic kept going by. Cars switched lanes to go around it, and traffic in the other direction slowed as drivers tried to see what was happening. People gathered on the sidewalks and ran along the street, and there were more police cars with their sirens and traffic started jamming up in both directions. The bulldozer driver and the foreman of the construction crew had tried to follow the bulldozer in a pickup, but they got stuck in traffic blocks away. People stopped at a light saw the bulldozer coming in their rearview mirrors and drove on through the red light. Others jumped out of their cars and ran.

What happened then scared everybody even worse. The bulldozer was out in the street and would have missed the light pole, except an Orkin truck it hit plunged into the pole and broke it off. The pole held not only a streetlight, but also the traffic light and powerlines. The lines fell right along the sidewalk sparking and smoking. People on the sidewalk screamed and ran. The lines hissed when they hit parked cars. Sparks fizzed and foamed at every place the wires touched.

When the bulldozer blade hit the wires, it seemed to rev the motor even higher. Smoke blasted from the pipe on its hood. Flames spurted from a car that had been overturned. There was a blinding ghost of light as the gas tank exploded. The fire station blasted its horn.

I watched the bulldozer lurching right down Main Street and tried to think what to do. I had only driven a dozer once, a little one, in the army. But I had driven a tank, which was similar. Cars stopped and tried to turn around in front of The Blue Guitar, and those behind rammed into the stopped ones. A Federal Express truck was caught in the jam and as the bulldozer approached the driver jumped from the cab and ran over the hoods of stalled cars.

"Somebody stop that thing!" Sheriff Dixon called.

People were running down the street on either side and a police car came roaring up the sidewalk.

"Why doesn't somebody do something?" Mary Lee said. She'd come out of The Blue Guitar with a hamburger platter in her hand.

"I'm going to shoot the engine," Dixon said. He took his pistol out of the holster and checked to see if it was loaded. He looked at the crowd and at the approaching dozer. "I'm afraid a bullet might ricochet," he said and put the revolver back in the holster.

"Somebody's got to do something," Mary Lee said.

If the bulldozer had been going slow that would have been one thing. You could have just climbed up and turned off the ignition. But the motor was going full throttle and didn't even slow down when a car or truck was hit. Every collision just seemed to make it roar louder. As the big Cat got closer, I saw what the worst difficulty was. To get up on the seat you had to climb on a track, and each track was about five feet high. Plus, it was moving so fast that soon as you climbed on the track you would be thrown forward and never reach the controls.

I saw the way to stop the big Cat was to jump on it from something higher. But you would have to be close enough so you wouldn't land on the track and get jerked forward. I looked around to see what was in the path of the dozer that I could climb up on. Mary Lee was watching me and I had to do something. I'd planned to ask her to marry me that night.

Just across the street from The Blue Guitar was Gosnell's fruit stand. It was a little outdoor market with boxes of tomatoes and peaches and cucumbers by the sidewalk and grapes and apples and cantaloupes on the tables. Watermelons were stacked along the front. Gosnell stood in his apron watching the dozer roar toward him. It appeared to be headed right at the stand. The crowd moved back past him and Gosnell started to grab a basket of peaches to move them out of the way. Then he remembered something inside the shed and started in, but it was too late. The bulldozer clanked across the sidewalk and Gosnell had to run just as the big blade turned over the first boxes of tomatoes.

The machine didn't go through the fruit stand. The blade just swept over the boxes and baskets in front, crushing cucumbers and cantaloupes, and busting melons like water balloons. The awning was swept away and the counter with the cash register spun over as coins and bills spilled among the fruit and were covered by the grinding track. Those who saw the cash register tip over ran behind the machine as soon as the dozer passed. Gosnell stood there in his apron watching.

The next thing down the street from the fruit stand was the drive-in branch of the Blue Ridge Trust Company. There was an automatic teller machine under the overhang as well as a drive-up window. A Toyota was stopped at the ATM and the driver was pushing the buttons on the panel. But as the dozer got closer, he pulled away, leaving his card in the beeping machine.

I don't reckon it took more than a few seconds for the big Cat to crawl from the fruit stand to the branch bank, but to us looking on, it seemed to take forever. The blade was aimed right toward the ATM and the dozer lurched on the boundary where shrubs and flowerbeds had been set out. The tracks crushed a low brick wall and banged to the paved parking lot. I thought if I could climb up on the roof of the drive-in I could jump down on the hood of the dozer and slide back under the canopy into the driver's seat while Mary Lee was watching me. But it was too late. The blade hit a post and the roof came crashing down just as the ATM was knocked over. People inside the branch bank poured out the door. The last to go was Sharon, the girl in the service window. She grabbed a canvas bag from the counter and ran out the front door just as the blade hit the main building.

One whole end of the branch bank was ripped open and bricks and glass, steel and sections of the roof, came crashing down. Right behind the dozer the crowd dived in, grabbing through the rubble for bills from the crushed teller machine and the drawer of the drive-in window. There was money fluttering among the crushed bricks and shattered glass and people pushed each other aside and fought over bills and tubes of coins. But some were waiting to see if the dozer hit the safe. As it came out of the collapsing building, I saw the blade pushing the safe like a heavy dog kennel. The door with its wheels and knobs and bars was open and packs and boxes of bills spilled out. The dozer pushed the heavy box through the rubble and across the driveway. The safe turned over and finally rolled aside. Sheriff Dixon and two policemen ran to it with their guns out and threatened people away from the twisted door. But there was nothing they could do about people picking through the glass and dirt and bricks for the loose bills. People swarmed over the mess like birds pecking for worms in a new plowed field.

That's when I saw where the bulldozer was headed next. Just beyond the wall around the bank was a high wooden fence. And beyond the fence was Carter's Buick dealership. The dozer was aimed right at the lot of new cars that covered most of the block.

I ran as hard as I could around the mess of the drive-in bank and the crowd shoving there, to the fence of the car lot. I figured if I could get up on top of a car I might be able to jump into the cockpit of the bulldozer. The problem was the blade was so wide it knocked everything close out of the way. But it was too late anyway. The bulldozer crashed through the wooden fence and rolled right on top of a new Regal. The car was shiny ruby red and I saw the top crumple like paper and the big tracks flatten the trunk and hood like a milk carton. Gasoline squirted from the crushed tank.

"No!" somebody shouted. "No!" It was one of the car salesmen, Franklin Ward I think it was. He stood in front of the dozer like he was giving it orders, and then he jumped to the side at the last second. The blade hit a little blue Skylark and turned it over. The dozer crawled on top of a row of Centuries and crumpled them. The windshields turned to frost and shattered into crumbs of glass. The polished metal skin was left as wrinkled scrap.

Ahead of the Cat was a new Riviera. It was the most beautiful car I'd ever seen. It was the car I would have bought if I was a rich man. It was the car I would have liked to drive Mary Lee to Asheville in. The Riviera was dark green, and looked carved from a solid block of emerald.

"No!" I shouted, and ran past Franklin Ward. Other salesmen and secretaries from the Buick office had gathered at the doorway and looked on in horror. The blade knocked a Le Sabre aside and smashed through the windshield of a Park Avenue. The tracks clanked on the paving of the parking lot the way panzers do in war movies when they enter the streets of a town. I think I closed my eyes as the blade crashed into the aircraft shape of the Riviera. The windows of the sleek car popped out and shattered as the Cat crawled right on top of the cab. One track went over the engine and I imagined I could hear the gaskets pop as cylinders broke apart.

Just beyond the Riviera ran a cinder block fence about six feet high. The bulldozer slammed into it and stopped. But the engine kept revving and the tracks going round. There was an awful screeching and clanking as the tracks ground into the pavement like ditch-diggers. I ran as hard as I could over the wrecks to the stalled machine. Where the tracks raked into the macadam, sparks and smoke and rocks and pieces of asphalt went flying. The bulldozer shook in convulsions.

There was no way I could climb on the tracks they were moving so fast. But there was a big hitch just behind the seat where they hooked cables for towing earthmovers. I leaped up on the hitch and swung myself around under the canopy into the seat. The exhaust and dust from the churning tracks were blinding. I felt along the panel for the key but couldn't find it. There was the lever for the left track, and the lever for the right track, and there was a brake pedal on either side. The panel was covered with dials and knobs. I felt all around the front for the key, and along each side. There didn't seem to be any key.

People were crowding around the dozer by then. Dixon hollered something at me, and Franklin Ward was hollering something. A man in a hard-hat—I figured it was the construction foreman—was motioning for me to turn the key. He kept putting his thumb on his first finger and turning his hand over. I felt around again on the panel, patting the dials and levers. The engine roar and the screeching of the tracks were so loud I couldn't hear a thing that was said. But I saw Dixon was ordering me to get off the dozer and let somebody else try to turn it off. The foreman pointed to the bottom of the panel. I felt there again and found the ignition switch. But the key had been broken off in the slot. There was nothing but a little twisted piece of metal sticking out of the keyhole.

Now if a key is broken off in a keyhole you can try to pull it out with a pair of pliers, or you can cut the wires leading to the switch. I tried to feel around for where the wires ran, but they were all behind the panel. To reach them I would need a screwdriver to take the panel off. I felt around again to the side, but I must have touched the lever that lifted the big blade for the next thing I knew there was a whining sound and the hydraulic bars pulled the heavy arms of the blade up against the cinder block wall, scraping steel on cement. Soon as the blade reached the top of the wall the dozer tilted in the pits the tracks had dug and began climbing right up the wall. I was slung against the back of the seat and just had time to grab the poles that held the canopy to keep from falling off.

It seemed the dozer was rearing so steep it was going to flip backwards on top of me. I was looking straight up at the wide blade against the sky. I closed my eyes thinking I was a goner. But somehow the big tracks caught on the top of the wall and pulled the dozer forward with a lurch and scream of metal on concrete. I was thrown forward, then back again. And the machine lifted itself right over the top of the wall and across the bank of red clay. Before I could do anything besides hold on, the dozer roared through another wooden fence and started downhill. Smoke and splinters and dust flew in my face.

The bulldozer speeded down the slope. I couldn't even see where we were going with the big blade raised in front. I knew the railroad tracks ran just beyond the car lot. There was a kind of freight yard, with a siding and loading docks where pulp wood and gravel were shipped. The trains came through about half a dozen times a day. There was one that arrived every day just after lunch hour.

It came to me that if I couldn't stop the bulldozer at least I could steer it. All Caterpillars steered the same way. You slow one side down to turn in that direction. The tank I drove in Vietnam twenty years before would turn in a space no longer than its length. While the dozer lurched and banged I tried to find the brake pedals with my feet.

I touched one pedal and pressed, and the dozer jerked around so violently I almost fell off. It was going too fast to steer easily. I would have to find the throttle and slow it down before trying to turn. Or maybe I could push both brake pedals and slow down that way. Above the roar of the diesel and the clanking of the tracks I heard the blast of a train horn. And looking to the right I saw a freight train coming toward us. The horn blasted again and again, and sparks and smoke started squirting from the train wheels. The engine wheels were frozen and hissing. And it was like I froze too. I couldn't even find the brake pedals with my feet as the dozer rocked across the rails and ties into the oncoming locomotive. The train blasted its horn and just kept coming. There was more smoke and sparks and dust around the wheels. The locomotive was even taller than the raised blade of the bulldozer.

It all happened in a couple of seconds, I guess, but it seemed to take hours. The train got closer and the bulldozer lurched and clattered on the rails. I watched the headlight on the train like it was going to hit me in the forehead. The front of the engine met the corner of the blade and the bulldozer spun to the side. The locomotive just nudged the track of the bulldozer as the train came to a stop with a hiss and the dozer jolted away onto the siding.

I was relieved, until I saw the cliff ahead. About fifty feet from the tracks was the bluff above the river gorge. The tracks ran almost along the rim. That was when I should have jumped over the back of the seat, but I was too addled to do anything except stomp the brake pedals and hold onto the poles with both hands.

"Whoa!" I hollered, like it was a horse I was riding. The bulldozer hit a telegraph pole and crashed through some sumac bushes beside the tracks. There was a wire fence there, and then nothing but the river valley far below. I saw Filson's barn way down by the river and a tractor out in Barrett's field pulling a haybaler.

As the bulldozer tipped over the cliff I could see above the blade the whole valley. I thought: this is what it's like to die. You live your life and then you die for no reason and none of it means a thing. The whole business is nothing but a shrug and a glance. I wondered if Mary Lee was watching me. Maybe I should have been praying, but I didn't think of that. I was too busy holding on as my belly shot up in my throat and I tasted shrimp and hushpuppies as things rushed by.

I expected to be falling and turning over, but the cliff was not as straight up and down as it looked. It was more a steep slope, steep as the steepest roof. What the bulldozer did was just run right down the side like a roller coaster knocking down trees and banging on big rocks. It plowed through cedars and the tops of poplars. I felt I was falling through tree after tree as limbs whipped by me.

The bulldozer plunged on through laurel bushes and banged on boulders and crushed logs. Several times I thought it was going to pitch over or roll to the side. But the heavy blade just pulled it down and down. Trees shot by, and loose rocks tumbled alongside.

When we landed in a hayfield the bulldozer kept going. It was only a little way to the river and I saw we were going right into the water if I didn't do something. I pushed down on both brakes, and the dozer slowed a little. And then I found the throttle and pushed that knob and the engine got quieter and quieter. Finally the motor started barking and coughing as a diesel will, and just stalled out. Maybe it ran out of fuel. It was so quiet in the hayfield I could hear the breeze, and the grasshoppers in the weeds. Somewhere there was the scream of a firetruck coming along the river road. I sniffed the stink of grease still on my knuckles, mixed with the smell of hay and fumes off the hot engine. I looked back up toward the cliff and saw a crowd had gathered on the rim, and it tickled me that Mary Lee was among them, still holding the hamburger platter, and looking toward me.

# HAPPY VALLEY

ANNIE WAS DETERMINED to escape from the Happy Valley Rehab Center and Nursing Home. She believed her son had imprisoned her there to get her out of his way. She couldn't remember that she'd fallen and broken her hip and that she still had trouble walking. And even when she was reminded of her condition she quickly forgot it. It seemed to her some of the time that she was back home with her mama and daddy. At other times it seemed she was waiting for her husband Muir to come for her in his pickup truck. When the nurse's aide appeared to change her diaper or bring her pills she'd say, "Hurry up, I've got to get dressed."

"Why do you have to get dressed, Miss Annie?" the aide, who was named Carolyn, said.

"Because I've got to start fixing supper."

"You don't have to fix supper. I'll bring your supper on a tray," Carolyn said.

"All those people are coming and I've got to help Mama fix supper," Annie said.

"Don't worry, Miss Annie, we'll take care of everything."

At times Annie believed it was the new preacher from Greenville who was conducting a revival at the church who was coming with his young wife for dinner. At other times it was all the cousins from Asheville who visited once or twice a year. And the problem was not just getting supper cooked and on the table, but gathering eggs, shelling corn for the chickens, making sure someone milked the cow. Nothing would get done if she didn't get out of bed, put on her clothes, gather her things, and reach home in time. Otherwise Mama would have to do it all herself.

Some days, when Annie could recall where she was and how she got there, she knew she'd have to be cunning to escape. If her son had incarcerated her here and the staff of Happy Valley was cooperating with him to keep her prisoner, following his orders, she'd have to outsmart them. When she was young she'd loved to act. She'd starred in several plays in high school. And she'd played one role or another all her life. Acting was her best talent. She smiled and made friends with everybody on her hall. When she was able to walk with the walker she explored the other hallways, and the lounge, the cafeteria, and the exercise rooms. There was a room decorated like a dairy bar where you could get an ice cream cone every afternoon. There was a little chapel with both a cross and a menorah. There was a library reading room with a fireplace. Annie spoke to everyone and pretended she remembered who they were as she made her rounds. She stopped in the beauty shop to chat with the beautician.

But all the time Annie was exploring the nooks and alcoves she was studying the exits. Some doors led only to a courtyard enclosed on all sides. One long hallway led to the hospice wing where they took those near death. Another door led through the lounge to the main entrance. But there was always someone on duty at the reception desk.

The door that seemed most promising was the one that opened to the far end of the parking lot. That door was the farthest from the central nurse's station. The hallway to it led past the physical therapy rooms, the room where they showed movies from time to time, and the showers for patients who couldn't stand. Beyond the door Annie could see a few cars and trucks, and empty spaces between white lines. She reasoned that if she could get out that door she could find someone in the parking lot who would drive her home. Or perhaps she could flag down a taxi, or one of those city buses that made their rounds. Surely there would be someone who would drive her away from Happy Valley.

To make her escape Annie thought the best time would not be in the middle of the night when all was quiet. Then someone would notice her moving about. The busiest time of day, when all the staff were stirring about, giving medicines, baths, changing beds, was her best chance. While nurses and orderlies and aides were rushing about the halls she would not be conspicuous. In preparation she hid her purse and shoes and a sweater in the basket on her walker. As soon as the nurse had given Annie her pills and the aide had changed her diaper she gripped the handles of the walker and entered the hallway. Nodding and smiling at all she passed she made her way around carts loaded with breakfast trays, laundry carts, nurses with clipboards, patients asleep in wheelchairs, janitors with brooms, all the way down the long corridor to the door near the far end of the parking lot.

A physical therapist named Gerald saw her go by and waved. But he was busy throwing a red beach ball back and forth to a patient, while around him other patients pedaled exercise machines. Annie knew that if she could get out of this place she would exercise in normal, useful ways, working in the garden, walking to the store, as she always had.

When Annie first pushed on the glass door it didn't give. She studied the door and realized she'd forgotten her glasses. There were red letters on the glass, but she couldn't read them. She touched the middle of the door and found a kind of lever. As she pushed the lever the lock clicked, and, using all her strength, she pushed the door. A bell went off somewhere, but without her hearing aid she hardly noticed it.

The difficulty was to push the door open and drive the walker through. After several tries she saw the only way was to back through the door. It took every bit of strength she had to shove the door with her behind and get far enough outside to let the door close. When she finally made it and the door shut on its own she saw people hurrying down the hall toward her. One was Gerald the physical therapist who motioned for her to stop.

Fast as she could Annie turned the walker around and aimed it down the walkway toward the parking lot. If she could only get to the cars surely someone would give her a ride. All she had to do was ask them. People had always been generous to her. If no one offered a ride there had to be a taxi or a bus she could catch. She wondered if she had enough money in her purse for a taxi or bus fare. She was pretty sure she did. Bus fare to town used to be twenty cents. Even if prices had gone up she had enough.

Annie was sure she would make it to the parking lot, until a wheel of the walker ran over the edge of the sidewalk and jammed in the groove between the turf and the concrete. Pushing hard as she could she slammed into the walker and fell over into the grass, spilling her purse and shoes and sweater on the ground around her.

The physical therapist got to her first. "Why Miss Annie, where are you going?" he said.

She could tell him she was going home, but it wouldn't do any good. She determined she would say nothing as the physical therapist and a nurse lifted her up. An aide brought a wheelchair, and they rolled her back inside and down the long hallway to her room.

Later that day a nurse checked Annie for broken bones, but found only bruises. "I have something pretty for you, Miss Annie," the nurse said. She held up a pink band that looked like a plastic watch.

"What is that?"

"You've been such a good girl we're going to give you an ankle bracelet."

"Why?"

"To show you're almost finished with therapy."

The nurse strapped the band to Annie's ankle and said, "Now doesn't that look pretty?"

Sitting in the wheelchair it was hard for Annie to see her ankle. But the nurses and the nurses' aides kept telling her how pretty the anklet looked. "Not everyone has one of these," Carolyn said. "This means you're somebody special."

Just because she'd failed once to escape from Happy Valley didn't mean Annie was defeated. She could see through their flattery. No matter what they said she knew she had to get home and help Mama feed the chickens and fix supper. There were beans to string and potatoes to peel. That very night, or maybe it was the next night, she began to plan another escape.

This time she would be more subtle. She'd wait until Sunday afternoon when there were the most visitors. The lobby would be full of people coming and going. She'd blend into the crowd and simply ask someone to hold the door for her, roll the wheelchair out to the loading area and then to the parking lot and catch a ride with someone leaving.

As she was planning this escape Annie forgot that her husband Muir had passed away almost twenty years ago. He'd died at the age of eighty-six. As she thought of leaving the nursing home and rehab center on Sunday afternoon it occurred to her Muir would be waiting in the pickup truck in the parking lot, as he always did while she shopped. He would be a little mad because he'd been there since church let out. When Muir got mad he would sulk. She'd have to talk sweetly to him, as she had so many times before, until he forgot his anger. Then she'd suggest that they go to Shoney's or McDonald's. Muir was especially fond of the big double cheeseburgers. Then on the way home they'd stop at the fruit stand by the river and buy a watermelon or two ripe cantaloupes.

That Sunday afternoon a preacher came by and spoke to Annie. He claimed he was her minister, but she didn't recognize him. She thought he meant well, but was confused. Her pastor was named Liner and she'd recognize him in a second if she saw him.

"How are you, Sister Annie?" the strange preacher said.

"I'm just fine," she said. "I'm going home today."

"Going home, already?"

"My husband Muir is coming for me."

The minister nodded and smiled and patted her hand. "That's just fine, Sister Annie. That's just fine."

When the preacher was gone Annie rolled her wheelchair to the chest of drawers and got out her purse. There were other things in the drawer she should take too, an extra sweater, a cosmetics kit, an extra pair of slippers. But she'd have to leave them. There simply wasn't room in the wheelchair to hide them. All her life she'd done without things and made do.

As Annie pushed herself out into the hallway she put on her biggest smile. She greeted every visitor carrying flowers or candy or a wrapped gift. She spoke to other patients nodding in wheelchairs whether they noticed her or not. At the nurse's station she made a right turn down the long hallway toward the lobby and main entrance. The administrative and business offices she passed along the way were mostly closed. It was Sunday.

In the lounge area there were several patients in wheelchairs surrounded by family, or sitting on couches with their walkers in front of them. Many visitors were dressed in Sunday best, as if they had just come from an Easter service.

"Hello, Miss Annie," the woman at the reception desk said. "How are you?"

"I'm just fine," Annie said.

"Are you expecting someone?" the receptionist said.

"Yes, I'm meeting my husband."

Just then a couple came through the door and walked to the reception desk. They asked for the room number of a patient, and Annie took the opportunity to roll herself to the entrance. She reached the doorway just as someone else came in.

"Would you please hold the door for me?" she asked as sweetly as she could.

"Certainly, ma'am," the man said.

As Annie pushed herself forward she knew she was almost home free. Muir was waiting in the pickup. They would drive right to town and have lunch and she'd never come back to Happy Valley. Because she'd thought it out carefully everything had gone as she'd planned.

But as she passed through the door a bell went off. It was that awful ringing she'd heard before, like a fire alarm. Someone took her wheelchair by the handles and pulled her back into the lobby. The receptionist bent over her and said, "You don't want to go out there, Miss Annie. You're not dressed for going outside today."

"Muir is waiting for me," Annie said.

"When the weather's warmer you can go outside," the receptionist said. A nurse's aide came and wheeled her back down the corridor to her room. There she gave Annie a pill in a tiny paper cup.

"Don't want no pill," Annie said.

"It's time for your medicine," the aide said. "Here, have some ginger ale." After she took the pill Annie slept. She must have been tired for she slept a long time. And while she slept she dreamed someone came by who said he was her son. But she knew it wasn't her son. This was an older man with graying hair, partly bald. Her son had thick blond hair. He'd put her in this place and left her. He'd tricked her into signing a paper, he and a lawyer. He wouldn't dare come to see her after what he'd done. The man who claimed to be her son must have been hired by the lawyer. They must have taken her money because she didn't have any money now except for a few dollars in her purse. She had just enough for a phone call, or maybe a taxi ride.

IT WAS SEVERAL days later when Annie began to think about the bell going off as she rolled through the entrance door. When other people entered or left no bell had sounded. That's when she remembered the strap buckled to her ankle. It looked like a cheap watch, but a watch would be strapped to her wrist. Why would something be buckled on her ankle where she couldn't even see it, much less reach it? Surely it didn't measure her pulse or blood pressure or temperature. A heart monitor would be on her chest.

It came to Annie that the pink band was put on her ankle *because* she couldn't reach it there. They were afraid she'd take it off if she got her hands on it. Why had she not thought of that before? The alarm bell had gone off just before she rolled through the lobby door, just as her foot had passed through the entrance. It was the band that had set off the bell. How clever they thought they were, with their pretty pink anklet.

Over the next several days Annie began to study on ways to get the strap off her ankle. She was simply too stiff to raise her leg or bend down to reach the anklet. And it had no ordinary buckle. Even if she could reach it she might have trouble with the buckle. Luckily the thing was made of plastic and plastic could be stretched or broken.

One day was so much like another in the nursing home she lost count of the days and weeks. Some days she mostly slept. Other days she was sure she was home, even though the room didn't look exactly like her bedroom. She worried that her children had gone out to play and hadn't come back in. She'd warned them to stay out of the pasture where the bull was, and to stay away from the river. She was afraid they'd wander into the weeds across the road where she'd seen a copperhead. And they were not to ride their tricycles near the road where a big truck might hit them.

Annie began to plan her third escape from Happy Valley. First she had to break or slip the band off her ankle, and then she had to roll herself down the corridor to the hospice wing. It was a long hallway. But once she reached the hospice where there were only patients near death and aides making them comfortable, she could find an unguarded door and go outside to that section of the large parking lot. She should have tried the hospice exit the first time.

Annie decided that the best way to break the band on her ankle was to catch it on something sharp. But then it occurred to her that when she curled up in bed at night she might reach the band. With her knees to her chin, lying on her left side, she could touch the band. They hadn't thought of that. So that night or the next, when she thought of it, she curled herself into a ball and reached for the anklet. Sure enough, she could feel the slick plastic. But as she ran her hands on the band it wasn't clear where the buckle was. It took many tries to find the buckle under a kind of sheath, and many more attempts to find the end and pull it loose. But before she went to sleep her ankle was free. She placed the band in the drawer of the stand beside her bed.

ONE OF THE reasons Annie blamed her son for placing her in Happy Valley was that she herself, when her mama got sick with a brain tumor, had stayed at home and looked after her. Annie had quit her job and moved in with her parents. Every night and every day for months she was there to cook and clean, to sit up at night, to give medicine, accompany Mama to the doctor, change bed clothes, make it easier for Papa. She'd accompanied Mama to the hospital in Winston-Salem for surgery and then on to Charlotte. She was with Mama in the recovery room when she died, her head bandaged where they'd shaved away her hair and sawed through her skull. For weeks afterward she'd dreamed about Mama falling off the gurney and her brains spilling out through the hole they'd cut.

But her son, after Annie had had a little fall and was recovering, had dumped her at the rehab center and never come back, claiming he couldn't miss any more days of work than he already had. He'd abandoned her. He didn't come to see her. Now it was up to her to get herself out of this jail called Happy Valley.

As Annie studied on a way to get to the hospice wing, she promised herself she'd learned from her mistakes. First she'd tried to escape into the parking lot at the busiest hour of the morning. But that had only landed her back in a wheelchair. Next she'd tried to make it through the front door on a Sunday afternoon while the lobby was crowded with visitors. That had only set off their damned alarm bell. Now that the band was off her ankle she had to be smart. She felt in her heart this would be her last chance to get away from Happy Valley.

This time she'd try to escape in the wee hours of the night when no one was stirring. The nurses and the nurses' aides would be at the station clicking their computers, eating snacks, reading magazines. All she would have to do was turn down the long corridor that led to the hospice wing. A door had to be opened there, but with the anklet off no alarm would sound.

Annie wasn't exactly sure what to expect once she reached the hospice. There would be someone on duty, but she'd tell them she'd come to visit a patient, if they saw her. With luck she could slip out the door into the parking lot without being seen. From there Muir with his pickup truck or someone else would drive her home. She knew there were risks in her plan, but there were risks in everything. The alternative would be to stay at Happy Valley forever.

When her son had placed her in the nursing home he'd given Annie a cell phone and told her she could call him any time. But she'd never learned to use the cell phone, and the phone had disappeared, either lost or stolen. Things disappeared all the time at the nursing home. The nurse's aide had looked for the cell phone, but with no luck. Annie knew that once she got outside the hospice she'd have to find a pay phone, if Muir wasn't there waiting in the pickup.

In preparation for her departure Annie placed her purse in the bag attached to the back of the wheelchair. She stowed the kit of her cosmetic things there too. She'd saved a cupcake from the supper tray and added that to her supplies. She could munch on the cupcake while waiting for a ride in the parking lot.

That night Annie waited until the digital clock beside her bed said 3:00 before rolling herself out of bed. Reaching out to the wheelchair she pulled it closer and twisted herself so she fell almost onto the seat. She banged her knee and almost slid to the floor, but caught her elbows on the armrests, and pushed with her feet until she was firmly in the seat. She listened for sounds in the hall. The nurse's aide had gone by at 2:45. It would be another hour before she made the next round.

Rolling herself to the door Annie looked up and down the hallway:

no one was in sight. She pushed herself into the hall, made a right turn, and headed down the long corridor as quietly as she could. Patients moaned or cried out in the rooms she passed. Through one door she saw a woman sitting up in bed, but hurried on, hoping the woman wouldn't call out.

As she approached the entrance to the hospice wing she saw the heavy doors were closed. If they were locked she was doomed. Turning the wheelchair around she backed against the doors and pushed as hard as she could. The doors gave a little, and with great effort she backed through. Once in the hallway of the hospice she noticed different smells from the nursing home. Instead of alcohol, Lysol, urine, she smelled carpets, and some kind of incense.

Annie had visited the hospice when her cousin Helen was dying of cancer there. She remembered it as a quiet, clean place, almost like a hotel. She tried to recall the pattern of the rooms and hallways. There was a reception room and a lounge area. She planned to go out through the front entrance, but any door to the outside would do.

On the carpeted hallway Annie stopped and listened. Someone was talking down the corridor, as if they were speaking on a phone. And then she heard the sound of wheels rolling, like a cart or gurney. It was hard to believe someone was working at this hour. Could it be a cleaning woman? A new patient arriving? With horror Annie realized the sound was getting louder. They were coming her way.

She looked to the left and saw an open door. Quickly she rolled herself through the doorway into a darkened room. Only a small lamp burned on a table in the corner. There was a kind of counter in the middle of the room and as the sound got closer she pushed herself into a corner behind the counter. And just in time, for two men rolled something into the room, and then left, closing the door.

Annie waited until she was sure they'd gone and wheeled herself out from behind the counter. A gurney sat in the middle of the room. In the dim light she could see a sheet draped over the gurney and white hair where the sheet didn't completely cover a head. Annie pushed her chair closer where she could see better. The hair was exactly the shade of Mama's hair, the hair that had been partly shaved away for the surgery. Had they pushed Mama into this darkened room after the operation? Annie got closer and pulled the sheet back a little, and sure enough it was Mama's face.

"What are you doing here?" she said.

It surprised her that Mama had ended up here too, at the hospice in Happy Valley, after all the care Annie had given her, all the days and nights of sitting up, cleaning up, the days of worry and waiting.

"I've got to take you out of here," she said and reached up to touch Mama's shoulder. An arm fell from under the sheet and she took hold of the hand and pulled it. "We've got to go now," Annie said. "Let's hurry."

She had to get Mama home in time to fix supper. Annie pulled as hard as she could and the body began to slide off the gurney on top of her. She felt she was going to be crushed under the weight. She was falling. And just then Annie heard voices behind her and a blinding light obliterated everything in the room.

# BIG WORDS AND FAME

I WAS ON STUDY LEAVE from the university and supposedly in Washington to research my next book. But I'd just turned fifty, and for the first time in my professional life found it hard to concentrate on utopian communities of the nineteenth century. As a graduate student in the 1960s I'd seen the parallels between my generation's counterculture and the idealists of Brook Farm and Fruitlands and New Harmony. My first book was a comparative study of contemporary radical philosophy and the utopian ideals of the century before. My professorship and my reputation had been earned by that study. Fellowships, visiting appointments, and consultantships came thanks to my early explorations in that specialty. It had been implicit in my writing that as the Civil War was the revolution following the idealism of the 1830s and 1840s, a similar cleansing reformation loomed in our near future.

But as I turned fifty in our apartment near the Capitol, I no longer recognized such radical winds stirring around us. In fact, Congress was more lethargic than ever, the administration more petty and timid and confused, the press more tabloid, and special interests owned government more completely than at any time since the presidency of Grant. The streets were dangerous, and the future ominous. I had at my fingertips all the materials of the Library of Congress, the Smithsonian, and the National Archives, but there was little I could do with that material. The only revolution that had occurred since the 1960s was technological. We now lived in a world of answering machines, cell phones, faxes, personal computers, email, and compact disks. We had radical means of communication, and nothing much to communicate.

"This is the age of information," my friend Jamison liked to say to tease me.

"I don't feel very informed," I said.

My wife Marjorie loved Washington. Our children were grown and on their own, and she had taken leave from her job at the community college to join me. "This is the most beautiful city in America," Marjorie loved to say. Through a friend from college she had gotten us invited to a reception at the British Embassy, and to a dinner given for environmentalists at the Vice President's mansion. I went along like a boy attending a tea dance.

"You'll snap out of this," Marjorie said. "Everybody has doubts turning fifty. I remember my dad did."

"What did he do about it?"

"He bought some tools and made furniture in the basement."

"I could take up drinking," I said.

"What you need is a change," she said and laughed.

What I felt was not exactly depression. It was more a disconnectedness, a sense of unease. Things were just not right. Nothing seemed to have meaning anymore. I lay awake at night and thought of my professional rivals and enemies. I recalled slights that were magnified by insomnia and darkness. And I remembered instances where I'd hurt the feelings of friends and colleagues for no reason at all and loathed myself afterward. My achievements were minimal, my failures immense. I saw many things I had not accomplished, and clearly would never accomplish.

"Anybody feels bad who thinks too much about himself," Marjorie said. "Focus on someone else's troubles for a change, and the world will look better."

"Thanks for the therapy."

She touched my shoulder as she left to meet a friend for lunch. I returned to my laptop and kept looking through the notes I'd made the winter before. None of my ideas seemed to connect up with anything interesting. I knew well how to build an article, but it was hard to see why I should bother to concoct and compile another version of the same idea. I'd done variations on the theme for thirty years. My arguments were no longer relevant or interesting. Every phrase I wrote wobbled and slipped out of place. The chain of logic would not lock into sequence. I read the newspaper most of the afternoon, until it was time to fix myself a drink.

"What you need is to get away," Marjorie said later that evening. "Get away from this apartment. Why not go over to the Blue Ridge Mountains and hike along the trail for a few days before the cold weather comes. It will clear your mind. You've wanted to do that for years."

It was not the kind of thing she usually suggested. Normally she would say we should have a few friends over, or give a party. Now she seemed to want to get rid of me for a few days. I was so surprised I was a little offended. "Sure, why not?" I said.

That weekend I packed a few things in the Volvo, my hiking boots, a backpack, a notebook and camera, and headed across the bridge to the west. It seemed I'd come to a watershed in my career, but I had no idea what it meant. I wasn't sure what lay ahead, and I wasn't even certain of what lay behind. But as I drove through Arlington and the suburbs of high-rise condos and corporate headquarters, I started to feel a little better. "This is the Open Road," I said and chuckled. In the distance the blue mountains rose and fell like dolphins on the horizon.

When I reached the Shenandoah Valley I decided to keep going. The farther west and south I traveled the better I seemed to feel. Why not hike in the bigger mountains far to the south? Marjorie thought I was a hundred miles away. Why not go three or four hundred miles away? In two more hours I passed Roanoke on the Interstate. In another two I'd reached the high mountains near North Carolina.

That night I stopped at a motel and watched a rerun of *Bridge on the River Kwai*. But the next morning I was out on the trail. I started slow, knowing how important it is not to tire yourself out at the beginning. Men over fifty have heart attacks from hiking when they're out of shape. Walking is an art, I told myself, like playing music or a sport. You have to find your pace each time you go out. Every time the rhythm is a little different. Only when you find the right pitch of attack can you begin to improvise, be spontaneous, get truly *inside* the action. It's like writing a book. And once you find that beat, the walking itself will take over as you stretch out across the miles of trail with strength and confidence. When a walk goes well you grip the ground with the soles of your boots. It's as satisfying as moving your hands over a woman's body one deliberate touch at a time.

When a walk goes well you feel compact, in the distances of the wilderness. In cool weather you're a seed of warmth in the stream of the breeze.

As you walk the mountains appear to move with you, keeping pace. You step among trees, upright as they are.

Thank goodness for old Benton MacKye, I thought, thinking of the visionary planner who first proposed the Appalachian Trail in 1921. MacKaye was another utopian dreamer, among all the rest.

The trees were turning, and yellow and orange leaves floated across the trail. It had rained the day before and puddles in miry places complicated the path. I met only two or three other hikers all morning. It was a Monday and I was already miles from the nearest road. I thought how few people in our society go anywhere more than a mile from the nearest highway or street. I doubted that one in a hundred got eight miles from their car. It was a cool October day and I was sweating a little under my pack, the kind of sweat that makes you feel more alive. I crossed a slight stream and climbed a long ridge. The highest mountains were ahead of me, a chain of ridges that ran southwest. On the next ridge I could see the balsams, dark pointed firs that belonged to Canada and Maine. I'd read the balsams in the South had been stranded on peaks since the last ice age by retreating glaciers. A phrase kept running through my head, *exiled by height*, and I wondered if it applied to me, somehow.

Across the top of the ridge the trail ran alongside an old field. Goldenrod and some kind of blue flowers were bright there. Red leaves and purple leaves had settled from oaks and gum trees across the broomsedge, and in the distance the mountains rippled high and gray as smoke. It was the most beautiful field I'd ever seen. I paused on the trail just to gaze at it. A section of rail fence ran along the far end of the field.

I walked into the field to see if the fence was made of chestnut. Since the chestnut trees here died around 1924 such a fence would be quite old. Under the weeds the field still had furrows and a few gray cornstalks. The fence was indeed chestnut, as I could tell by the grain and hardness. And beyond the fence stretched another field, with a few apple trees scattered over it. At the end stood some kind of cabin or shed.

I started across the farther field, avoiding clumps of blackberry briars. The air was scented with ripe and rotting apples. As I got closer the building appeared to be a house, not a barn or shed. There was a glass window and a chimney almost hidden by a walnut tree. I listened for the sound of a dog, or dishes rattling, or an axe chopping. I stepped a few yards closer and wondered if someone had a shotgun trained on me that very instant. There were voices in the house that sounded like a conversation conducted in mutters and whispers. I listened, then stepped closer. The yard had been bare once, but was grown up in tufts of weeds. There was an old chair beside the door and a coat or blanket hung from a nail. Across the yard a chicken house or woodshed was half buried in weeds.

"Anyone home?" I called. That seemed like the polite thing to do. The house looked like a place where a hermit from an earlier age might live. A pan lay on the porch, but it was turned over and rusty. I waited a few moments and then called again.

There was a stir inside and I expected someone to appear in the doorway. The door was open, hanging on one hinge. Something fluttered or flashed behind the window. "I just want a drink of water," I said.

The mumbling and muttering inside continued. I stepped up on the porch making as much noise as I could and knocked on the door post. "Hello," I yelled.

As I leaned into the doorway something swung at me like a hand in a white glove. I leaped back and the hand followed me and shot past my head. It was a dove that must have been roosting inside. I stood on the porch as my heart went crazy with surprise and the bird fluttered out through the apple trees.

"I'm taking a census," I called. "I'm here to count toes and divide by ten."

"Ten, ten," the echoes came back from the shed and the woods beyond.

Stepping inside, I expected to see another bird or animal, but the abandoned house was quiet. I squinted into the gloom. It was a large room with a kind of hayloft above, the sort you see in pictures of pioneer cabins. There was an overturned chair on the floor, and cans and dishes scattered around. The place looked like a hurricane had swept through it. Rusty lanterns hung from the walls, and soot had blown across the floor from the fireplace.

As I stepped to the table covered with oilcloth I tripped on something. It was a big book. I picked up the volume and caught a whiff of pungent mildew. The pages were damp and stuck together. It was a dictionary, one of the best dictionaries of forty years before. The pages were glued together with black mold. Dampness had ruined the volume.

And then I saw other volumes scattered on the floor. As my eyes adjusted to the gloom I saw books under the table and piled by the cot in the corner. There were big volumes and little volumes, magazines, and newspapers. The numbers of an encyclopedia lay like wide bricks fallen from a wall. Wondering why so many books would have been left so far back in the mountains, I picked up a volume and saw it was poetry, a book famous back in the 1960s when I was in graduate school. There were books in French, and a well-known work by Wittgenstein. A volume of essays by Charles Pierce almost melted in my hands as silverfish and little yellow spiders shivered over it.

The smell of the cabin was overwhelming. I remembered descriptions of bombed-out London during the Blitz, the smells of rotten clothes and food, papers and bodies and broken sewers. Here was the mustiness of corn meal left to sour in a bin, and canned things that had rusted through their tins and spilled. Old clothes hung on the walls and rotted on the floor among the dust and soot and bird droppings.

But the greatest surprise still awaited me. I pushed a dusty quilt aside and saw manuscript pages scattered on the floor. A sheaf of papers was stuck together by dampness. Others had been soiled by mold and muddy boots and birds. Many of the bird droppings were purple as wine. The doves had been eating pokeberries. On the table lay a thick manuscript tied with a string but so furry with mildew it was impossible to read. There were candy wrappers and soda cans and bottles that must have been left by recent hikers.

Something scurried at my feet, and I saw a rat disappear through the open door. My foot crushed something in the shadows and I bent down to find a pair of broken glasses. There was another pair of spectacles on the table, the lenses frosted with dust.

This rough mountain cabin had been somebody's study, but I couldn't imagine who it might have been. Would it have been a scholar escaping from academia to work here in summer? Had a dropout from the 1960s come here to avoid the draft and returned to the world twenty years later, leaving behind all his books and papers?

A ladder led to the loft, and I shook the shafts to see if it was solid. One of the rungs had broken, but I mounted with caution, careful to place my feet near the sides where the rungs were strongest. I was almost afraid to look in the loft. It was even darker up there, with the only light coming from a kind of louvered ventilator.

Straining to see in the dark, I was dizzied by the smell of mold and bird droppings. The loft had rotten straw in it, and an old trunk and piles of newspapers yellowing and composting together. The trunk was covered with leather, cracked and rotting.

The boards of the loft creaked as I stepped on them. I imagined a movie comedy scene of me crashing through the floor and being stuck, my backpack still on, in a haunted, bird-harried cabin no one knew about except the monster that hibernated in the cellar. I reached for the trunk and pulled it toward me. The box was not as heavy as I expected. The lock on the trunk had been broken, and the hasp torn out by the screws. I pried the lid loose and raised it, but it was too dark to see inside. A smell of dust and ancient tobacco and corroded brass rose from the depths.

I thought if I could slide the trunk over the lip of the loft and hold it by the strap on its end, I could lower it to the floor a step at a time. But no sooner had I pushed the trunk over the edge than the clamps holding the strap broke and the box flung away spilling its contents and crashing to the floor below. I almost fell off myself before grabbing a beam of the loft.

When I reached the floor the first things I saw were several pens and water-damaged photographs. The pictures were so spoiled I could only make out parts of faces and clothes. There was a stained diploma from a correspondence school, but I couldn't tell what the subject was. A great pile of notes had spilled out. They were rejection slips from magazines, hundreds of them, stuck together and faded, stained by corrosion from coins and rifle cartridges.

Then I saw a big blacksnake lying near the door as if it had just appeared there out of air. It sparkled in the light and looked at least six feet long. I'd read that blacksnakes were territorial. When I stood and took a step forward the big reptile raised its head and hissed. The head backed like a cocked hammer. I could smell the stink it gave off in anger. The cabin was its castle and I had invaded it.

I looked around for something to use as a weapon. Blacksnakes are not poisonous, but I knew they could bite. This one was between me and the door. It hissed again and I picked up a chair that had fallen among the dusty rags and books and held it out the way a lion tamer at the circus does. I didn't know exactly what I would do with the chair if the snake crawled toward me. Perhaps I could hit it on the head with a chair leg. But the black giant got bored with me and lowered its head and crawled out the door. It looked limp as a silk rope as it pulled over the doorsill and rough boards of the porch and poured itself into the weeds.

My hands were damp and my pulse spurting. Watching the movement of even a harmless blacksnake makes you feel hypnotized and afraid. A spot ran across one of the dirty pages at my feet. It was a spider and I stepped back, then crushed it with my boot. I picked up the page its juice had smeared. "Dear Mr. Evans," it began, "I regret to inform you..."

I picked up another page. It was typed, though the ink had blurred from age and moisture. I could barely make out the words in the dim light. "The most expressive thing about the mountains in winter is their silence," it said. "Across the ridges and high fields, even across the valleys, there will not be one sound. A hawk whistle, or the whisper of an airplane, will break the stillness maybe once every two..." And then the page was rusty with mold and unreadable. I picked up another sheet, but it was so rotten it turned to paste on my fingertips. Where rain had blown through the door, water had stood in a puddle and soaked the pages to pulp. Whatever had been written on those sheets had been melted and composted into a kind of sludge.

I looked at my watch and saw it was almost lunchtime. I was less than halfway toward my planned camping place. I might as well have a bite here and then hike faster that afternoon to make up for lost time. I wanted out of the dampness and darkness of the cabin. The place seemed to press its coldness into me.

Outside the sun was high as ever. I had to shade my eyes as I looked for the blacksnake in the weeds before the porch. And then I stumbled over a heap of books somebody had thrown out into the yard. The volumes had rotted and were chewed by mice. Honeysuckle vines threaded through the faded pages. I wanted to find a sunny place to sit and headed toward the shed.

Papers and books had been dumped in the shed also. There were scholarly journals and copies of the *Times* of London. There were also issues of *The Hudson Review* and *The American Scholar*. The shed smelled of sour glue and mildew. I tromped down the weeds around a weathered bench and sat down. A rusty crosscut saw lay in the grass. While I ate I watched the birds in the apple trees. A hawk whistled far across the field. As I finished my granola bar I heard a jet muttering in the sky far above.

I wondered who Mr. Evans could have been. He must have lived there a long time to have collected so many books and magazines and journals. How could he have gotten so much mail so far from a post office? I wondered if he'd been someone who was fired or blacklisted, or was hiding out from the police. Nothing I'd seen among the pages and pictures offered a clue. None of the items of information would connect. I picked up one of the journals and saw the date, July 1954. But that didn't prove he'd lived there that long ago. He might have collected old magazines later. I tried to guess how one would carry that many hundreds of volumes this far up the mountain. There might have been a road at one time, or the mailman could have ridden on horseback.

I wished I had some coffee, but didn't take the time to boil water. I stood up and put the wrapping papers from my sandwich and the granola bar in the backpack, and took a drink from my canteen. I was ready to head back to the trail when I realized I felt more alive and curious than I had in months. My blood was charged with the excitement I used to have when looking through old documents and letters in libraries and finding surprises. My detective instincts had been revived. I would love to find out who had written all those pages, who had read all those books. But I had to get back to the trail if I was going to keep to schedule.

Parting the big weeds I started across the field toward the rail fence and the trail beyond. The sun on the goldenrods was dim compared to the brightness of my curiosity. It was farther to the trail than I remembered. I stopped to catch my breath at the rail fence.

The first people I met on the trail were a couple in their late fifties or early sixties. They looked alike, as some couples do. They were both lean and tanned, with shiny gray hair and identical leather and canvas backpacks. They carried staffs of strong hickory. "A beautiful day," I said to them and stopped walking.

"Yes, lovely," they said and stopped out of politeness.

"Have you been walking far?" I said.

"From the Smokies," the woman said.

"We want to make it to Stone Mountain," the man said.

"Do you know this area?" I said.

"We lived near Damascus for ten years," the man said.

"Do you know the cabin off the trail here?" I said.

"We've never seen it," the woman said, "but we've heard about it."

"Do you know who lived there?"

"Some hermit," the man said. "It's called The Hermit's Cabin by the Park Service. He lived there for years and years, but that's all I know."

"When was this?"

"Oh years and years ago," the woman said. "Before we ever moved here."

"I hear it's haunted," the man said.

I thanked them and they hurried on, as though my questions had aroused their suspicions. Perhaps they thought my curiosity was a cover for some ulterior purpose. I watched them negotiate the rocks and turns in the trail with the bounce and strength of real fitness. They were in far better shape than I was.

I was about to head south again when it occurred to me I was more interested in finding out who lived in the cabin than in just logging miles on the trail. Hiking would tire me out and take me away from my anxieties. But I would rather be going *toward* something than merely walking. My scholarly instincts had been aroused. But where would one start? I could find rangers or Park officials and talk with them, or I could go to the local courthouse and look up deeds and records. I got out my map to see what county I was in, and what the nearest town was.

Since I'd walked about eight miles that morning, I wasn't close to any town at all. I could head back to the car and drive into the burg called Jackson. Or I could keep walking and stop at the village of Hooper, which appeared to be about a mile off the trail. I looked for a road up to the place I guessed was the location of the cabin, but there was nothing except topographical contours in the area. If I knew what post office served the section I would know where to start looking.

And then I saw I would have to go back to the Volvo anyway. Without the car I couldn't do much looking. Instead of camping high in the mountains I needed to be closer to the sources for investigation. I folded my map and turned on the trail to follow the athletic couple.

I must have walked faster than usual for within ten minutes I had the couple in sight again. They walked at a slow but steady pace, and looked back at me from time to time as I gained on them. When I reached them I saw they were afraid of me. Their fear embarrassed me.

"Don't mind me," I said a little out of breath. "I decided to go back and do a little detective work."

"Are you a detective?" the woman said. She glanced at me as she might a potential mugger. But she and her husband kept walking as though I hadn't disturbed them.

"I want to find out who really lived in that cabin," I said.

"All I know is he was a hermit," the man said.

"Someone must know."

"Perhaps," the woman said.

I was almost even with them, and then I saw them decide without a word how to get rid of me. They slowed down and I had to slip past them. "I'm afraid there's a rock in my shoe," the man said.

"Good luck," I said. It was all I could think of to say as I hurried on. But I knew they were relieved to get rid of me. A perverse voice whispered I should pause and ask them another question, but I resisted it.

I got back to the car by mid-afternoon and it felt good to sit down. I'd walked more than fifteen miles with the pack on my back, and I was out of shape. My shirt was damp when I took the pack off. The warm interior of the Volvo felt welcome though, after being out in the cool wind. I was trembly all over with fatigue and excitement.

THE NEAREST RANGER station was several miles down the highway. It was an office building made of logs, with a visitor center, exhibits of mountain minerals and local crafts, and a book and souvenir store. The clerk at the desk wore a uniform. I asked if she could give me any information about the cabin on the trail about ten miles to the south.

"I'm sorry, I can't," she said.

"Do you mean you don't know, or you're not allowed to give out information?" I said. My voice sounded stiffer, more professional, than I intended. A frown passed over her face. "I can ask my supervisor," she said and picked up the phone. I saw I'd taken the wrong tack in my fatigue and hurry. I was going to have to slow down and sound friendly and casual.

When the ranger came out of his office he was clearly expecting trouble. "What can I do for you?" he said, looking me in the eye.

"Hello, I'm Bill Lance of Colgate University," I said. "I'm doing research on this area and wonder if you could help me."

"What do you need, sir?"

I told him about the cabin and asked if he knew who had lived there. "It's called the Evans Cabin, or the Hermit's Cabin," he said. "It was abandoned long before I came here. They say some hermit named Evans lived there. I know it was filled with all kinds of junk, but we left it as it was. It was never our plan to restore the cabin as any kind of exhibit."

"Do you have any records of the cabin or its inhabitants?" I said. I took a piece of paper from my pocket, as though to make notes.

"I'm afraid not. You would have to write to the Park Service in Washington. I can give you the address."

"I'm living there now," I said. "I can go there in person." I thanked him and left.

It was after four-thirty and I would just have time to reach Jackson before offices started closing. But I had no idea where to look first. The courthouse? The public library? The local newspaper? I decided to try the courthouse since it was right in the middle of town and easy to find. After I parked and got out I discovered my legs were already stiff and sore.

The courthouse was built like a brick Victorian mansion, except someone had thought to add a dome. The result was almost surrealistic, as if two buildings had been jammed together to create a mongrel of architecture.

The Registrar of Deeds office was to the left of the courtroom. No one was there but an ancient secretary. I told her what I was looking for. "You're welcome to look in the deed books," she said, "if you know the location of the parcel of land."

"It's up near the trail," I said. "I don't know exactly."

"Then it's owned by the Park Service."

"Yes, I think it is," I said. "But I want to know who owned it before."

She glanced at the clock on the wall and my eyes followed hers. It was five minutes till five. Her purse was already out on her desk.

"I think it's called the Evans Cabin," I said.

"Why didn't you say so?" she said. She took a scarf from her purse and tied it around her hair. "The deeds won't tell you much, for the Evanses settled that land a long time ago. There's not much of a record. They claimed the land was given to them by the Indians."

"They were settlers here?" I said.

"They're mostly gone now," the woman said. She picked up her purse and turned off the desk lamp. "Who you want to talk to is Shirley Mc-Graw, down at The Rosebud. Shirley Evans McGraw. She grew up there."

The clerk turned out the overhead lights and locked the door. The courthouse seemed entirely deserted except for us. I walked out with her and when we reached the street I asked where The Rosebud was. "Just over there," she said and pointed. "Over on Third Street by the shoe store."

She hurried away as if afraid I would follow her. I wondered if my hiking clothes and trail boots made me look suspicious. I hadn't brought any other clothes, since I'd planned to spend my time on the trail. Then I looked down and saw the hunting knife strapped to my belt. I'd forgotten it completely. I returned to the Volvo and slipped the knife from the belt and placed it in the trunk with the backpack.

There were only three customers in The Rosebud. I figured I might as well have a cup of coffee while I was there. But I saw no waitress in the diner, only a man wearing a white cap and a dirty apron who stood by the grill frying a hamburger. Grease bubbled and crackled around a wire basket of fries in the deep fryer.

"Is Shirley McGraw here?" I said.

"No, she ain't here," the cook said. I ordered a cup of coffee and he brought it.

"I understand Shirley works here," I said. But the cook didn't answer. He returned to the grill and turned the hamburger. Then he lifted the french fries out of the oil and set the basket on a rack. I sipped the bitter coffee and added a splash of cream to smooth it.

"I'm interested in the Evans family," I said. "I'm doing research on the area." The cook carried the hamburger to the customer at the other end of the counter. When he returned he stopped directly in front of me.

"You insurance people have give Shirley enough trouble," he said. "Why don't you lay off?"

"I'm not in insurance," I said and felt my face get hot. "I have nothing to do with insurance."

The waiter returned to the grill and emptied the french fries onto a plate. After he took them to the customer he stopped in front of me again. "Shirley works here in the morning," he said, "six o'clock till two."

I thanked him and finished the coffee. Then I drove to the Holiday Inn on the by-pass south of town.

At the motel I watched the news and then had shrimp at the restaurant. Later I watched TV and drank ginger ale. I thought of calling Marjorie back in Washington, but instead dropped off to sleep. Early next morning I showered and shaved and headed for The Rosebud.

THERE IS A liveliness in diners in the early morning. It's thrilling to see the world begin to go about its business again even before the sun is up. "Good morning," the waitress called as I came through the door. "Find yourself a seat, honey." There was a free stool at the end of the counter.

"Coffee, darling?" she said, and had already poured the cup and slapped down two thimbles of cream before I could answer.

"Shirley, could we have the sugar?" a man wearing a feedstore cap hollered down at the other end.

"Sweetie, what can I get for you?" she said, holding the coffee pot over the counter.

"Shirley, make that hash browns," another customer called. They were all men. There wasn't a single woman sitting at the counter.

"Hold your tater, sugar," Shirley called, and looked back at me.

"Two eggs over easy with bacon and biscuits," I said. "And some orange juice."

"Two easy and bacon," she shouted to the man at the grill. She turned back to me. "Hash browns?" she said.

"No, grits," I said.

"That's a sweetheart," she said and then hurried to the other end of the counter.

When she brought the plate I asked if she was an Evans. "Yeah, honey, and who are you?" she shot back. I told her I was trying to find out about the Evans Cabin.

"Darling, that ain't nothing but a junk pile," she said and was gone again.

I'd finished eating and was ready for more coffee when she came back again. "It won't do you any good to ask, sweetheart," she said, "for I'm not paying any more taxes and I'm not asking for any insurance..."

"I'm a historian..." I said, but she was gone again. Several of the men at the counter turned to look at me. The coffee and hot grits made the diner seem very bright. Outside it was getting light. When Shirley returned she tore a page off her pad and dropped it in front of me.

"Who left all the books and papers in the cabin?" I said.

"That was my uncle Stephen," she said. "But don't worry about him. He never made a nickel out of all those books and writings. And besides, he was partly handicapped. He was a kind of cripple. And he's long dead." She was gone again.

The clientele on the stools had turned over at least once while I'd been in The Rosebud. Everyone was in a hurry to get to work except me. The cook at the grill gave me a hard look. "Could I talk to you sometime?" I said to Shirley when I went to the register to pay.

"You've been talking to me, sweetie," she said. She gave me the look of someone who knows every pick-up line there is.

"I want to find out about your uncle," I said.

"Right," she said and glanced over her shoulder at the man at the grill.

"I would appreciate a little of your time," I said.

"Uncle Stephen never amounted to squat," she said. "But he could be a sweet guy." She told me she got off at two, and I promised I would meet her then.

AFTER LEAVING The Rosebud I walked up the main street of Jackson. Only a few stores were opening. The newspaper office was deserted except for one receptionist at the counter who was looking at her smart phone. I told her I was searching for information about Stephen Evans who'd lived in the old Evans Cabin up near the trail.

"I've heard of him," she said.

"I'm looking for anything about him," I said. "Is there a county history?"

"He was a kind of hermit," the girl said. "But that was before my time."

"Was there anything about him in the paper? He must have been a character."

"I think he used to write for the paper, but that was years and years ago."

She wouldn't let me look at the newspaper files. She said only employees of the paper were allowed in the morgue. I asked if she would look for me. "I'm the only person here to answer the phone until eleven," she said. "I have to take care of the desk. But you can go to the library. I reckon they have the papers on file."

Back on the street I watched the storekeepers roll up their blinds and crank out their awnings. A man at a little grocery store was setting out crates of apples and pears on the sidewalk. The newsstand smelled of tobacco and ink stained pages. A school bus passed with children shouting from the windows. A police car cruised down the street and stopped in front of The Rosebud. I found the library on the other side of the courthouse. It was a new building of cream-colored brick with high windows. They had just opened and the woman at the front desk still had on her jacket. Her hair was blue as monofilament fishing line. "I turned up the heat," she said, shivering.

"I'm looking for information about Stephen Evans," I said. I told her what I knew about the Evans Cabin and that I was looking for the local newspaper files.

"Afraid I'm just a volunteer," the woman said. She had a Boston accent. "The regular staff will be here at nine. I've heard of Hermit's Cabin, but we're new to this area. My husband and I just retired last year."

"Is there a county history?"

"Local books are over there," she said and pointed to a shelf near the rear of the library.

I found the blue volume of county history on the shelf and saw it had been published in the late 1940s. It had a number of photographs and drawings of county pioneers and early buildings. There were only two entries under Evans in the index, and when I tracked them down I found they referred to the Evans family as among the early settlers in the Balsam Creek section of the south end of the county. On the shelf of local books there were thin privately printed volumes of poems, ghost stories done by vanity presses, Summers' *History of Southwest Virginia 1746-1786,* and a book of photographs of flowers of the Great Smoky Mountains. There was another book on waterfalls in an adjoining county, a volume of top-ographical maps, and another volume about South Carolina planters who built vacation homes in the mountains in the 1830s and 1840s. I looked around at the stacks and saw folios of bound newspapers in a far corner.

Sure enough, it was the files of the local paper going back to the year 1928. I pulled out a volume and smelled the aged yellowing pages. It was a familiar scent. In my years in graduate school, and while I was writing my first two books, I'd spent many hours in the basements of libraries sifting for articles and references to Brook Farm and Fruitlands, to Fouri-erism and the first Mormons. I wanted to know how their contempo-raries viewed the utopian movements. I became familiar with the parlance of local cattle shows, society columns, and political hatchet work of the era. I saw the beginnings of modern advertising in the drawings for harness makers' shops and hoop skirts, and the first engravings of photographs to appear in local newspapers in Massachusetts.

There is an under-scent to newsprint kept on file in air-conditioned libraries. It's hard to describe because it isn't like anything else. It must be some chemical they use to keep the paper from turning brown. The result is the bound pages smell slightly rotten and a little like medicine. The smell can make you nauseous after a while.

I turned the brittle pages of the first volume, skimming over the wedding announcements, notices of auctions, and articles on Herbert Hoover's campaign of 1928. In page after page I saw nothing by Stephen Evans or about him. I began to turn the pages faster. There were ads for Model-A Ford trucks and Black Draught laxative, for liver pills and squirrel rifles. I read announcements of bank failures and bank re-openings. The National Recovery Act was condemned by the Supreme Court. I was about to give up when a tiny item caught my eye. "Local Author Wins Writing Contest" it said. It was only a couple of inches long. "Stephen Evans, who lives on Balsam Creek in the southern end of the county, has been awarded honorable mention in the essay contest sponsored by the Virginia Association of Writers, in cooperation with the Federal Work Projects Administration. He was recognized for his contribution called 'Spring Notes.' Stephan is a shut-in who many of you will remember carried mail on the Star Route to Balsam Creek before his accident a few years ago."

I read the notice three times to glean what information there was. The date was November 1935. It was the first mention of any accident I'd heard, though Shirley McGraw had said her uncle was partly crippled. And no one had said anything about his carrying mail. At last I was beginning to get somewhere.

But there were no other references to Evans in the rest of the 1935 volumes. Or in the next ones. It wasn't until late 1937 that I finally came across Evans's name again.

"Our correspondent from Balsam Creek has sent us this description," the leader read. It was a short article set in small type. "When autumn comes to the mountains," it began, "the weeds harden and shrink. Leaves begin to look metallic and turn to foam in the wind. Thistle-down smokes from the goldenrods hit by frost..."

For about a year the column was repeated monthly. The little essays followed the seasons, and sometimes mentioned politics and world events. I had the feeling they were selections from much longer articles, made of vivid sentences clustered together. There were pieces about gritted bread, and drying apples in the sun. There were articles about spring water, and about terracing mountain fields. Evans wrote of infare parties given after mountain weddings, and about the first churches in the county. He recounted stories of Civil War times told by his grandfather, and described the bands of outlaws who roamed the mountains while the men-folk were off in the Confederate or Union armies. The column stopped suddenly in 1939. I thought I should Xerox some of the articles, but I could always come back and do that later.

What I wanted most was information about Evans himself, something that told me how he lived and who he really was, and what he did after he stopped writing the column. But combing through the weeks and months and years that followed I found nothing but a few letters to the editor complaining about taxes and coverage of a murder trial, and questioning the paper's advocacy of war bonds. They were letters of an intelligent eccentric.

Why don't you give this up? I said to myself. There was little I could do professionally with the story. I was supposed to be relaxing and refreshing myself on the trail, not buried among whiffy old newspapers reading about a cranky invalid whom even his family never paid much attention to. My eyes burned from the strain of looking at the faded newsprint, squinting at the tiny type. If I kept it up I would have a headache. I could have been out walking in the autumn sunlight along the summit trail. I could have been halfway to Tennessee if I'd stayed on the trail.

But there was something about the Evans story that made me continue. I think it was the sight of all those ruined books and papers with mold and bird droppings on them. I'd known so many people in academia who had started out with brilliance and promise and been ground down by competition, by teaching and tedium and jealousy. The cabin suggested a ruined utopia, a destroyed ideal, as much as Brook Farm or Fruitlands. Evans had probably never had a chance at all, self-educated and self-made, and for all I knew self-defeated.

I had to find out more about him. I had to know what happened to him. I looked at my watch. It was almost eleven o'clock. There were more people in the library now. I hadn't even noticed the new arrivals or the staff working to reshelve books and answering the phone. Instead of the volunteer at the desk with blue hair there was a young man with wide red suspenders sitting behind the computer. "Can I help you?" he said when I approached. I introduced myself and asked if there were any papers that belonged to Stephen Evans in the library. He pushed some keys on the computer, and then some more keys, and shook his head. "I don't see a thing," he said. "Our papers are mainly the papers of local politicians and judges. Also we have a collection of Indian artifacts."

"Stephen Evans lived in a cabin up near the trail," I said.

"Oh yes, I've heard of that," the librarian said.

"He wrote for the local newspaper back in the 1930s."

"Is that so?"

The librarian said he'd moved there from Richmond within the last year. I asked him if there was some older citizen in the town who might remember Evans.

"There's the retired mayor, Mr. Simpson, who lives over on Vine," he said. I thanked him and left.

After the strain to my eyes of the newsprint, the sunlight was blinding. It rushed at my face like a high-pitched sound. But I was glad to be back in the open air. Before returning to the newspaper office I walked up Main Street and around the block to clear my head. I thought I should call Marjorie that evening to let her know where I was.

The editor of the paper was in when I returned to the office. I introduced myself and he invited me to sit. His name was Locklin. "I'm interested in Stephen Evans," I said. "I'd like to find someone who knew him."

"I never actually met him," Mr. Locklin said. "But he was still alive when I moved here from Florida."

"But he no longer wrote for the paper?"

"I came here in 1953," Mr. Locklin said. "Evans was just somebody who sent crazy letters to the paper about everything under the sun. Sometimes we even printed one. I heard he wanted to be a writer. He was one of the few people who sent us typewritten letters back then. I remember that. Yes, his letters were always typed and corrected."

"He must have been self-educated."

"If he was educated at all. Maybe he'd taught school way back then, in some little one-room schoolhouse. But by the time I came up here he was just known as a crank. He complained about tourists and retirees buying up land on the mountainsides, and building houses on mountaintops. He was angry that paper mills polluted the air and water. He acted like he thought the modern world was out to get him. You know the kind."

"He had some sort of accident," I said.

"That was before my time," Locklin said. "But he had a gimp."

I saw I'd gotten all out of Locklin I was going to. I stood up and thanked him.

"I'm just an old-fashioned newspaperman," he said, leaning back in his swivel chair, folding a sheet of paper into a paper airplane. "I know how to throw a dart when I have to, and how to call it sunny when the egg hits the fan. But don't ask me to judge all the people back in these hollers who think they know how to write and have a personal hotline to the truth." He sailed the airplane into the wastebasket.

It was time to head back to The Rosebud for lunch.

The crowd at the counter looked almost the same as the one at breakfast, except there were a few women and children, in town for their weekly shopping. Shopping bags sat on the floor beside their stools.

"I don't want a Pepsi, I want a cherry Coke," a little boy whined.

I didn't know if Shirley had taken a break that morning or not. It was more than five hours since I'd left the diner, but she moved just as fast and shouted a loud as before. But from her makeup you could tell she was tired. It wasn't that her mascara had smeared or her lipstick had faded. I suppose the powder on her cheeks had dusted off a little. There was something blurred about the makeup, as though it had been touched up along slightly different lines and the fit was not perfect.

"What'll you have, sweetie?" she said a few seconds after I'd sat down.

"The fish sandwich with coleslaw and onion rings," I said.

"Fish and rings," she called over her shoulder to the man at the grill.

"Drink?" she said.

"Coffee with..." Before I'd finished she had put a cup in front of me and was pouring from the pot. "There you are, honey," she said.

"You get off at two?" I said.

"At two," she said and was gone. She looked like the kind of woman

148

who might have played basketball in high school and softball on the company team. She could have been anywhere from forty to fifty-five. It was hard to tell. Her figure was strong and lean in the white uniform. She poured coffee for a customer while busing a dirty plate and glass and crumpled napkin from the counter nearby. She called an order over her shoulder while setting a new place with silverware, napkin and glass of water.

"What can I get for you, darling?" she said to the man who had just sat down beside me, as she placed the plate of onion rings and little bowl of coleslaw and steaming fish sandwich before me. As soon as she wrote down his order she refilled my cup.

Later, while I was waiting until two, I had a piece of pecan pie from the glass case in the middle of the counter.

"I don't see how you do it," I said to Shirley when she finally took off her apron and sat down beside me. The cook brought her a cup of coffee and she lit a cigarette.

"I found out a few things this morning," I said. "I went to the library and read articles Stephen wrote for the newspaper back in the 1930s."

"He was always scribbling something," Shirley said.

"A note in the newspaper said he was a shut-in."

"He fell off his horse when he was carrying the mail up the mountain," Shirley said. "I reckon his leg never healed right."

"So he didn't carry the mail after that?"

"I don't know. That was long before my time." Shirley sipped her coffee. I could see I was boring her.

"Did you grow up on the ridge?" I said.

"So far back we raised hoot-owls for chickens."

"In the same house with Uncle Stephen?" I said.

"No, no, we lived down the ridge a little way in Daddy's house, the one he built when he married Mama. I just saw Stephen from time to time. He lived on the old Evans Place."

"Did he travel at all? Could he get around?"

"If you come for him in a truck or wagon he could get around. But it was hard to take the pickup truck all the way up to his place. The old road had washed away and grown up. Mostly he didn't go anywhere. We youn-guns thought he was quair."

"Why did he seem quair?"

"Because he talked funny, and never did go anywhere. And because he read books all the time. We had a name for him. We called him 'Big Words' because he used so many big words when he talked." She laughed and crushed out her cigarette. "He was weird," she said, and laughed again.

"How was he weird?"

"He just was. He wouldn't go to church, and when the preacher come to visit he just grinned at him, sat there and grinned. And then one day he got mad and drawed his gun on the poor preacher. Just like that, he pulled out his gun." Shirley held her lighter against her forehead as she leaned on the counter. She seemed a little embarrassed to be talking about her family.

"Who owns the cabin now?" I said.

"The government bought it back ten years ago at least. They just left it like it was, to rot."

"And the family didn't want his things?" I said.

"They took what they wanted, Stephen's gun, and his razor, things like that. But mostly what he had was old books and papers that nobody had any use for."

"It looks like the place has been looted," I said.

"It was, soon after Uncle Stephen died. People just come in and took what they wanted. There was some rusty steel traps and pictures that got gone. Hunters and bums slept there, and hippies went there for drug parties. Some people said the place was haunted."

"What a waste," I said. Shirley was silent for a moment. She looked at her pack of cigarettes and decided not to have another. I noticed how beautiful her hair was. It was golden brown and sparkled like she'd put egg rinse on it. Close up I could see she was younger than I'd thought. It was the makeup that made her seem older.

"Are you married?" she said.

"Well, yes," I said.

"People will talk if they see me around town with a married man," she giggled. "I'm just going through a divorce. That's why the insurance people and tax people are after me. They're trying to collect my ex-husband's bad debts. Well let people talk. It won't be the first time." She slid from the stool and reached behind the counter for her purse. "Let's get going," she said.

I left a ten dollar bill on the counter and followed her. When we reached the street I asked where we were going.

"You need to talk to Maude," she said. "Aunt Maude's the only person left who really knew Stephen."

"Where is Aunt Maude?"

"You'll see."

We got in my Volvo and I lowered the windows. It was a windy sunny day, perfect Indian summer. As we drove by the school, children were just being let out. They ran across the lawn and up the sidewalk. One little fellow dashed right in front of us and I had to slam on my brakes. But the boy didn't even notice; he kept running.

"Younguns want to get away from school as quick as they can," Shirley said. "I did, that age."

We drove past the seed and feed store and the old depot, and then out to the truck route south of town where the motels and restaurants and shopping malls were. There were car lots between the fast food places, and a bowling alley and miniature golf course.

"This used to be the country," Shirley said, "back when I was a girl."

"This could be anywhere," I said.

"Or nowhere," Shirley said.

About ten miles south of Jackson, Shirley told me to turn to the left on a county road. We passed cornfields bleached by frost, with pumpkins bright in the stubble. Every old farmhouse seemed to have a trailer in the yard. In the fields hay bales were wrapped like great rolls of toilet paper, lined up along a fence. The mountains loomed ahead, colorful as opals in their orange and yellow and purple leaves.

"Turn here," Shirley said, and pointed to a dirt road that led off into the trees. The road was covered with yellow leaves except for places where puddles had splashed mud over the ruts. The Volvo climbed up a steep stretch and descended toward a creek, lurching over rocks and bumps.

"You can't drive all the way there," Shirley said. "We'll have to leave the car up here and walk the rest of the way."

I crossed a creek at a shallow ford and drove along a flat stretch through sycamore trees.

"Park here," Shirley said. We were at the edge of a meadow with a table and wash pot at one side. "This is where Aunt Maude used to do her washing," Shirley said. She pointed to a trail up the mountainside.

"Where does Aunt Maude do her washing now?" I said.

"She has a washing machine. We all pitched in and bought her a machine about five years ago."

I got a small notebook out of the backseat. "Wish I had a tape recorder," I said.

"You're lucky you don't," Shirley said. "Somebody from the Oral History Project at the community college come out to tape Aunt Maude and as soon as the machine was turned on she just clammed up and wouldn't say another word. You might as well put that notebook away too."

The path up the mountain was deep as a trench between rhododendrons and tulip poplars. It curved around trees and switched back and forth up the steep slope. Leaves had drifted in the deep places and we made a lot of noise splashing through the drifts. A power line had been run up the mountain beside the trail.

"Good gracious alive," I heard someone say as we reached the edge of the yard. I looked around to see who had spoken. The yard was swept dirt with watering cans and sardine cans scattered among the flowerpots. There were large boxwoods at the margins and cats everywhere. Cats slunk around the shrubbery, and lay in the sun near the water cans. A black and white cat sat on the steps and other cats lay on the porch. There were cats on the high bank behind the house watching us approach.

"If it ain't Shirley," the voice said. And this time I saw the speaker behind the screen door. An old woman stood in the shadows. The screen door opened, and Aunt Maude stepped into the doorway wearing a many-colored crocheted shawl. Her hair was in braids but not pinned up. "You all come on in," she said.

It was the oldest house I'd seen in the region. The doorsill and steps were worn smooth as bars of soap scrubbed thin. The house smelled of coffee and ancient wood smoke.

"Come set by the fire," Aunt Maude said.

The living room was tiny as a closet. Aunt Maude pointed to chairs with blankets draped over them. A big gray cat slid out of the way and another that had been sleeping on the hearth got up and stretched.

"Let me get you some coffee," Aunt Maude said. "I just made a new pot."

"No thank you. We just had some at The Rosebud," Shirley said.

In the dark living room by the smoldering fire Shirley looked young and fashionable, a visitor from the modern world. She introduced me and told Aunt Maude I was interested in finding out about Stephen, Uncle Stephen.

"How do you know about Stephen?" Aunt Maude said.

"I was hiking on the trail and found the cabin," I said.

"That place is a wreck and ruin," Aunt Maude said.

"His books and papers are all scattered and rotting," I said.

"The poor boy," Aunt Maude said, lowering herself into the chair right by the fireplace. "Nothing ever seemed to go right for him." She paused. I could see she was hesitant to talk to a stranger about family misfortunes and failures. Perhaps she thought it was bad manners to discuss Stephen's difficulties, or bad luck. I decided not to begin with a question.

"I saw some of the articles he wrote for the newspaper," I said.

"That was way back yonder," Aunt Maude said. "He didn't do that for too long."

"He was a good writer," I said. 'He must have worked hard."

"Honey, he never worked much at anything else," Aunt Maude said, as though admitting a sad fact. "I never seen a boy that hated work so. All he wanted was to keep his nose in a book. He was the laziest boy I ever seen, even if he was my brother."

"How did he get hurt?" Shirley said. "He never could walk too good."

"He could walk as well as anybody till that horse throwed him. He finally got a job carrying mail on the Star Route up the mountain. Didn't pay much, but at least it was something he could do. He got the contract for carrying the mail three times a week from the depot in town to the houses up here on the ridge. Wasn't much mail except around Christmas time. People ordered things from Sears and Roebuck and he had to carry the packages up the mountain. Sometimes it took two days to finish a haul, one to get the boxes and packages from town, another to carry them around to houses. By the time he finished it was time to go back for another load."

"And the horse threw him off?"

"Seen a rattlesnake on the trail and spooked I reckon, bucked Stephen clean over the bank and way down in the holler."

"And he broke a leg?" Shirley said.

"He did break a leg. But that wasn't what done him in. He hit a tree and the doctor said that lick hurt some kind of nerve in his spine. That's what fixed him. The leg mended up in a few months, but the nerve never did. He couldn't walk even with a crutch, except to drag hisself holding onto a chair. And the government wouldn't give him a thing because it was a Star Route and he wasn't a regular employee."

"So he stayed in the cabin?" I said.

"Didn't have much choice, did he? He could drag that chair out in the yard and prop hisself on it to chop a little wood and kindling. But George or Scott or one of his brothers had to saw the trees and drag the wood to him. Now the thing was, he put in a little garden with a hoe. Every year he'd take the chair out in the plot and set in it while he pulled weeds or thinned his corn. He did it every year by leaning on that old chair. Only problem was if he fell he had a terrible time getting up. He'd have to crawl to the house and pull hisself up on the bed.

"I don't think nobody ought to have to suffer like Stephen did, no matter what they have done. His life was finished after that fall, except he kept on reading books and trying to write things that would sell. He was always writing something. You'd go there any day of the week and he would be scribbling in a notebook or on a pad of paper. It looked like the whole house was covered with sheets. It looked like a paper tree had shed its leaves."

Aunt Maude paused and spat into the fireplace. That was the first time I noticed the sweet smell of snuff on her breath. A golden trickle of snuff juice ran from the corner of her mouth.

"What did he write?" I asked. "Was he writing a book? I saw papers in the house but they were so stained and faded I couldn't tell much about them."

Aunt Maude took a little stick from the table beside her chair. It was bigger than a toothpick and she worked it behind her lower lip. "Why he wrote everything, I reckon," she said. "He wrote poems and stories and articles for the papers. He wrote letters to the paper. I don't think he wrote no sermons, for he didn't hold much with church things. But he tried everything else, though I don't think he sold much. He sent stuff off to Chicago and New York and Boston and all the cities up north, but I don't think they cared much for what he done. Stephen never had been off to a university and he didn't know what the world wanted."

"Did he live by himself?" I said.

"He didn't have no choice. After Mama died and my youngest brother Luke got married—that's Shirley's daddy—he stayed there in the old cabin batching and looking after his garden. It must have been cold in winter. The cabin was built before the Confederate War and had nothing but a fireplace and lots of cracks in the walls. I don't think Stephen ever had a cookstove. And it was hard for him to carry water from the spring. He had to do it in a little syrup pail or lard bucket, hobbling along and leaning on that chair."

Aunt Maude stopped and looked around at the coffee cup on the table beside her. "Let me get some coffee," she said.

"I'll get it," Shirley said, and took the cup to the kitchen.

"I reckon Shirley is used to doing for folks," Aunt Maude said.

"She's a good waitress," I said.

Shirley returned with a steaming cup and handed it to Aunt Maude. "Got to have my coffee," Aunt Maude said. She took a sip and then another. "Stephen never could get married," she said. "Who would marry a man that was crippled and lived in an old cabin? I don't even know if he wanted to get married."

Wind sighed in the hemlocks outside and made the fireplace smoke a little. "Are you a writer?" Aunt Maude said to me.

"I'm a scholar," I said. "I write books about American history." I wasn't going to tell her I'd started out to be a fiction writer myself, while I was in graduate school.

"I don't know where that boy got it," Aunt Maude said, looking into the fire. "He just always wanted to write. It's all he ever wanted to do."

"Where did he get a typewriter?" I said.

"Bought it off Judge Shipman. It was an old wore-out thing they'd used in the law office for years. Stephen spent half his time trying to keep the thing fixed. He had a little screwdriver he used to fix it and an old toothbrush to clean it. He oiled all the parts the way you do a sewing machine and he even dabbed ink from a bottle on the wore-out ribbons to make them last longer. He was always babying that machine, and half the time it wouldn't work. I think he would have done better if he'd had a good typewriter."

"People have to do the best they can," Shirley said. "Since he couldn't sell any of his writings he couldn't afford a better typewriter."

"He was always coming up with crazy ideas," Aunt Maude said. "He would allow he didn't think there was any such thing as time. He would talk out of his head like that. He'd talk about things that happened a long time ago and hint that they was still going on somewhere. I don't know where he got such ideas, maybe from magazines and books he read. Maybe he dreamed them up when he had a fever."

"Is that what he wrote about?" I said.

"I don't know what all he wrote about. I just heard him talk. But I guess he wrote about the same things. I seen some of his newspaper pieces, but they wasn't so crazy. Maybe he just liked to shock people."

"And he kept writing to the end of his life?" I said.

"I reckon so. At least until he had a stroke. His cabin was littered with pages and pages the last time I ever saw him. It's a wonder it didn't catch fire."

"What did he live on?" I said.

Aunt Maude held the cup of coffee in both hands and sipped from it. A cat slipped between the rungs of her chair, a big golden cat with white feet. "That's a beautiful cat," I said.

"Tiger is spoilt," Aunt Maude said. "He's too used to having his own way. The thing is I like cats, but I wouldn't have them around if there was anybody to live here with me."

"Did Stephen have any animals?" I said.

"He kept chickens after Mama died. I reckon he even sold a few eggs during the war when the price was up."

"But he didn't keep a cow or pig?"

"No, how could he have took care of anything except that little garden? And I never knowed how he was able to do that. He sold shoes to people that come by. He had a catalog that he sold them out of. I think he made a little bit off each pair that was sent by mail to the customer. But during the war people quit stopping by. And that was the end of his shoe business."

"Why did they quit?" I said.

"He talked such foolish things, like how it was crazy to go to war. After the boys started getting killed people didn't like the way he talked, and they quit coming by."

"He was independent in his opinions," I said.

"He got crankier and crankier," Aunt Maude said. "Even if he was my brother I have to say it. Happens to anybody that lives alone. Sometimes I think I must be getting quair myself, living here with nothing but cats and the TV."

"You're sharp as a briar," Shirley said. "Aunt Maude, you put us all to shame."

"I'm just like everybody else, trying to make it through from one day to the next."

"You're fit as you ever were," Shirley said.

"I ain't fit for much," Aunt Maude said. There was a low mournful sigh in the hemlocks outside.

"What did people in the community think of Stephen's writing?" I said. "I mean people outside the family."

"They just thought he was quair, if they thought of him at all," Aunt Maude said. "If you're a shut-in people forget about you. But they didn't mind him or pay attention to him until he started talking against the war. After the world war broke out he just seemed to get worse and worse. He talked all kinds of crazy ideas, like we didn't have no reason to hate the Japanese, and that all people was the same race. He'd say that what people really wanted to do was to destroy theirselves. Nobody likes that kind of talk."

"He talked about race?"

"He talked about how everybody had the same blood, and things like that. People got sick of it. Even the preacher quit coming to see him. And the arthritis hit."

"Arthritis?"

"He already had trouble getting around, but when the arthritis come he was too stiff to move at all. His joints swelled up and he was in pain. I think it was the rain that done it. I always said it was the rain."

"What rain?"

"Some boys played a trick on Stephen. It was because he started talking against the war. You know how mean big old boys can be. One Saturday night they slipped up to his cabin and stirred up his chickens. They throwed a firecracker or something into his chicken house. When he hobbled out to see what was wrong they run and nailed his cabin door shut. There he was out in the yard and couldn't get back in. And it come up the awfullest rain. Took him almost until daylight to get the door prised open, and by then he was soaked and chilled. It was after that that the arthritis come."

"Did anybody look after him?" I said.

"I took him a dish from time to time," Aunt Maude said. "People in the family would go up there and wash his clothes. But he didn't want us to disturb any of his books and papers. Even though he couldn't hardly move he didn't want you to clean up the mess. The welfare people from town said they wouldn't help him as long as he owned the old place. He would have to sell it and use up the money before they put him on their rolls. And he wouldn't sell. It fell on the family to do what they could, for Stephen wouldn't go to no hospital, and he wouldn't even go to the doctor. And by then you couldn't get a doctor to ride back up there on the mountain. And who could blame them?"

Aunt Maude finished the coffee and set the empty cup down.

"I want to go back and look at the cabin," I said. "I want to see if there are any papers that can be saved."

"When Stephen died nobody knowed about it for almost a week," Aunt Maude said. "He was found dead all swole up like a balloon by a surveyor for the government."

Aunt Maude sank back into her chair as though she'd made a great effort and exhausted herself. The wrinkles on her face seemed pulled down by fatigue.

Shirley stood up. "I think we'd better go," she said. I stood up too.

"I'll tell you about some of the stuff Stephen wrote," Aunt Maude said. "I read a page or two of it one time. It was about strange beings coming from outer space and living underground. They played games by controlling people's minds, making them go to war. We was their toys, and their amusement. It was terrible stuff." She closed her eyes.

"Thank you for talking to us," I said.

"Get me started and I don't know when to stop," Aunt Maude said. She never opened her eyes again. Shirley wrapped the shawl more tightly around her shoulders and gave her a hug. We left her there by the fire, drifting into a nap.

Cats rubbed against our legs asking for attention as we crossed the yard. I turned down the trail, but Shirley caught my arm. "No, this way," she said. "You can't drive up there anymore."

"I want to go back to the cabin," I said.

"This is the only way," she said.

At the edge of the yard a haul-road ran up the mountain. It was drifted full of leaves in places, with briars arching over the sides. The tracks were washed out, and limbs had fallen in the ruts. Beyond the hemlocks the track ran through the oaks and along a grownup field.

"You mean this was the way Stephen had to go if he wanted to reach the highway?" I said.

"It was in better shape then," Shirley said. "In fact, this was a regular road back when I was a girl."

As we climbed the rough path I thought about the stories Aunt Maude said Stephen wrote, about the beings from outer space who lived underground and watched human activities as a spectator sport. I meant to find some of those stories if I could. Stephen had looked for an explanation for the craziness of human behavior. He had worked more than thirty years with little or no reward. After the accident he had few choices, and after the arthritis he had none. From my own experience I knew that failure makes everything, time, weather, other people, seem difficult, insurmountable. The more you fail the bigger the obstacles become, and the way to the future seems lost. I saw why I'd wanted to find out more about Stephen Evans. I needed to find out more about him. His griefs made my own failures seem negligible. Compared to his frustrations my impasse was hardly anything at all. Just thinking about him had lifted a great burden off me.

When I got back to the cabin I wanted to smell the mildew, the rot of the old pages, the sour cloth. I needed to see the dead ink and moldy words, dust and musty rags. I had not felt so alive in years. If I wrote an article about Stephen, and published even a few pages of his stories, I might begin my career all over again. But if I never wrote or published another word that would be all right too. Whatever happened I was going to go easy on myself, and follow my curiosities.

When we came out of the woods below the cabin long shadows stretched from the old apple trees and hedgerow. The air was chilly bright.

"It's a shame you had to walk so far," Shirley said.

"It's no trouble," I said. "Believe me, no trouble at all."

# THE CALM

WHEN DADDY SAID he'd shoot me if I didn't leave him alone I had to make an impossible choice: let him get sicker still, or risk being killed myself. He had the pistol in bed with him and was so mad he might well use it. And he had a bottle of vodka too; in fact he had several bottles on the night stand beside the bed. It was so dark in the bedroom I couldn't really count the bottles. He probably had others also, under the bed or in the closet. The Mexicans who worked for him in the fields brought him the liquor when I wasn't around and there didn't seem to be any way to stop it.

"I love you, Daddy," I said. "And I think you should go to the hospital."

"You leave me where I am," he said. "Touch me and I'll kill you."

"Just want to help."

"You can help me by leaving me alone." Daddy laid the .44 magnum on the covers in front of him.

Daddy had always been bad to drink, especially on weekends and holidays. He and his buddies would get a six-pack or two and drive around in their pickups and drink. And he liked to go down to South Carolina and buy white lightning, before there was an ABC store in Hendersonville. After that he could get all the legal liquor he wanted just by driving to town. When I was a boy I dreaded to see him come home drunk, hollering at Mama and throwing things around.

And then after Mama left him and took my sister Mary to live with her folks down at Tryon, Daddy drank even more. I stayed with Grandpa and Grandma most of the time. And I pretended not to be embarrassed when Daddy got arrested for DWI and his name was in the paper and my friends at school would tease me. "Your daddy is famous," they'd say and laugh, and I would laugh loudest.

Grandpa would be so mad at Daddy after he was arrested he wouldn't even talk to him. When they were watching television and Daddy would drop down on the couch Grandpa would go out and sit in his car and listen to the radio. During election time Daddy made fun of Grandpa for being a Democrat. Daddy and Grandma were Republicans.

But when things really got bad for Daddy was after he was diagnosed with arthritis. I don't know if it had been the bean dust that caused it, or the drinking, or something else. But after he turned forty-five he got these awful pains in his joints and swelling that wouldn't go away. Pain medicine didn't do much good for long, and his joints hurt so bad it was hard to move. He got too stiff all over to work much, and he couldn't sleep either. That's when he started drinking on week day nights, and then in the day-time too.

The doctor in Asheville said there was a treatment with gold that might help him, though he'd have to go down to Duke for that. But the gold could have bad side effects too. Some people had even died when they got the gold treatment. Even so it was his best hope. The doctor gave Daddy a brochure that described the gold therapy and he showed it around to people and asked their advice. But the side effects scared Daddy, and instead of going down to Duke he just drank more than ever.

About the same time Grandpa died of a heart attack. It was a surprise to us, no warning at all. Grandpa just stopped his tractor in the field and got down saying he didn't feel good. He dropped to the ground right at my feet by a bag of fertilizer, and I tried to wake him up, but he was already gone. He was laying right there beside me, but he was gone.

Though he'd quarreled and cussed Grandpa, Daddy took his death the hardest of us all. Grandma and I grieved, but we grieved quietly. Daddy cried at the funeral and kissed Grandpa on the lips in the coffin. And he sobbed up at the graveyard too, like he couldn't help himself. And then after the funeral it was like Daddy got mad that Grandpa was gone. Grandpa had always run the farm and looked after business. Now Daddy had to keep things up in spite of his arthritis and his drinking.

"Human life don't mean nothing," Daddy said. "You're born and live and die just like that, and it don't mean a thing."

Daddy bought Grandpa the most expensive tombstone he could find, and he brooded for months. And he cussed the preacher when he came by to visit. "Don't talk to me about no heaven," Daddy said. "I'd rather listen to my hound dogs holler after a possum or coon than hear a sermon."

Grandma would try to stop Daddy from drinking. She'd try to talk to Daddy the way Grandpa had. "Throw that bottle away or I'll throw it out for you," she'd say. But Daddy would just ignore her, or he'd snarl, "Don't nobody touch my medicine," for he called vodka his medicine.

I'd gone off to North Carolina State to study agriculture, and every summer I came back to work on the farm. It's a good thing I did for Daddy was drinking so much he couldn't really look after the Mexican work crews or the equipment or bookkeeping. Grandma did all she could, but I had to keep track of the payroll, carrying produce to market, keeping machinery repaired. Daddy would sit in his truck watching us work and sipping from his bottle.

After the arthritis got worse, Daddy didn't go to the fields anymore. He'd drive down to the store and sit on a bench, or drive around in his truck with one of his buddies. They'd go up on Pinnacle and sit and drink and look down on the county spread out below them. And sometimes they'd drive to bars in Greenville or Atlanta. But as the arthritis got worse he didn't even do that. Mostly he just stayed at home and nursed himself with a bottle.

AFTER DADDY threatened me with the pistol I stayed away that day. The Mexican work crews were stretching wire in the bean fields down on Gap Creek and I had to be there anyway. And then I had to run to town to get more wire for them to stretch the next day. By the time I returned to the house it was near dark. When I walked into the living room and turned on the light I saw Daddy laying on the couch.

He'd passed out holding a bottle to his chest, and the pistol had fallen to the floor. I thought I would hide the pistol, before carrying him to the bedroom. But when I reached down for the gun his hand shot off his chest and grabbed my wrist.

"Don't you touch that," he said.

The vodka bottle fell to the floor and he let it go, and took the pistol instead.

"You need to go to bed," I said.

"Can't you goddamn leave me alone?" Daddy said.

"You need a doctor."

"You call a doctor and I'll blow your damn college brains out," Daddy said.

"I'll just carry you to the bedroom."

"I can walk," Daddy said. I stepped back and he tried to sit up. He held the gun in his right hand and pushed himself with his left. But he was too weak or drunk to raise himself. And I could see the pain in his face. He winced with the force of the pain. He lifted himself a little and then fell back. I reached to help him but he waved me away with the .44 magnum. There were tears in his eyes.

When Daddy dropped back on the couch he tried one more time to raise himself and failed. He started to sob and turned his face away to the back of the couch. "Don't call the goddamn ambulance," he said.

"I won't, but I have to put you to bed."

It was all I could do to lift him off the couch. He was dead drunken weight. Once I got him in my arms I almost tripped over the bottle which rolled on the floor. Walking carefully I carried him into the dark bedroom and laid him on the bed. He was still crying as I wrapped the covers around him.

"Can I get you something to eat?" I said. "You need to eat."

"Get out of here," he said.

IT WOULD NOT be fair to say that Daddy always avoided work. It's true that when tedious things like tying bean strings or hoeing corn had to be done he always found something else to do. Back before we had Mexican hands, we all of us had to work in the fields, Mama and Mary, Grandma and Grandpa. Daddy would drive us to the field in the morning and say he had to go after something, more poles or string or fuel for the tractor. And he'd go to the store and drink Co-Colas and talk to his buddies until it was dinner time. And then he'd bring us hotdogs and drinks and candy bars and peanuts to eat before he disappeared again.

But what Daddy liked to do, the work he really enjoyed, was anything to do with machines. Whether it was oiling a planter or fixing a posthole digger, he would let nobody else touch it. He seemed to have a natural talent for machines and tools. And what he preferred more than anything else was driving the tractor, any kind of tractor, from a garden tractor to a Farmall Cub. But it was the big diesel he loved most. In the spring he could hardly wait to get it cranked up again, blowing out blue smoke and winter farts, driving it like a prancing horse down to the bottomland along the river.

Sinking plow blades into the winter stubble, he turned the moist soil two big ropes at a time. Sometimes he liked to plow at night and sing so loud you could hear his voice over the roar of the diesel. Round and round the field he went, more times than a driver at the Daytona 500. By morning the field was turned over all new and looked like fresh corduroy.

Daddy had a knack with mechanical things. Even when drinking he could fix anything, lawn mower motor or a gearbox. Anything made out of metal with an engine delighted him. He could start a chainsaw when nobody else could. He said motors ran on gasoline or diesel the way he ran on vodka.

I DON'T KNOW if Grandma called the preacher or if he just dropped by the house the following afternoon. But when I came in from work there was a Buick in the driveway and in the living room there was the preacher talking to Grandma. Preacher Bob looked and talked like a car salesman. In fact, he had once been a car salesman in Greenville.

"Brother Ray," he said and shook my hand. "I've come by to see your daddy."

"I don't think he's well enough to see anybody," I said. We never mentioned Daddy's drinking to anybody outside of the family.

"Perhaps I could just pray with him," Preacher Bob said. "A short prayer might do him good."

I knew it was impolite to disagree with the preacher or try to turn him away. But I didn't want anybody to see Daddy in the shape he was in. And I certainly didn't want Daddy to point his pistol at the preacher or maybe even try to shoot him.

"Uh, maybe another time," I said.

"A prayer might ease his mind," Preacher Bob said.

Now Daddy hadn't been to church in years, and he had a special scorn for preachers. The last person I wanted there was preacher Bob. But while I was thinking about what to say Grandma told the preacher, "You go on in and say a few words."

It was dark in the bedroom and as we shuffled in Grandma flicked on the light. Daddy must have been sleeping but he opened his eyes and winced in the glare.

"How are you, Brother Howard?" Preacher Bob said. "I dropped in to see about you."

My stomach felt like it was full of sharp-edged rocks. I knew I was an idiot for letting this scene happen.

"Who are you?" Daddy said.

"I'm Preacher Bob, the pastor. Can I offer up a prayer for you?"

"Is this a hospital?" Daddy said, looking around at me and Grandma.

"You're at home," I said.

"I just want to offer up a prayer," Preacher Bob said.

Daddy's hand came out from under the covers, holding the .44 magnum. His arm was so weak the gun trembled. "Get your praying ass out of here," he said.

Preacher Bob reached out his hand like he was protecting himself, but he backed toward the door. We followed him into the living room

"I will pray for him," Preacher Bob said and slipped out the front door.

GRANDMA FIXED SOUP and cornbread that evening and as we sat at the table in the kitchen I pondered what could be done. If I could get the pistol away from Daddy I could call the ambulance and take him to the hospital. It would be the only way to save him. That was my moral duty and

possibly my legal duty also. It would be against all his wishes. I didn't know exactly what was the right thing to do and there was nobody to help me. Did Daddy have a right to die any way he wanted to? What was my ultimate responsibility? Was Daddy in his right mind enough to know what he was doing? Was I guilty already for not taking the pistol away from him?

By the time I finished the soup I was determined to get the gun away from him and call the ambulance. There was no use to call the ambulance until the .44 magnum was out of his hands. If I didn't get Daddy to the doctor I'd blame myself for the rest of my life. You don't really have a choice, I told myself. I'd have to take the gun and somehow the rest would fall in place.

But I didn't want to get shot myself. In his pain Daddy was a light sleeper. It would be almost impossible to slip up on him, and even if I did the pistol would be in his hand. Soon as I touched the gun he'd wake up and point it at me. I was just going to have to take my chances, grab the pistol from Daddy and hope he wouldn't shoot me. For I thought he didn't really want to hurt me. It was a risk I had to take.

"I'm going to get the pistol," I said to Grandma.

"Don't do that," she said. She was so embarrassed by the preacher's visit she'd hardly said anything through supper.

"It's the only way," I said.

My plan was to slip into the bedroom and put my hand on Daddy's hand before he knew what I was doing. I'd jerk the gun away and throw it as far as I could before he realized what was happening. Then when he was unarmed I'd hold him down and yell to Grandma to call 911. Sick as Daddy was, I could hold him there until the First Responders arrived.

I was so tense I hardly breathed as I approached the bedroom. I stopped at the door to listen, but heard nothing. Are you making the worst mistake of your life? I said to myself. But I'd made up my mind and there was nothing to do but go through with it. Stepping as quietly as I could I hurried to the bed and put my hand where I thought Daddy's hand would be under the covers. Sure enough, I felt the barrel of the pistol and gripped it hard.

But there was no resistance. The .44 magnum came loose in my hand

and I flung it toward the door. I expected Daddy to grab me or hit me, but he was still.

"Daddy, are you all right?" I said. I could smell vodka. There was no sound from the pillow. I shook his shoulder but there was no response.

"Daddy," I said and ran to turn on the light. Grandma stood in the doorway. Daddy lay still in the bed. He wasn't breathing, but the look on his face was relaxed, like the pain had gone, calm, a way I hadn't seen him in years.

# THE JAGUAR

WHEN THE WAR was over Nathaniel wasn't sure where to go first. There was a girl in Virginia named Rebecca that he wanted to marry, if she would agree to marry him. The thought of her long red hair and lightly freckled cheeks had helped him through long marches in mud and snow, in the cold nights with the Virginia militia. His company had been with General Morgan at Cowpens on January 17th and at Guilford Courthouse in March. They'd followed Cornwallis into Virginia, then returned to the Carolinas to join up with Lighthorse Harry Lee at Fort Ninety-Six or somewhere farther south. Then word reached them that the Virginia legislature had disbanded their unit. Cornwallis had surrendered at Yorktown on October 17th. The colonel called them together and thanked them for their service and told them they'd be paid later with tracts of land. Now the state was broke and they were on their own. There was still some fighting farther south, but for them the war with the King was over.

The obvious thing would be to return to Virginia and ask Rebecca to marry him. It would take about two weeks to reach Culpeper. But if he returned now he'd have nothing but his ragged clothes, a rifle, and one worn blanket. Not much to offer the prettiest girl in the county who had many beaux. He could only blame himself if she turned him down.

Throughout the campaign Nathaniel had kept glancing at the chain of blue mountains to the west. They rose in soft and rumpled shapes out of the foothills and followed one another toward the southwest like a caravan of giant animals. In the foothills where the militia camped before and after the battle of Cowpens he saw deer and turkeys, the tracks of raccoons and foxes. On the morning of the battle there Tarleton's army had driven deer and turkeys, foxes and a bear, and even a panther, before it onto the pasture which became the battlefield. If there was that much game in the foothills

169

where the armies had been moving, it thrilled him to think how much more there might be higher in the mountains.

Nathaniel knew the mountains were Cherokee country. But rumor was that the Cherokees had withdrawn much farther west across the mountains. Some Cherokees had fought for the British and would stay far from the patriots. It was said land in the mountains would be divided among those who'd fought against the Crown.

As a boy Nathaniel had trapped mink and muskrats. He'd even caught four or five bobcats. He'd shot deer for their hides as well as for their meat. The wealth of the forest was in furs and hides and ginseng. With the war over there would be a market for furs again. Instead of returning to Culpeper and begging the beautiful and coy Rebecca to marry him, ragged and broke, he'd find a valley in the mountains and trap through the winter. By spring he'd have enough furs to sell to make Rebecca a respectable offer. She was not a girl who would choose to live in poverty.

A number of horses had been captured from the British and kept at the pasture called Cowpens after the battle there. The colonel had said each man could take one horse on condition he sign a note agreeing to pay the Continental government later. Also lead and powder, hatchets and knives, could be purchased from the supply wagons with the same kind of promissory note.

Nathaniel chose a small, compact mount black as Bible leather called Pearl. And he took from the wagon as much lead and powder as he could carry. A keg of rum was opened and the men drank to each other's health, to their sweethearts, and to General Washington, and the end of the war. Nathaniel slipped away early next morning while everyone but the sentry was still sleeping.

Five miles north he came to the Broad River, and followed a trail along its western bank, through river birch and sycamores and past clumps of hazelnut bushes. It was late October and the trail was covered with new fallen leaves. Early sun shot through the trees in horizontal shafts, sparkling on the frosty edges of leaves.

"Pearl, old girl," he said to his mount, "we're off to make our fortune." Nathaniel hoped the trail would lead into the mountains and all he'd have to do was follow it. For two years he'd followed orders from the colonel, the captain, the sergeant. Now he'd have to make his own decisions. The thought both scared and thrilled him.

Nathaniel came to a smaller river that plunged into the Broad, and had to make his first choice. The bigger stream came from the north, but the smaller river flowed from the northwest, directly out of the closest mountains, its water a clear green, as though issuing from a thousand mountain springs and branches. It was the kind of stream that would have many mink and muskrats along its banks. Maybe even otter. It must come out of remote valleys and hidden coves far back in the ridges. He longed to camp in a peaceful valley, far from the ugliness and filth of war, the dirt and endless boredom of the militia. He turned left to follow the smaller stream.

The trail along the green river was hardly a trail at all. It skirted cane-brakes and disappeared in meadows of grass and wild peavines. Sometimes a track veered away from the river, and ran higher on the side of a ridge. Then it dropped back into the mud near the water. There were tracks in the mud, deer tracks, raccoon tracks, possum tracks, fox tracks. And once Nathaniel saw what looked like a human track, with no heel mark, the print of a moccasin. Could there still be Indians on this side of the mountains? Of course there were white hunters and traders who dressed like Indians, wore moccasins like Indians.

As Nathaniel continued up the stream he wondered if he'd imagined the moccasin track, for he didn't see another, only sign of deer and other animals. Late in the day he came on a flock of turkeys among the vines by the river and shot one as it took flight. While it was still light he decided to camp beside a spring, and started a fire with his flint and steel. After dressing the turkey he roasted it over the fire, basting the body with its own grease caught on a piece of bark. The bird was so big all he could eat was one leg, relishing the dark meat. It was the best meal he'd had in weeks, in months. Then he lay on his blanket and looked up at the stars, and wondered where he would find steel-traps. Indians could catch mink and muskrats without metal traps. They used snares and dead-falls, but he never had. There were supposed to be trading posts all over the frontier. Surely there was a station somewhere in the region that would sell traps.

Next day he followed the river higher into the hills. The stream that had been so smooth and easy between its banks ran louder as it struggled over rocks. Stretches of lullwater alternated with shoals of white water. Water tumbled and crashed over logs. He entered a gorge so deep there was no sunlight on the river until near the middle of the day. Everywhere he looked for moccasin tracks, and wondered how he would acquire traps. The brush along the trail became so thick he dismounted and led Pearl around boulders and up steep inclines.

It was near the end of the long ravine where he saw the red berries on stems near the ground. First he saw one plant and then others beyond. It was the first time he'd seen ginseng since he volunteered for the militia. Tying Pearl to a sapling, he got out his hunting knife, cleared away leaves and sticks, and dug up the bulging, fat roots. He'd never seen so much sang. People said a ginseng root was supposed to be shaped like a man, but Nathaniel had always thought of testicles when he saw a fresh root.

Before it began to get dark he'd dug more than a dozen ginseng roots. That much would bring him several shillings or dollars if there was any place to trade. He washed the roots in the river and put them in one of his bags. When he reached a level place, a kind of plateau, he camped for the night. Taking the saddle and bridle off Pearl, he tethered her in a peavine meadow and started a fire near a spring.

After eating more roast turkey he lay on his blanket and tried to recall the price of ginseng. Before the war roots had been worth more than a shilling a pound. He had no way of knowing its value now. As he lay by the fire he heard a fox bark and another answer. Later he was awakened by an owl in the trees, and another owl that seemed to be down by the river. There was a howl of a wolf far away on the ridge. When he woke and restarted the fire he wished he had some coffee. If he could find a trader's store he'd trade the ginseng for traps and coffee. All he had now was more turkey meat.

Nathaniel expected to hear Pearl cropping grass, but the meadow was silent. In the dim light he couldn't see her. Had he forgotten where he had tethered the horse? He grabbed his rifle and tiptoed along the edge of the clearing. The horse was gone. The animal calls in the night must have been Indians signaling to each other as they approached his camp and untied the tether line from its stake. As it grew lighter he could see the tracks leading not up the river but up the side of the mountain.

Without a horse to carry his baggage Nathaniel felt stranded. What he couldn't carry in his bags he'd have to bury and come back for later, the saddle, some of the cooking utensils. He would not leave the cask of powder. All his plans had depended on a horse, to carry supplies, to pack furs and hides out of the mountains in the spring. Now all he had was shank's mare. He could give up and hoof it back out of the mountains, or he could hoof it deeper into the mountains.

Burying what he couldn't carry, slinging bags of ginseng and shot over his shoulder, tying the cooking pot to his waist, he held the cask of power under one arm and carried the rifle in the other. He'd entered a kind of bowl, surrounded by mountains. The river was smaller now, really just a big creek, or run, as they'd call it in Virginia. In the distance he saw smoke, and when he crossed a rise a cabin came in view on a high bank above the stream. An Indian woman on her knees scraped a deer hide stretched on the ground and held by pegs.

As he approached, lugging his bags and the cask of powder, the woman looked up at him. She was younger than he expected, and plump. She wore a bright blue calico dress and had many strands of beads around her neck. She stared at Nathaniel for a moment without greeting him, and then returned to her work. Her black hair fell across her face as she scraped the hide.

"Anybody here?" Nathaniel called to the cabin. A bear hide was pegged on the side of the building and several rattlesnake skins hung from the eave. Two horses looked at him from the pen in back. Steel-traps hung from the wall of a shed by the woodpile. A man with long gray hair and beard appeared in the cabin door.

"I'm Nathaniel."

"McIver," the man said and looked at the bags Nathaniel was carrying.

"My horse was stole," Nathaniel said.

"So I see."

McIver ducked back into the cabin and reappeared with a jug. "Have a drink, stranger," he said and handed the jug to Nathaniel. Holding the jug with his thumb and slinging it over his shoulder Nathaniel took a swallow. The corn liquor was so strong his throat burned and his eyes smarted.

"Ain't got no horse to sell," McIver said. Nathaniel handed the jug back to him and the trader took a drink.

"What I need is steel-traps," Nathaniel said. "I have sang to trade." He opened the leather bag and showed McIver the roots he'd dug.

"Sang ain't worth nothing because of the war. The harbors are blocked. Besides, that's not even been dried."

"The war is over."

"I knowed the rebels would be defeated," McIver said.

"The rebels won. I was in the militia."

McIver looked at Nathaniel as if he suspected Nathaniel was lying. Like other Tories, he must have stayed back in the mountains while war raged in the piedmont. The trader shook his head and took another drink. The news seemed to make him look older.

"I can give you one trap for them roots," McIver said and squinted at Nathaniel.

"For all this sang?"

"Best I can do, take it or leave it."

Nathaniel had no choice but to take it. As far as he knew there was not another trader within a hundred miles. Without traps he could catch no fur, and winter was about to set in. One trap was better than no trap. He handed the bag of ginseng to McIver and the trader called to the Indian woman and told her to take the bag to the shed out back. McIver offered another drink from the bag to seal the deal, and handed him a steel-trap.

When the Indian woman brought the bag back to Nathaniel it felt a little heavier than an empty bag, but Nathaniel didn't mention it. The woman didn't look at him, and returned to her work on the hide.

"Cherokee?" Nathaniel asked.

McIver shook his head. "Bought her from the Cherokees for a musket and a jug of applejack."

McIver said Nathaniel's horse was likely stolen by the Cherokees. They'd been hunting in the region, but with winter they'd return to their villages over the mountains.

"Might be a while before you see that horse again," McIver said. From the wrinkles around his eyes Nathaniel guessed the trader was fifty or more.

As NATHANIEL headed up the river he found the path well marked around a canebrake and then below a laurel thicket. Horses had passed this way recently. Most of the tracks were made by unshod horses. But one had shoes the size of Pearl's foot. Surely McIver must have seen his horse if they'd passed this way, yet he hadn't said so.

When Nathaniel stopped for the night he looked into the leather bag the Indian woman had handed him. There was a small steel-trap in the bottom, just big enough to catch a muskrat. Now he had two traps, and it pleased Nathaniel to think the Indian woman had helped him. As he made a fire he tried to recall what the Indian woman had been wearing. It was a blue calico dress, and her leggings were buckskin with beads on them. Her skin was the color of new molasses. She'd not spoken to him nor looked him in the eye, but she'd given him the extra trap.

That night as Nathaniel slept with his rifle at his side he dreamed about Rebecca. In the dream she stood beside a well and as he approached she drew a bucket from the well and with a dipper scooped fresh water from the bucket. If she offered the dipper to him that meant she would marry him. But as he got closer and waited for her to hold the dipper out to him he woke. Stars gleamed through the trees. A moon thin as a reaping hook hung straight above.

All the next day Nathaniel followed the stream. There was no trail now, and boulders made the bank so difficult to follow he climbed up on the mountainside and skirted thickets of laurel. The river valley narrowed for several miles and the pinched stream tumbled and crashed on rocks. From the ridge he could see the mountains far ahead, lavender and brown now that the leaves had fallen, blue in the distance, then gray in the further distance where summits seemed almost to merge with the sky. Somewhere in those higher mountains he'd find the cove or hollow where he could camp and trap throughout the winter. With only two traps it would take him all winter to catch enough furs to ask for Rebecca's hand.

It was late the third day after he left McIver's that he came to the head-spring of the river. He'd followed the stream as it got smaller and smaller, and then he followed a branch to where the fountain came right out of the mountainside. Three or four inlets in the spring, like nostrils, made sand dance at the bottom of the pool. He cleaned leaves and sticks away from the basin and saw mica and quartz glittering in the sand. He drank from the spring, water that tasted like it had run through silver and emeralds deep in the earth. He'd never tasted water with exactly that flavor. He wondered what special mineral might be inside the mountain.

With winter so near Nathaniel only had time to build a three-sided shelter called a half-face, a low cabin open on the side facing south where a fire would be kept burning. With the hatchet he'd bought from the militia it took him most of a day. He covered the structure with poplar bark spread on poles, then laid rocks and brush on the bark to hold it down. The half-face blended so well with the woods and thickets it would not be noticed from a distance.

When the structure was done Nathaniel took his rifle to look for a turkey or squirrel. He would settle for a rabbit if he had to. As he crossed the branch below the spring he saw a large track in the sand, a cat track, much bigger than a bobcat's, bigger than any panther track he'd ever seen in Virginia. It must be a panther track, and yet it didn't look exactly like a panther track. If there was a cat that big in the area he'd have to take extra care, especially if he was out before sunrise or after sunset. Big cats usually did their stalking in the dark. He shot a turkey in a peavine meadow a little farther down the branch.

With only two traps Nathaniel chose the sites to set them with great care, ranging downstream to places where he found tracks of muskrat and mink in sand and mud. Traps had to be in water deep enough to drown the caught animal before it could gnaw its foot off to escape. If water was too deep over the trap the muskrat or mink would swim right over it. Best spots were near slides on the banks where the animals came down to the water. He caught two muskrats the first week, and a mink and three muskrats the second week. He stretched the hides on frames of sourwood sprouts to cure.

It was in the third week when he saw the big cat. He'd killed a deer and dressed it and hung the meat from an oak limb out of reach of bears and wolves and other animals. It was just before dawn when he woke and was about to build up the fire. As he reached for kindling wood at the entrance of the half-face he saw an animal standing under the deer carcass where it hung, about twenty paces away. He froze and watched. It was a big cat, but it had *spots* and looked heavier than a panther. And when it turned he saw its face was round with whiskers like a tiger, not a panther. But tigers he'd seen in pictures had stripes. He felt for his rifle beside the blanket. The big cat circled beneath the deer carcass, looked toward the half-face, sniffed the air, and then strolled away toward the branch.

Nathaniel didn't realize until the cat was gone that he'd been holding his breath. He gasped, and breathed out. If the big cat was not a panther, what was it? Its face looked like a tiger, but it had spots. Leopards had spots, but they were sleek and trim. This animal looked heavy and powerful. He'd been worried about bears and wolves and panthers, but who ever heard of a tiger in the Carolina mountains.

By the time of the first snow Nathaniel had more than a dozen muskrat hides and two mink skins. He also had two deer hides he'd stretched on pegs on the side of the half-face. Before the winter was over he was sure he'd be able to add a bear skin to his collection. Now bears had gone into caves or dens or hollow logs to sleep through the cold weather. He could understand that tendency to sleep through the winter. On the coldest days he didn't go out to check his traps, but lay by the fire and dreamed about Virginia and Rebecca.

He had the dream again of Rebecca standing by the well and holding out the dipper of water to him. Her red hair glistened in the sun. But when he got closer he saw her face was wrinkled. Instead of freckles there were warts, and when she opened her mouth gaps showed in her teeth. He recoiled in astonishment and then woke up. He blamed the bad dream on the greasy turkey meat he'd eaten.

Later, in mid-winter, there was a thaw. Nathaniel decided to take the furs and deer hides he had to McIver for more traps, some corn meal, salt, and maybe coffee. He wrapped the furs in deer skins and tied them all in a bundle he could carry on his back. He calculated it would take him three

days to reach the trader's cabin. It made sense to go before he'd accumu-
lated more furs than he could carry.

He'd not traveled more than a mile downstream when he saw in the
sand a large cat's track. It looked even bigger than the one the tiger cat
had left near his camp in the fall. But perhaps he'd forgotten just how big
those tracks were. The giant feline had not returned since it had tried to
reach his deer meat. He knew panthers roved over wide circuits in their
hunts. Maybe this cat did the same. That night Nathaniel kept his rifle close
as he lay in a small clearing near the river.

Two days later, as he approached McIver's station, he saw several
horses in the pen behind the cabin. One of them was black and looked a
lot like Pearl. He hurried to the cabin to ask who had brought the horse
there. No one was outside and no one came to the door when he called.
"McIver!" he shouted and pushed open the door.

It was so dark inside he saw nothing at first. Then he made out the
Indian woman sitting by the fireplace sewing something from buckskin.
Bolts of cloth lay on the shelves and steel-traps hung from pegs on the
wall. Barrels and bins of corn meal, gunpowder, and whiskey lined the
wall. McIver lay on a bunk bed with a bearskin over him.

"What do you want?" the trader said.

Nathaniel dropped the bundle of furs and hides on the floor. "I need
more traps, some corn meal, and my horse," he said.

"I'm sick," McIver said. "The winter fever has got me."

"That black horse is the one stole from me."

"I bought that mare from an Indian," McIver said. "You got no proof
she was yorn." His hand came out from under the bearskin holding a
pistol.

Nathaniel looked at the Indian woman, and then back at McIver. "I
need five more steel-traps, some corn meal, and lead and powder," he said.

"Fur ain't worth nothing now," McIver said.

"I have five mink here."

McIver spoke to the Indian woman in words Nathaniel didn't recognize. She put her sewing down and stood. With the pistol McIver pointed
to the barrel of corn meal and the traps hanging on the wall. The woman
handed Nathaniel two steel traps and scooped meal into a leather bag.

"I need five traps," Nathaniel said.

"Two is all you get," McIver said. He started coughing, a cough so deep it might have come from underground. He heaved and spat onto the floor. McIver's face was flushed and he appeared to have lost a lot of weight. He coughed again, and spat again. "Take your stuff and git," he said and pointed the pistol at the door.

The Indian woman handed Nathaniel the bag of corn meal, a bag of shot, and a small cask of powder. She didn't look at Nathaniel at first, and then she stared straight into his eyes. Her eyes were dark as brandy.

"Be gone," McIver said, and with the pistol motioned him again toward the door.

Outside Nathaniel tied the cask and bags together and slung them on his back. He glanced at the horse pen and saw Pearl watching him. It appeared McIver was dying of consumption, or something like consumption. Nathaniel wanted to pause and think about the best way to reclaim his horse. But he heard McIver shout again, telling him to get away. The Indian woman stood in the doorway staring at him.

Nathaniel shouldered his burden, and holding the rifle in his right hand started up the trail. Once he got into the woods he had to stop and readjust the pack. The cask of powder kept slipping loose from the straps. He dropped to his knees and was retying the bundle when he heard steps behind him. As he turned he saw the Indian woman leading Pearl. Deerskin bags hung on either side of the horse. Nathaniel stood up and the woman handed him the reins of the bridle. She stared directly into his eyes and then looked away.

"Do you mean I can take her?" he asked.

The woman nodded and started back down the trail. He watched her blue calico dress disappear around a bend. Nathaniel wondered if this was a trick. Would McIver accuse him of stealing the horse? But McIver seemed too weak to even get out of bed and his hand trembled when he held the pistol.

The deerskin bags over Pearl's back were big enough to hold all his baggage. Nathaniel packed everything, dividing the load between the two sides. Then he spoke to Pearl and caressed her nose. He imagined she remembered him, but couldn't be sure. Taking up the reins he led her carefully up the trail, picking a way around boulders and over logs. Now that he had his horse back, he couldn't risk her stumbling and breaking a leg. It seemed too good to be true that the Indian woman had given Pearl back to him.

That night as he camped by the river, with Pearl close by, he dreamed of Rebecca for the first time in weeks. It was the same dream as before, but as he approached her by the well and her face showed all the wrinkles of age, she began to laugh at him like he'd made a fool of himself. Instead of handing him the dipper, she flung the water in his face, and the water was not cool but scalding hot. He wiped it out of his eyes and then he woke up.

When Nathaniel looked through the trees the stars were gone. It had clouded up in the night, and gotten colder. Something faint as the breeze from a mosquito's wing touched his lips and cheek. Then he felt the wetness and knew it was snowflakes. It was snowing in the silent woods and the thaw was over.

Next day Nathaniel led Pearl through deepening snow along the river. In places it was hard to see ahead because of snow on limbs and brush. Once or twice on steep ground it looked as though Pearl was going to slide into the river. In some places it was easier to walk in the stream itself than to keep a footing on the bank. Once they passed the tracks of a large animal. But he couldn't tell if it was a panther or the track of the other large cat because of the falling snow.

At day's end Nathaniel decided not to make a fire. He tied Pearl to a tree, and seated himself against an oak, blanket over his head and shoulders, rifle in his lap under the blanket to keep the powder dry. Snow continued to fall, whispering and ticking on branches, seething faintly as flakes meshed together. He chewed a piece of dried turkey, melted snow in his mouth for something to drink. Pearl munched corn from a bag slung over her ears.

Nathaniel was twice wakened as he leaned against the tree. Once he thought he heard an animal scream, a panther, and once a long note like a wolf or dog might make. But mostly it was the faint hiss of falling snow. Snow, especially snow in darkness, created its own world, muffled, cushioned, almost silent, almost beyond time. Deepening snow made you want to burrow under and sleep with the ground hogs and other animals, with the sap in deep roots, with the seeds, and salt in stones, and dream of spring.

When he woke the blanket weighed on him. More than a foot of snow had fallen. Snow had built on Pearl's back but she shivered it off. Nathaniel knew he was only half a day's walk from his camp, but in the deep snow it would take him most of the day to get there. And when he reached his camp before dark he saw tracks all around the half-face, wolf tracks, deer tracks, tracks of the big tiger cat. Something had climbed the oak tree and jumped down on the hanging deer carcass and eaten from it. He wasn't sure what animal would have done that, a raccoon, a bobcat?

It took him some effort to get a fire started at the entrance of the half-face. Snow had blown and drifted into the shelter and he had to clean the drift away from the circle of rocks. To find kindling he split some pine limbs to expose the resiny heartwood. He shaved curls and found a few dry leaves and twigs in the corner. With flint and steel he finally got a fire going and fed it carefully with shavings and pine splinters until the flames were hot enough to catch the larger sticks. In the deep snow his only choice was to break lower limbs from pines and knock the snow off and lay them one at a time on the fire.

When he emptied the bags slung over Pearl's back he found a bag of coffee beans. Whether it had been put there by mistake he couldn't know. But gratefully he crushed some beans between two rocks and boiled coffee until it was black and strong and scalding. As he sipped the brew it warmed his belly and bowels, and sent light out through his veins to the tips of his fingers and toes.

As he drank the coffee and gnawed turkey meat and looked out at the snow beyond the fire, Nathaniel knew he had much work to do. He had to build a real cabin for himself, with four walls and a fireplace, and he had to make some kind of shelter for Pearl. She'd need a stall built of poles and logs. Pearl could not be left outside, tied to a tree all winter, as wolves and panthers, Indians and the tiger cat, came prowling.

Nathaniel expected the snow to melt, but instead the weather grew colder, and more snow came. Snow and ice on the stream made it hard to find his old traps, much less set the new ones. Every day snow fell, and he cleared a yard around the half-face and shot turkeys and a deer that wandered near. He didn't even have to go out into the woods to hunt. It was so cold turkeys died from suffocation as ice clogged their breathing holes. While the snow was so deep it was hard to get started cutting logs for a cabin and horse stall.

One night in late winter he heard Pearl whinny and her whinny rose to a scream. Nathaniel grabbed his rifle and a blazing stick from the fire. Pearl was jumping and kicking and he saw something spotted on her back. The horse thrashed and reared and bucked, but the animal stuck to her back. It had to be the big tiger cat he'd seen before. The weeks of blizzard had made it desperate for a kill. He couldn't raise the rifle while holding the burning stick.

Pearl swung from side to side in terror and the giant cat gripped her flesh and bit her neck. Nathaniel stuck the burning stick into the snow-bank where it blazed like a torch. He raised the rifle, but how was he to shoot in the flickering light without hitting Pearl? He had only one shot. If he missed the tiger would kill Pearl before he could reload, and if he merely wounded the cat it might turn on him. With the end of the rifle barrel he followed the rising and falling, the lurch from side to side, of the horse and cat. It was too dangerous to risk the shot.

Stepping closer, just a few feet from the horse, he pointed the barrel behind the cat's shoulders and fired. Pearl wheeled away, jumped and bucked, kicked out behind, and swung out of the light. The tiger cat clung to her back and Nathaniel thought he'd missed. There was no time to reload. Raising the rifle by its barrel he clubbed the cat on the head. The head fell to the side, and slowly the spotted body slid off the horse into the snow. He pounded the head with the butt of the rifle and the big cat lay still.

Blood seeped from the places on Pearl's neck and withers where the cat's teeth and claws had ripped the flesh. He rubbed grease on the wounds, and whispered to the horse to calm her. Nathaniel was trembling so he could hardly reload the rifle. Throwing more wood on the fire he made coffee and sat to calm himself until it was daylight.

When he looked closely at the carcass of the tiger cat he saw the spots were in clusters of four, almost in circles, around a central spot, like the leaves of four-leaf clovers or the petals of a flower. It was the most beautiful hide he'd ever seen. Nathaniel ran his fingers over the fine hair. He'd never touched anything like it. The cat must have been an individual that had wandered into the mountains from far to the south or west.

It took Nathaniel most of the day to skin the tiger cat. It was a male and must have weighed over two hundred pounds. The body was heavier and thicker than that of a panther, though not as long. He peeled the hide off with great care. No telling what he could get for such a skin, maybe enough for a new rifle, more traps, supplies for another season. When the big carcass was skinned he stretched the hide on the wall of the half-face with pegs stuck between the poles.

Nathaniel dragged the carcass to the edge of his yard and left it there. He shot a wolf that came at dusk to eat the flesh. The next evening he killed a bobcat that came to feed there. But when buzzards arrived on the third day he let them peck their fill. It took about a week for the scavengers to pick the bones clean.

A few weeks later the rains started. Never had he seen it rain harder or longer. Hour after hour, day after day, the water came down like an ocean dropping out of the sky. The great drifts of snow turned sodden, gray, and drained away. The yard filled with water and mud. Water seeped into the half-face. The spring flooded as snow on the ridge above melted and poured downhill. The branch spread far beyond its banks.

The corn meal he'd brought from McIver's was ruined by water and had rotted. So had the turkey meat he'd dried over the fire. Water had gotten into his keg of powder. All he had left was the amount in his horn. With a piece of deerskin he rubbed water off the big cat hide. To cure it must be kept dry.

It was only when the rain stopped that Nathaniel realized a terrible flood must have swept through the valley below. The melting snow and endless rain would have scoured the river valley. When he went to look for his two traps they were gone. He'd not been able to set the new traps because of the heavy snow. Now it was too late in the season to catch fur in its prime. Soon it would be spring.

The only thing Nathaniel had to trade was the hide of the tiger cat. With so little powder left he had no choice but to go back to McIver's to see what the trader would give him for the unusual hide. Folding the big skin, he tied it on Pearl's back. As he led the mare down the valley he saw the effects of the flood. Trees had been torn out by the roots and piled up against other trees. Raw banks had been cut at the bends. The farther he traveled the more devastation he saw. Debris was left in meadows and trash caught in the tops of trees still standing. The flood had cut a swath up to the sides of the mountains.

There was no path now. He had to find a way around heaped brush, uprooted trees, boulders washed out of the mountainside. Landslides had piled mud and dammed the stream in places. He slogged through mud up to his knees. It took Nathaniel four days to reach McIver's station, and when he came into the clearing he saw everything was wrong. The cabin was not where it had been, but was turned sideways and leaning toward the river and the roof had fallen in. The fence of the horse pen had washed away, and the horses were gone. The storage shed had been knocked over by the flood. Dead trees littered the yard.

Something moved to his right, and he turned and saw the Indian woman digging in the hillside. Nathaniel led Pearl in that direction and noticed a body lying on the ground wrapped in a bear skin. It was McIver. As he approached, the Indian woman ignored him and kept digging. McIver's face was white as wax, almost blue.

"Can I help you with that?" Nathaniel said.

There was a trail in the mud and grass where she had dragged the body to the spot on the hill. She dug slowly, as though worn out.

"Give me the shovel," Nathaniel said. The Indian woman stopped digging and he took the shovel from her. Underneath the sod the dirt was red clay with only a few rocks and roots. He cut the corners of the grave hole square and carved the walls straight. Digging dirt was something Nathaniel had always been good at. Added strength always came to him when he cut into the earth. The Indian woman held Pearl while he worked. When the hole was deep enough they lowered the body into it.

Standing at the foot of the grave the Indian woman looked up at the sky and said some words Nathaniel didn't understand. She reached out a hand toward the west, and then laid the hand over her heart. They both stood silent for a moment and then Nathaniel began shoveling red clay back into the grave.

As they walked toward the tilted cabin Nathaniel said, "I see the flood was bad."

"Flood took everything," she said. Her calico dress was smeared with mud and her moccasins and leggings were muddy.

Nathaniel looked into the leaning cabin and saw barrels of meal and tobacco, gunpowder, whiskey, kegs of bear grease, had been broken open and ruined. A few traps hung on the wall, already beginning to rust.

"Did McIver drown in the flood?" Nathaniel said.

"McIver dead," the woman said. She looked away toward the mountains.

"What is your name?"

"McIver call me Sarah."

"Are you a Catawba? Cherokee?"

The woman turned and looked him in the eye. "Coosa," she said.

"Coosa?"

The woman pointed toward the southwest. "Cherokee burn my village, take me, sell me to McIver." She sounded sad but not angry. She stared at the tiger cat hide on Pearl's back, and stepped closer to stroke the spotted skin. "Jaguar," she said.

"Jaguar?" It was a name Nathaniel had heard, but thought that animal belonged to the tropics.

"Jaguar," she said again, and it was clear she had seen such a big cat before. Wherever she was from it must be far south where there were jaguars to hunt.

"Where will you go now?" Nathaniel said.

She looked away toward the mountains. "I go with you," she said.

Nathaniel was surprised.

The death of McIver, the flood, the jaguar, had changed everything. Should he go back down to the foothills and head for Virginia? He had nothing but the jaguar hide to show for his winter's work. Should he help the Indian woman rebuild McIver's cabin? Should he send her down to the settlements?

As he studied his options, the Indian woman stepped into the ruined cabin and came out with a dozen rusting steel-traps which she tied to Pearl's back. Then she returned to the cabin and came back with a bundle of hunting knives and a leather bag of lead. On her next trip she brought several cooking pots and tied those to Pearl's back also.

"Did McIver have any money?" Nathaniel said.

"Money wash away," she said. Then she reached into a bag tied to her neck and took out three gold coins. "My money," she said. Then she returned to the cabin and came back with a small cask of gunpowder.

"Is the powder dry?" Nathaniel said.

"Sealed with tar," she said and showed him the seams filled with pitch.

As he watched her lash the keg to Pearl's back Nathaniel knew a decision had been made. She'd made the decision for him. Or he'd made the decision when he chose to return to McIver's. Or the flood had made the decision.

They started up the washed-out river valley by mid-afternoon, Nathaniel in front leading the mare, Sarah behind carrying a pack of muskrat hides and sewing things, beads and needles, knives and salt and herbs on her back. Redbud and sarvis were beginning to bloom. The scoured river banks were starting to dry.

When they stopped for the night Sarah started a fire and put a pot of water on to boil for coffee. Then she took a fish hook and thread from her pack, found white grubs under a log for bait, and caught three trout in the river. For supper they ate fresh trout and drank strong black coffee. After they ate Sarah bowed her head and said a prayer. She said missionaries had come to her village when she was little and taught her to pray after every meal. Then she washed the pot in the river and unrolled a bearskin on the ground.

"I make you a coat," she said and pointed to the jaguar hide.

"A coat for me?" Nathaniel sat with his loaded rifle beside him. Bears, wolves, panthers, Cherokees, might be prowling. But because the woman was with him he felt more at ease, a confidence he hadn't expected. With another person the woods seemed different.

"I don't know where we can sell furs now that McIver's gone," Nathaniel said.

"McIver sell his furs to Davis," she said and pointed to the east.

"Maybe you can make a coat for yourself from the jaguar," Nathaniel said.

"No, for you," she said and put a hand on his cheek.

186

Later that night as he lay beside Sarah listening to the murmur of the river he thought of Rebecca and tried to recall her face, but couldn't be sure he remembered any features except the red hair.

# ACKNOWLEDGMENTS

The author thanks the editors of the following journals for first publishing the stories indicated.

*Appalachian Heritage:* "The Burning Chair,"

*Epoch:* "As Rain Turns to Snow," "The Wedding Party," "Big Words and Fame"

*Greensboro Review:* "Halcyon Acres"

*Meet Me on the Plaza:* "Happy Valley"

*Negative Capability:* "The Calm"

*North Carolina Literary Review:* "The Cliff"

*Pembroke Magazine:* "The Church of the Ascension"

*Roanoke Review:* "The Jaguar"

*Shenandoah:* "The Dulcimer Maker"

*Southern Review:* "The Distant Blue Hills"

*Story:* "Dans Les Hautes Montagnes de Caroline"

This book has been set in Matthew Carter's Galliard
with display in Matthew Carter's Mantinia

Design & typesetting by Jonathan Greene.

Printing & binding by Thomson-Shore.